Gold And Glory
Or, Wild Ways Of Other Days A Tale Of Early American Discovery

by

Grace Stebbing

Double9
BOOKS

Gold And Glory
Or, Wild Ways Of Other Days A Tale Of Early American Discovery
by Grace Stebbing

ISBN: 978-93-61425-60-8

Published by

DOUBLE 9 BOOKS

2/13-B, Ansari Road
Daryaganj, New Delhi – 110002
info@double9books.com
www.double9books.com
Tel. 011-40042856

ABOUT THE AUTHOR

Grace Stebbing contributed to the literary scene with her stories by frequently writing in particular genres or eras. Stebbing's stories may have been influenced by cultural themes, historical occurrences, or her own experiences. Even though her biography isn't very detailed, her works like "Gold and Glory or Wild Ways of Other Days: A Tale of Early American Discovery" demonstrate the influence of her writing. Her passion for history, exploration, and narrative is probably evident in this work, which provides readers with a fictional window into several historical periods and cultural contexts. Even though Grace Stebbing's literary contributions may not be well known, her stories may have offered readers amusement, wisdom, and escape.

CONTENTS

INTRODUCTION

Only an apology for having written this historical tale.

My private opinion is, that all writers of historical tales should return me thanks if I apologize for them with myself, all in a body, the truer the tale the ampler being the spirit of the apology.

While I have been writing this tale, sometimes in its most important or serious portions, I have been startled by detecting my own mouth widening with an absurd smile, or by hearing a ridiculous chuckle issuing from my own lips, and have suddenly discovered that I was quite unconsciously repeating to myself the famous old Scotch anecdote of the old woman and the Scotch preacher—"That's good, and that's Robertson; and that's good, and that's Chalmers; ... and that's bad, and that's himsel'."

Turning the old woman into the more learned among my possible readers, and the Scotch preacher into myself, I read the anecdote—"That's good, and that's Prescott; that's good, and that's Robertson; that's good, and that's guide-book; that's good, and that's Arthur Helps; and that's bad, and that's hersel'."

I can only wind up my apology by pleading, that at least my badness has not gone the length of distorting a single fact, nor of giving to this wonderful page of history any touch of false colouring.

G. S.

CHAPTER I
A POISON-FLY FOR THE HEART OF ARAGON

In an apartment, gorgeous with a magnificence that owed something of its style to Moorish influence, were gathered, one evening, a number of stern-browed companions.

A group of men, whose dark eyes and olive complexions proclaimed their Spanish nationality, as their haughty mien and the splendour of their attire bore evidence to their noble rank.

The year was 1485: a sad year for Aragon was that of 1485, and above all terrible for Saragossa. But as yet only the half, indeed not quite the half, of the year had gone by, when those Spanish grandees were gathered together, and when one of them muttered beneath his breath, fiercely:

"It is not the horror of it only, that sets one's brain on fire. It is the shame!"

And those around him echoed—"It is the shame."

During the past year, 1484, his Most Catholic Majesty, King Ferdinand of the lately-united kingdoms of Castile and Aragon, had forced upon his proud, independent-spirited Aragonese a new-modelled form of the Inquisition. The Inquisition had, indeed, been one of the institutions of the noble little kingdom for over two hundred years already, but in the free air of Aragon it had been rather an admonisher to orderliness and good manners than a deadly foe to liberty. Now, all this was changed. The stern and bitter-spirited Torquemada took care of that. The new Inquisition was fierce, relentless, suspicious, grasping, avaricious, deadly. And in their hearts the haughty, freedom-loving Aragonese loathed its imperious domination even more than they dreaded its cruelty.

"It was not the horror of it only," said Montoro de Diego truly, "that made their eyes burn, and sent the tingling blood quivering into their hands. It was the shame."

And those others around him, even to Don James of Navarre, the King Ferdinand's own nephew, echoed the words with clenched hands, and between clenched teeth—

"It is the shame!"

But what cared Torquemada, the Grand Inquisitor, that mortal wounds should be inflicted on the noblest instincts of human nature? or what cared his tools in Aragon? Crushed, broken-spirited men would be all the easier to handle—all the easier to plunder or destroy.

Montoro de Diego had been one of the deputation sent by the Cortes to the fountain-head, as it was then believed, of all truth and mercy and justice, to implore release from the new infliction; for whilst one deputation had gone to the king himself, to implore him to abolish his recent innovation, another, headed by Diego, had gone to the pope. But the embassy was fruitless. The pope wanted money, and burning rich Jews, and wealthy Aragonese suspected of heretical tendencies, put their property into the papal coffers. The pope very decidedly refused to give up this new and easy way of making himself and his friends rich. The king's refusal was equally peremptory, and the deputations returned with dark brows and heavy hearts to those anxiously awaiting them.

The burnings and confiscations had already begun.

Soon after Diego and his companions entered the city of Saragossa they encountered a great procession, evidently one of importance judging from the sumptuousness of the ecclesiastics' dresses, their numbers, and the crowds of attendants surrounding them, crucifix-bearers, candle-bearers, incense-bearers, and others. There was no especial Saint's Day or Festival named in the Calendar for that date, and for a few moments the returning travellers were puzzled. But the procession advanced, and the mystery was solved.

In the centre of the gorgeous train moved a group so dismal, so heart-rending to look upon, that it must have rained tears down the cheeks of the Inquisitors themselves, had they not steeled their hearts with the impenetrable armour of a cold, utter selfishness.

Deadly pale, emaciated, unwashed, uncombed, with wrists and fingers twisted and broken, and limping feet, came the members of this group clad in coarse yellow garments embroidered with scarlet crosses, and a hideous adornment of red flames and devils. Some few of the tortured victims of base or bigoted cruelty were on their way to receive such a pardon as consisted in the fine of their entire fortunes, or life-long imprisonment; the others— they were to afford illuminations for the day's ceremonies with their own burning bodies. For each member of the wretched group there was the added burden of knowing that they were leaving behind them names that were to be loaded with infamy, and families reduced to the lowest depths of beggary.

"And all," muttered a voice beside Diego's elbow, "for the crime, real or suspected, or imputed, of having Jewish blood in their veins."

"Say rather," fiercely muttered back the noble—"say rather, for the crime of having gold and lands, which will so stick to the hands of the Inquisitors, that the king's troops in Granada will keep the Lenten fast the year through, before a sack of grain is bought for them out of those new funds."

"Ay," answered the unknown voice, "the Señor saith truth, unless there shall be hearts stout enough, and hands daring enough, to rid our Aragon of yon fiend Arbues de Epila."

Montoro de Diego turned with an involuntary start to look at the speaker of such daring words. For even though they had been uttered in low cautious tones they betokened an almost mad audacity, during those late spring days when the very breath of the warm air seemed laden with accusations, bringing death and ruin to the worthiest of the land, at the mandate of that very Arbues.

But Diego's eyes encountered nothing more important than the wondering brown orbs of a little beggar child, who was taking the whole imposing spectacle in with artistic delight, unmixed with any idea of horror, and who was evidently astonished at the agitated aspect of his tall companion, and irritated too, that the Señor should thus stand barring the way, instead of passing on with the rest of the rabble-rout trailing after the procession.

Whoever had ventured to express his fury against the new Inquisitor of Saragossa, it was evidently not this curly-headed little urchin, and with a somewhat impatient gesture of disappointment the noble turned away in search of his companions. But they also had disappeared. Carried away by the excitement or curiosity of the moment, they also had joined in the dread procession of the Auto da Fé.

CHAPTER II
CONSPIRATORS

"It is the shame," that was the burden of the low and emphatic consultation that was being held by the group of men, gathered privately in the palace of one of the indignant nobles of Aragon. Little more than twenty-four hours had passed since the disappointed deputation to Rome had returned, in time to witness the full horrors of the cruel tribunal they had so vainly tried to abolish, and the feeling of humiliation was keen.

And shame, indeed, there was for the brave, proud Aragonese, that the despotic tyranny of the Inquisition should hold sway amidst their boasted freedom and high culture.

"We are not alone in our indignation," added Montoro de Diego after a pause, and with a keen, swift glance around at the faces of his companions to satisfy a lurking doubt whether the muffled voice at his elbow, yesterday, had not indeed belonged to one of them.

But every face present was turned to his suddenly, with such vivid, evident curiosity at the changed and significant tone of his voice, that the shadowy supposition quickly faded, and with a second cautious but sharp glance, this time directed at doors and windows instead of at the room's occupants, the young nobleman replied to the questioning looks by a sign which gathered them all closer about him as he repeated:

"No; we are not alone in our just resentment. The spirit of disaffection is rife in Saragossa."

"The Virgin be praised that it is so," muttered one of the grandees moodily, while another asked hastily:

"But how know you this? What secret intelligence have you received?"

"And when?" put in a third questioner somewhat jealously.

The new system was already beginning to grow its natural fruit of general suspicion and distrust. But Diego speedily disarmed them as regarded himself on this occasion. His voice had been low before, it sank now to a scarcely audible whisper as he answered:

"One, I know not who—even the voice was a disguised one I believe—spoke to me yesterday in the crowded streets; one who must have marked the anger and mortification of my countenance I judge, and thence dared act the tempter."

"But how?" "In what way?" came the eager, impatient queries.

"In the intimation that the world were well rid of Arbues de Epila."

As those few weighty words were rather breathed than spoken, those self-controlled, impassible grandees of Spain started involuntarily, and stifled exclamations escaped their lips.

Arbues de Epila! The day was hot with brilliant sunshine. Even in that carefully-shaded room the air was heavy with warmth, and yet—as Montoro de Diego muttered the hinted threat against Arbues de Epila, the crafty, cruel, unsparing Inquisitor—those brave, dauntless, self-reliant men felt chill. They were in a close group before, but involuntarily they drew into a still closer circle, and looked over their shoulders. In open fight with the impetuous Italians or with the desperate Moors of Granada, no more fearless warriors could be found than those grandees of Spain, but against this new, secret, lurking, unaccustomed foe their haughty courage provided them no weapons. To be snatched at in the dark, torn secretly from home, fame, and family, buried in oblivion until brought forth to be burnt; and branded, unheard with the blackest infamy—these were agonies to fill even those stout hearts with horror.

Stealthy glances, of which until the present time they would have been altogether disdainful, were cast by each and all of them at one another. Who should say that even in their own midst there might not be standing a creature of the Inquisition, bribed to the hideous work by promises of titles, lands, position, or Paradise without Purgatory?

Quailing beneath these strangely unaccustomed fears all maintained a constrained silence for some time. But meanwhile the suggestion thrown out yesterday, and now repeated, worked in those fevered brains, and at length the fiercest of the number threw back his head, folded his arms across his breast, and spoke. Not loudly indeed, but with a concentrated passion that sent each syllable with the force of an alarum into the hearts of his hearers.

"The stranger was right. We have been cravens—children kissing the rod, with our petitions. Now we will be men once more, judges in our own cause, and Arbues shall die."

As he pronounced that last dread word he held out his hand, and his companions crowded together to clasp it, in tacit acceptance of the declaration. But there was one exception. One member of the group drew back. Montoro de Diego stretched forth no consenting hand, but stood, pale and sorrowful, gazing at his friends. They in turn gazed back at him with mingled astonishment, fear, and fury. But he never blenched. His lip indeed curled for a moment with something of scorn as he detected the expression of terror in some of the gleaming eyes turned on him. But scorn died away again in sadness as he said slowly:

"Is it so then, truly, that we nobles of Aragon have already yielded ourselves voluntarily for slaves, accepting the despicable sins of slaves—cowardice and assassination! Now verily it is time then to weep for the past of Aragon, to mourn over its decay."

But bravely and nobly as Montoro de Diego spoke, he could not undo the harm of his incautious repetition of the stranger's fatal hint. Some of his companions had already their affections lacerated by the loss of friends, torn from their families to undergo the most horrible of deaths, the others were full of dark apprehensions for themselves, or for those whose lives were more precious to them than their own. And the thought of getting quit of the cruel tormentor took all too swift and fast hold of the minds of that assembled group.

"It is very evident," muttered one of the party with a scarcely stifled groan—"it is very evident, my Diego, that you count amongst the number of your friends none of those whose names, or position, or country, place them in jeopardy."

"Ah! indeed," added another, without perceiving the flush that suddenly deepened on the young noble's cheeks, "and it is easy enough to discover, even if one had not known it, that Diego has neither wife nor child for whose sake to feel a due value for his life and lands."

Again that sudden flush on the handsome face, but Montoro stood in shadow, and none marked it. The gathering of men, now turned into a band of conspirators, was more intent on learning from Montoro de Diego whether he meant to betray their purpose, than in taking note of his own private emotion, and once assured of his silence they let him depart, while they remained yet some time longer in secret conclave, to concert their plans for destroying Arbues and the Inquisition both together.

"There cannot be much difficulty one would imagine," muttered one of the conspirators, "in compassing the death of a wretch held in almost universal odium."

But others of the party shook their heads, while one, more fully acquainted with the state of affairs than the rest, replied moodily:

"Nay then, your imagination runs wide of the mark. The difficulty in accomplishing our undertaking will be as great as the danger we incur. The cruel are ever cowards. Arbues wears mail beneath his monastic robes, complete even to bearing the weight of the warrior's helmet beneath the monk's hood. And his person is diligently guarded by an obsequious train of satellites."

"Then we must bribe the watch-dogs over to our side," was the stern remark of the haughty Don Alonso, who had been the first to seize upon the suggestion thrown out by the unknown voice in the crowd.

Immediately after that declaration the noblemen dispersed, for it was not safe just at that time for men to remain too long closeted together.

CHAPTER III
RIVALS AT DON PHILIP'S HOUSE

When Montoro de Diego quitted the palace of Don Alonso his face betokened an anxiety even greater than that warranted by the conversation in which he had just taken part. To say truth his secret belief was, that the deadly decision arrived at by his friends was the frothy result of recent disappointed hopes, and that with the calming influence of time bolder and more honourable counsels would prevail. As he left the palace, therefore, he left also behind him all disquietudes especially associated with the late discussion, and the settled gravity of his face now belonged to matters of more private interest.

Don Alonso had declared, that it was easy enough to see that Don Diego had no friends amongst those looked upon with evil eyes by the authorities of the Inquisition. But Don Alonso was wrong. The two friends whom Don Diego valued more highly than any others upon earth were reputed of the race of Israel. Christians indeed, for two generations past, but still with a true proud gratitude clinging to the remembrance that they had the blood in their veins of the "chosen people of God." They were Don Philip and his daughter Rachel.

Don Miguel had remarked with something of a sneer that it was easy enough to remember, from his present action, that Don Diego was unencumbered with family ties. And Don Miguel was so far right that Montoro de Diego was as yet a bachelor. But he was on the eve of marriage with Don Philip's daughter, and the words of his fellow-nobles had rung in his ears as words of evil omen. As he paced along the streets he tried in vain to shake off his dark forebodings, and it was with a very careworn countenance that he at length presented himself at the home of his promised bride.

To his increased disturbance, upon being ushered into the presence of Don Philip and his daughter, the young nobleman found a stranger with them; at least, one who was a stranger to him, though apparently not so to his friends, with whom he appeared to be on terms of familiar intercourse.

Don Diego at once took a deep aversion to the interloper, for he had entered with the full determination to press upon Rachel and Don Philip the expediency of an immediate marriage, in order that both father and daughter might have the powerful protection of his high position, and undoubted Spanish descent and orthodoxy. But it was, of course, impossible to speak on such topics in the presence of a stranger. So annoyed was he that his greetings to his betrothed bride partook of his constraint, and the girl appeared relieved when her father called to her:

"Rachel, my child, the evening is warm; will you not order in some fruit for the refreshment of our guests?"

As the beautiful young girl left the apartment in gentle obedience to her father's desire the stranger followed her with his eyes, saying with studied softness:

"Your daughter is so lovely it were a pity that she had not been dowered with a fairer name."

The old man sighed before replying: "Perchance, Señor, you are right. And yet, in my ears the name of Rachel has a sweetness that can scarcely be surpassed."

"It might sound sweeter in mine," rejoined the stranger still in tones of studied suavity, "if it were not one of the names favoured by the accursed race of Israel."

A momentary flash shot from the eyes of Don Philip, but hastily he dropped his lids over them as he answered with forced quietude: "Doubtless I should have bestowed another name upon my child had I foreseen these days, when it is counted for a crime to be descended from those to whom the Great I Am, in His infinite wisdom, gave the first Law and the first Covenant."

He ceased with another low, quiet sigh, and a short silence ensued, during which Don Diego felt rather than saw the sharp, searching glances being bestowed upon himself by the stranger, who at length rose, and said coolly:

"Ay, truly, Don Philip, a crime it is in the eyes of Holy Mother Church to have aught to do, even to the extent of a name, with the accursed race, and so, to repeat my offer to you for the hand of your fair daughter. I support my offer now with the promise—not a light one, permit me to impress upon you—to gain the sanction of the Church that her old name of Rachel shall be cancelled, and a new and Christian one bestowed upon her?"

As he finished speaking he turned from Don Philip with a look of insolent assurance to Don Diego, who in his turn had started from his seat, and stood with nervous fingers grasping the hilt of his rapier. As the nobleman met the sinister eyes, full of an impertinent challenge, he made a hasty step forward with the haughty exclamation:

"And who are you pray, sir, who dare ask for the hand of one who is promised to Don Montoro de Diego? Know you, sir, that the daughter of Don Philip is my affianced bride?"

"I have heard something of the sort," was the reply, in a tone of indescribable cool insolence. "Yes; I have already learnt that you have had eyesight good enough to discover the fairest beauty in Saragossa. But you had better leave her to me, noble Señor. She will be—" and the speaker paused a moment to give greater emphasis to his next slowly-uttered words—"she will be safer with me than with you—and her father also." And with a parting look and nod, so full of latent knowledge and cruel determination that Don Diego's blood seemed to freeze in his veins as he encountered them, the new aspirant for the beautiful young heiress took his leave.

As the great iron-bound outer door clanged to, behind him, the head of the old man sank forward on his breast with a groan. His daughter re-entered the apartment at the moment, and the smile which had begun to dawn on her countenance at the departure of the unwelcome guest gave way to a cry of dismay. Flying across the floor she threw herself on the ground beside her father with a pitiful little cry.

"Oh! my father, are you ill?—What ails you, my father?"

For some seconds the old man's trembling hand tenderly caressing the soft hair was the only answer. At last he asked with a choked voice:

"My daughter—couldst thou be content to wed yon Italian?"

The words had scarcely passed his lips when the girl sprang to her feet, gazing with wild eyes at her questioner.

"Kill me, my father, but give me not to yon awful, hateful man. Besides—" and with a look of agonized entreaty she turned towards Don Diego—"besides, am I not already given by you to another?"

"And to another who has both the will and the power to claim the fulfilment of the promise," exclaimed Montoro de Diego, coming forward, and clasping the girl's hand in his with an air of iron resolution.

Once again there was a heavy silence in the darkening chamber, and when it was broken the hearers felt scarcely less oppressed by the sound, although the words themselves seemed to speak of happiness.

"My son," said the old man in low and urgent tones, "it is true, I have given you my child—my only one. Fetch the good old priest Bartolo now, at once, and secretly, and let him within this hour make my gift to you secure."

A faint protest against this sudden, unexpected haste was made by the young bride, but Don Diego needed no second bidding to the adoption of a course he considered to be dictated as much by prudence as affection. Two hours later Montoro de Diego wended his way to his own palace with his young wife, Rachel Diego, by his side.

"Do not weep so, my Rachel," entreated the young nobleman as he led his bride into her new home.

But the tears of the agitated girl flowed as bitterly as ever as she moaned, "My father—oh! my father! If but my father had come with us!"

"He has promised to take up his abode with us, if possible, within the next few weeks, my Rachel," returned Montoro de Diego, in the vain endeavour to give her comfort. But she dwelt upon the words, "if possible," rather than upon the promise. She guessed but too well the fears which had dismissed her thus summarily from her father's home. She had heard but too much of the hideous tragedies of the past two months, and her husband himself was too oppressed with forebodings to give her consolation in such a tone of confidence as should secure her belief.

Don Philip had offered his life for his daughter's happiness, and his daughter well-nigh divined the fact.

Had the Christianized Jew consented to give his daughter, and his daughters princely fortune, to the vile informer of the Inquisition, he would have escaped harm or persecution, at any rate for that season. But he counted the cost, and taking his life into his hand, for the sake of his child's happiness, he committed her henceforth to the loving charge of the noble-hearted Don Diego. The fulfilment of the sacrifice was not long delayed.

The days went by, and the weeks—one—two—three. The second day of the fourth week was drawing to its close, since the group of Spanish noblemen had muttered their passionate resolves to rid their Aragon of Arbues de Epila. They had not been idle since then. Time had not quenched their burning indignation, but rather fanned it fiercer as they gathered fresh adherents, and gold, that ever needful aid in all enterprises. But the one adherent Don Alonso and Don Miguel most longed for still held aloof.

The lengthening shadows of that day belonged also, as the reader knows, to the second day of the fourth week since Don Diego's marriage, and his new ties made him but increasingly anxious to keep in the most careful path of rectitude, for the sake of expediency now as much as honour.

The name of Montoro de Diego was hitherto so unblemished, his rank was so important, that he might well believe himself a safe protector for his young bride, and for his new father-in-law, even though it was not wholly unmixed, pure Spanish blood that flowed in their veins. And he was firm in his refusal to have any part in schemes of danger. His wife was safe, hidden up in the recesses of his palace; and his father-in-law, he trusted, had secured safety in flight.

On the day succeeding that on which Don Philip had refused to purchase peace at the price of his daughter's welfare, Rachel Diego had received a few hurried lines of farewell from him, saying that he was going into exile until safer times for Saragossa, and bidding her be of good cheer, as all immediately concerning themselves now promised to go well.

Under these circumstances Don Diego might be pardoned, perhaps, if for a time he forgot the miseries surrounding him—forgot his hopes to infuse a bolder, nobler spirit of upright resistance to evil, into his comrades, and rested content with his own happiness.

But there came a dark awakening.

The day had been one of dazzling heat; and as the sun's rays grew more and more slanting, and the shadows longer, Don Diego bid his gentle young wife a short adieu, and sauntered forth to draw, if possible, a freer breath out-of-doors than was possible within.

He had been more impatient in seeking the evening breeze than most of his fellow-citizens, for the streets were still almost deserted. There was but one pedestrian besides himself in sight, and Montoro de Diego was well content to note that that one was a stranger, for he was in no mood just then for parrying fresh solicitations from his friends by signs, and half-uttered words, to join their secret counsels. He was sufficiently annoyed when he perceived at the lapse of a few seconds that even the stranger was evidently bent on accosting him. Determined not to have his meditations interrupted he turned short round, and began to retrace his way towards his own abode.

But not so was he to secure isolation. The rapid pitpat of steps behind him quickly proved that the stranger was as desirous of a meeting as he was wishful to avoid it; and scarcely had the Spanish nobleman had time to entertain thoughts of mingled wonder and annoyance, when he shrank angrily from a tap on his arm, and faced round to see what manner of individual it might be who had dared such a familiarity with one of the grandees of Aragon. The explanation was sudden and complete.

A low, mocking laugh greeted the involuntary widening of his eyes. Don Diego stood face to face with the man he had seen but once before; but that was on an occasion never to be forgotten, for it was the evening of his marriage, and the man before him was the one who had dared try to deprive him of his bride. For that he bore him no love, nor for the hinted threats then uttered; but now his blood curdled with instinctive horror as he gazed at the sinister, cruel face mocking his with an expression on it of such cool insolence.

Don Diego's most eager impulse was to dash his companion to the ground and leave him; but for the first time in his life fear had gained possession of him. Fear, not for himself, but for those whom he held more precious.

"Why do you stay me? What would you with me?" he questioned at last, in tones that vainly strove for their customary accent of haughtiness. The cynical triumph of the Italian grew more visible.

"Meseems, my Señor," he replied with a sneer; "meseems from your countenance, and your new-found humility of voice, that your heart must have prophesied to you that matter anent which I have stayed you, that counsel that I would, for our mutual advantage, hold with you. It is of Don Philip and his daughter Rachel that I wish to speak with you."

Montoro de Diego inclined his head in silent token of attention, and the foreigner continued in slow, smooth speech:

"Doubtless, my Señor, you remember that in your presence, some few weeks ago, I made proposals of marriage for the fair, rich daughter of Don Philip. The night of the day on which I made these proposals the birds flew from me, and from my little hints in case of contumacy, out of Saragossa. That was a foolish step to take, my Señor, was it not?"

He paused for an answer, and the dry lips of Don Diego replied stiffly: "Don Philip asked me not for counsel in his actions, neither did I give it."

"Ah!" resumed the Italian with a second sneer, "that may perchance be a true statement, Don Diego; but I shall be better inclined to accept it worthily, when you shall now reverse your professed behaviour, and accept the post of adviser to the obstinate heretic."

"I cannot," was the hasty exclamation. "Don Philip is no heretic, but a faithful son of the Church, and I have no clue to his retreat."

"Then I can give you one," was the low-spoken answer. "Don Philip has been tracked, and brought back. But his daughter is not with him. He refuses to confess her hiding-place, although he is now in the dungeons of the Holy Inquisition, and can purchase freedom by the information."

"Cruel, black-hearted villain!" exclaimed Don Diego, shocked and infuriated at length beyond all prudence; "know this, that Rachel, daughter of Don Philip, is now my bride. And know this yet further, that the nobles of Aragon are not yet so ground beneath the feet of a new dominion that they cannot protect their wives, and those belonging to them, from the perjured baseness of dastards who would destroy them."

Once more the young nobleman turned to quit his abhorred companion, but once more that hated touch fell upon his arm, and the Italian again confronted him with a face literally livid with malice as he hissed out:

"The nobles of Aragon are doubtless all-powerful, my Señor, and yet for your news of your bride I will give you news of her father. Ere this hour to-morrow the burnt ashes of his body will have been scattered to the four winds of heaven. Take that news back to your bride to win her welcome with."

Don Diego was alone. Whether he had been leaning against the walls of that heavy portico five seconds, five minutes, or five hours, he could scarcely tell when he became conscious of his own painful reiteration of the words, "Ere this hour to-morrow—ere this hour to-morrow."

"What is the matter, Montoro? rouse yourself. What about this hour to-morrow?" asked the voice of Don Alonso at his elbow. And Montoro shudderingly raised himself from the wall, looked with dazed eyes at his friend, and repeated:

"Ere this hour to-morrow. Will she know?"

"Will who know?" again questioned Don Alonso, as he passed his arm through his friend's and drew him on, for the street was no longer empty. Doors were opening on all sides, and the people pouring forth to the various entertainments of the evening. Some curious glances had already been cast at Don Diego, as he leant there stupefied with horror and anguish for his wife's threatened misery.

In the early part of the evening the Italian tool of the Inquisition had sought Don Diego. When evening had given way to night, Don Diego sought the Italian, and as a suppliant.

"It ill suits an Aragonese to sue to the villain of a foreigner," said the wretch, with malicious sarcasm. "It makes me marvel, my Señor, that you should deign thus to condescend."

"I marvel also," murmured the Spaniard, rather to himself than to his unworthy companion. "When the sword of the Moor was at my throat I disdained to sue for mercy; when I lay spurned by the pirate's foot I felt no fear; but now—ay now, if you will—I will give you the power to boast that one of the greatest of the nobles of Aragon has knelt at your feet to sue for a favour at your hands."

"And you will not deny the humiliating fact if I should publish it?" demanded the Italian, with a half air of yielding, and Montoro Diego, with a light of hope springing into his face, exclaimed:

"No, no. I will myself declare the deed, if for its performance you will obtain me the life and freedom of Don Philip."

Like a drowning man stretching forth to a straw, Montoro had snatched at a false hope. With that low, mocking laugh that issued freely enough from his thin, cruel lips, the Italian said slowly:

"Ah! your wish is very great, my Señor, I see that—truly very great to save a heart-ache to your bride. But—see you—you have hindered Jerome Tivoli of his desire, and now it is his turn, the turn of the 'base, black-hearted villain,' Jerome. And he takes your desire into his ears, he tastes it on his palate, it is sweet to him, sweetened with the thought of revenge, and then—he spurns it—spits it forth from him—thus!"

The Aragonese tore his rapier from its sheath, and darted forward, his fierce southern blood aflame with fury at the insult. But his companion stood there coolly with folded arms, content to hiss between his teeth:

"We are not unwatched, my Señor. I have plenty to avenge me if you think Doña Rachel will be gratified to lose husband now as well as father."

The mention of his wife was opportune. It restored Don Diego to his self-control. With a mighty effort mastering his pride, he collected his thoughts for one final attempt on behalf of the good old man doomed so tyrannically to an awful death.

Before seeking this second interview with the foreigner Montoro de Diego had schooled himself to bear everything for the sake of his one great object, and although for a moment he had allowed self to rise uppermost, he now once more crushed it down, and returned to the attitude of the humble suppliant.

He did not indeed repeat the offer, so insultingly rejected, to kneel to the informer, but he appealed earnestly to more sordid instincts. The man had alluded to Don Philip's daughter as rich as well as beautiful, and he now offered him the heiress's wealth as compensation for the loss of the heiress herself.

As he spoke a sudden gleam of satisfaction shot into the Italian's eyes, and a second time a hope, far greater than the first, rose in the petitioner's heart; but yet again it was dashed to the ground. Just as he was prepared to hear that his terms were agreed upon, his companion's countenance underwent a sudden change. A shadow had just fallen across the floor, and with a heavy scowl replacing the expression of greed he bent forward with the hasty mutter:

"Fool of a Spaniard, has that idiot tongue of thine but one tone, that thou must needs screech thy offers, like a parrot from the Indies, into all ears that choose to listen?" Then aloud, as though in continuation of a widely-different theme: "And so, as I tell thee, thy offers go for nought, for the wealth will of right flow into the coffers of the Sacred Office when the accursed Jew shall have suffered in the flesh to save his soul. And now," insolently, "I have no more time to listen to thy prating, and so go."

Whether he went of his free will, or was turned out, Montoro de Diego never clearly remembered, but on finding himself beneath the starry sky, he dashed off to the palace of the dread Arbues himself. Well-nigh frantic with despair, as he thought of the torments that the aged prisoner was even then all too probably undergoing, he forced admittance, late though the hour was, to the presence of the stern ecclesiastic, who was prudently surrounded by guards even in the privacy of his own supper-room. Nothing short of the great influence of Don Diego's high rank would have enabled him to penetrate so far, but even that did not protect him from the Inquisitor's rebuke, nor gain him a favourable hearing for his cause.

"It is our blessed office," said the bigoted supporter of Rome's worst errors, "to purge the Church, to—"

"If Don Philip die, others will die with him," sharply interrupted the young Spaniard, with fierce significance, and he left the Inquisitor's palace as abruptly as he had entered it, half determined, in that bitter hour, to throw in his lot with the conspirators. If there were none to listen to reason, none to obey the dictates of justice or mercy, why should he maintain alone his integrity?

So passion and despair tried to argue against his conscience, as he retraced his steps to his own home and the waiting Rachel. But the events of that night were not yet over.

CHAPTER IV
THINKING OF EXILE

As Montoro de Diego entered the deep portico of his palace entrance, he stumbled against some obstruction in the way. He stooped, and found there was a man dead, or in a deep swoon, lying at his feet.

Before he could ascertain more, or summon his servants, a third person stepped out of the obscurity and muttered rapidly:

"Remember, the gold is to be mine. It is not my fault that he has thus suffered before release."

Then the whisperer of those significant words was gone, and the young man was alone with the prostrate form of his father-in-law. Relinquishing his intention to call for aid, he lifted the inanimate body in his own strong arms, and bore his burden into a small inner apartment, reserved for his own devotion to such learned studies as were then flourishing in Aragon under the fostering care of royal encouragement. Something of medicine and surgery he had also acquired, but he soon discovered with bitter sorrow that in the present case his skill was useless. The old man was dying. Every limb had been dislocated on the rack.

"They tortured me to try to extort the secret of my child's hiding-place," murmured the old man quietly. "But thanks be to the Lord, He gave me strength. This day I shall be with Him. They have but hastened my coming home, my children."

And so, with forgiveness and love in his heart, and the light of coming glory on his face, this rescued victim of the Inquisition died in his daughter's arms, just as the sun's first golden rays were brightening the streets of Saragossa. Those rays that were glowing on the walls of the dungeons, within which slept, for the last time on earth, those innocent ones who were that day to be burnt in one of the awful Autos da Fé; those rays that were glowing on the walls and windows of the palace where Arbues the Inquisitor still slumbered.

"For so He maketh His sun to shine on the evil and the good."

The morning was still young when Don Diego received two visitors. The first, Jerome Tivoli, was quickly dismissed with the curt but satisfying speech:

"A noble of Aragon ever keeps his word. The miserable treasure you crave is yours."

His interview with Don Alonso was far longer.

"Surely now you must join us," urged that fiery spirit with impatient indignation. "You cannot refuse to aid in avenging the wrongs of your father-in-law."

"His mode," murmured the other, "of avenging his own wrongs, was to pray for light for his murderers."

But Don Alonso was marching with hasty strides up and down the apartment, and did not hear the words. His own conscience was ill at ease, as the head of conspirators having assassination for their object, and he had an unacknowledged feeling that he would be more comfortable in his mind if the upright Montoro would throw in his lot with them. But Don Diego was firm in his refusal. That recent death-bed scene had given him back his faith in the wisdom and love of God, in spite of the darkness now around him, and he ended the discussion at last, by saying:

"No, Alonso, I will keep my honour whatever else I may be forced to lose. But, although I will not join you, I will tell you whom I would join, were my Rachel a man, or, being a woman, had she but been inured to hardships as a mountain peasant. I would suffer exile thankfully, so embittered to me has my native land become."

"Embittered indeed to us all," almost groaned the other, adding, "But whom then is it you would join in your exile? Any of our friends, or one I know not?"

"One you know not, nor I either, personally," was the reply; "but one whom we both know well by reputation. That Christopher Colon, the Genoese, who, for the past six months almost, has been wearying our Queen Isabella of Castile to provide him means to find some strange new world; some vision of wonder that has risen in his imagination, brilliant with lands of gold and pearl, and perfumed with sweeter spices than the Indies."

Don Alonso uttered a short laugh of contempt.

"Ah, ha! And you mean to tell me that you would be willing to throw in your lot with that beggarly, visionary adventurer! Our King Ferdinand knows better than to waste his maravedis on such moon-struck projects, or to let his consort do so either."

"And yet," said Montoro, somewhat doubtfully, "and yet, although of course new worlds are foolishness to dream of, some islands might perchance fall to our share, if we adventured somewhat to find them, as such good and profitable prizes have been falling, during the past fifty years, pretty plentifully, to our clever neighbours, the Portuguese."

"Ay, and even they won't listen to this Genoese, you may recollect. Besides, the Pope has given everything in the seas and on it, I have heard, to those lucky neighbours of ours, so of what use for Spaniards to jeopardize lives and treasure to benefit the Portuguese?"

"Nay," answered Don Diego, "the Pope's grant to them is only for the countries from Cape Horn to India. Why should not we obtain a grant for lands in the other hemisphere?"

And so the poor young nobleman tried to stifle grief and apprehension in dreams of other lands, of whose discovery he would not live to hear, although his son would one day help others to found new homes on their far-off soil.

CHAPTER V
DEATH FOR ARBUES DE EPILA

The days went by; the days of that year, 1485: and still the hideous spectacles of the Auto da Fé continued to be witnessed with shame and anguish by the inhabitants of Saragossa. Still the cry of the tortured victims ascended up to heaven, and still Arbues de Epila lived in his case of mail.

Those were busy, agitating days for Spain. The war with Granada was still in progress. King Ferdinand was much exercised in mind with various jealousies connected with French affairs, and, more than all important for future ages, the Queen's confessor, Ferdinand di Talavera, together with a council of self-sufficient pedants and philosophers, was taking into consideration that request of the Genoese, Christopher Colon, or, as we call him, Columbus, to be provided with such an equipment of ships, men, and necessary stores, as should enable him to find and found countries hitherto unheard of, and only thought of, most people declared, by crack-brained dreamers.

"Besides," finally decided Talavera and his sage council, with pompous absurdity; "besides, if there were nothing else against this scheme, such as the convex figure of the globe, for instance, which, of course, would prevent vessels ever getting back again, up the side of the world, once they got down, there was the impudence of the suggestion. It was presumptuous in any person to pretend that he alone possessed knowledge superior to all the rest of the world united."

And such impertinent presumption was certainly not to be encouraged in an "obscure Genoese pilot." And so, for that while, after weary waiting, and the weary hope deferred that maketh the heart sick, Columbus and his splendid plans were dismissed. But this result was not arrived at until four years after the months with which we are, for the minute, more immediately concerned; and so to return to the thread of our narrative, and to add yet further—and still the men of Saragossa gathered into secret bands, discussing rather by tokens, than by words, the unspeakable cruelties that were being committed in their midst, and the proposed destruction of their arch-instigator, Arbues de Epila.

All was ripe at length for the fulfilment of the fatal plot; fatal, alas, not only to the Inquisitor, but to his murderers also, and to many and many another wholly innocent of the crime.

All day long Don Alonso, Don Miguel, Don James of Navarre, with the rest of the conspirators, many of them with the noblest blood of Aragon flowing in their veins, watched with a fierce, hungry eagerness for the moment in which to strike the blow. The hours wore on, the evening came. In low-breathed murmurs one and another rekindled their own fury, or revived the flagging courage of a companion, by recalling the generosity of character, the blameless life, of some friend or relative snatched out of life by this barbarous persecution.

Night fell over the city of Saragossa, and gradually the conspirators stealthily, silently drew round about the walls of the cathedral. It was approaching midnight. The fierce persecutor of his fellow-men was on his knees before the great altar of the cathedral, on his knees before Him who has said, "I will have mercy, and not sacrifice."

Arbues knelt there in the flood of brightness from the lighted altar, and his enemies gathered up around him in the gloomy shadows of the surrounding darkness. Suddenly there was a muffled shout—a cry. He raised his head;—too late,—escape was impossible. Already the arm and hand were streaming with blood that had signed so many warrants for the torture and death of others. Then came the fatal blow.

Arbues knelt there in a flood of brightness from the lighted altar. Suddenly there was a muffled shout—a cry. He raised his head;—too late,—escape was impossible.

A dagger shone, gleaming red with life-blood, in the light, from the back of the victim's neck, in the flesh of which its point was firmly embedded.

Who gave that final thrust none knew but the giver. Only Don Miguel, who stood by in the fierce crush and *melée*, heard the words hissed out as the deadly weapon was darted forth:

"So dies the fiend, Arbues de Epila!"

And he, too, cast a hasty glance beside him, as Montoro de Diego had done when those words were uttered behind his ear in the Auto da Fé crowd some weeks ago.

But Montoro de Diego had found no one at his elbow but an innocent, wide-eyed child; and Don Miguel only found a crowd of terrified, cringing priests, who with pallid faces and trembling limbs bore off the dying superior to his own apartments, where he lingered two days, blindly giving thanks to God that he had been accepted as a martyr in His cause!

"The enemy of our liberty, our honour, our security is dead," muttered Don Alonso in fierce triumph to Montoro de Diego, as he sought temporary shelter from the dangers of pursuit in his friend's palace. But Don Diego shook his head with prophetic sadness as he answered:

"May the Holy Virgin grant that you have not called down worse evils upon our unhappy city!"

All too soon his fears were realized. The Church was offended, and the sovereigns, at the assassination of the great Inquisitor, and terrible was the vengeance wreaked far and wide upon all who had been, or were supposed to have been, implicated in the impious deed. Hundreds upon hundreds of people died, by torture, in the dungeons, at the stake, by persecutions innumerable, and starvation; and the whole province of Aragon was still further cruelly humiliated in the persons of its nobles, who were condemned in crowds to do penance in the Autos da Fé.

Don Alonso and Don Miguel were hanged instead of burned, not in mercy, but in sign of greater infamy, and that they might feel themselves ground to the very dust by the intense degradation of their punishment. And Don Diego did not escape the general ruin of his friends.

The heat of the search for victims had somewhat abated, when the covetous desires of one of the members of the Inquisition turned upon the possessions of the wealthy nobleman.

A path to the coveted riches was soon found. Montoro de Diego's words were suddenly remembered that he uttered on the night of Don Philip's death—"If Don Philip die others will die with him." On these words he was condemned, first to lingering months in a loathsome dungeon, then to death; and his young wife was driven forth from the gates of Saragossa in widowed penury and despair. The second Montoro de Diego was born a beggar and fatherless, but he had the brave, upright spirit of his father in him for his portion; and with his fortunes our tale is, for the future, concerned.

CHAPTER VI
SANCHO'S BROKEN VICTUALS

Poverty and pride do not go well in company, and so a Spanish lad of some fourteen or fifteen years of age had begun to learn. But the lesson was hard, and one badly learnt, when one evening some broken victuals were flung to him as they might have been to a famished dog, and accompanied by the exclamation:

"There, starveling, be not squeamish, but feed those lean cheeks of thine, and give me thanks for thy supper."

"I'll give thee that for thy base-born impudence," was the passionate retort, as the youth seized the package of broken meats and was about to use it as a missile to hurl at the donor's head.

But as the muscular young arm was raised it was suddenly grasped from behind, and a sweet, soft voice said hurriedly:

"My son, bethink you. For those of noble blood to be street-brawlers brings as great disgrace as beggary. You have never yet so far shamed me, or forgotten the due restraints of your rank."

As the slight, pale woman spoke the lad's clutched fingers loosened their hold of the parcel; it dropped back into the dusty gutter; and with burning cheeks he suffered himself to be led away from the neighbourhood of the half-angry, half-contemptuous man whose well-intentioned gift had been so spurned. When the mother and son had disappeared the man turned, with a short laugh, from watching them, and addressed himself to a neighbour.

"Easy to see who they are. Holy Mother Church has had something to say to their belongings in the past, I wager. But noble though they may be still, and rich though they may have been once, they are clearly starving now, and had better accept good food when they can get it."

And in this declaration the worthy Sancho was certainly most right, although the bread of charity, even when most delicately bestowed, tasted bitter in those hungry mouths; for the man was further right in his belief that mother and son were of high birth, and the mother had also been reared in luxury.

However, the little incident over, with the alms-giver's comment upon it, the worthy burgess of the small town of El Cuevo, upon the very borders of Aragon, turned his thoughts to matters of greater interest and importance.

"What thinkest thou, friend Pedro, of the new expedition preparing to set out for yon troublesome new-found island of Hispaniola—has it thy approval?"

The friend Pedro thus addressed was busily engaged in inspecting various samples of foreign spices. He now raised a solemn pair of eyes from his aromatic treasures as he replied:

"Troublesome it may be to those who govern it; but so long as my son doth continue to send me home a sufficiency of these marketable commodities, it is not he nor I that shall grumble at its finding."

The burly Sancho laughed.

"Ay, ay, neighbour, I know thee of old. A well-lined pocket thou ever holdest good recompense for a few thwacks. Would that the grand old Admiral Columbus could find comfort for ingratitude and sorrows with such ease!"

"But so he might do if he would but try," was the shrewd answer. "You see our brave Genoese hath ever been more needful for empty-handed honour and glory, than for gathering together good store of worldly spoil, to fall back upon when men should begrudge him the shadow-prizes he desired. Now it seemeth that he may chance to have neither."

"Well, well, I know not," continued Sancho. "The queen hath ever a good will to the great man. And although he is not to be commissioned to go himself to the punishment of that Jack-in-office Bobadilla, men say that the Commendador of Lares, Don Nicolas de Ovando, who is now preparing to set out thither, hath all the virtues under the sun. Wise and prudent and abstemious, and of a winning manner."

"Umph!" grunted the spice-dealer. "Don Ovando had needs be a second St. Paul if he is to win justice and mercy for the poor natives out yonder, at the hands of the off-scouring of our streets; and that is what our gentle-hearted queen hath most at heart."

Master Sancho nodded his head gravely.

"Ah, friend Pedro, I say not but you are right. And that minds me: if my head were not so thick, I might have bethought me to advise yon lad, with the great eyes and the short temper, to seek fortune, like many another of his peers, in those far-off lands across the ocean. I daresay he would have accepted that advice with a better grace than he did my scraps."

His neighbour looked up this time more fully than he had yet done, and let his hands rest for a few moments idle on the samples with which he had been so occupied, as he exclaimed with genuine astonishment:

"Why, friend Sancho, verily it seems to me that you have taken some queer true interest in yon ragged piece of impudence. I have noted you more than once, ay, than twice, watch him of an evening as he went by till out of sight. And now, when he would have flung your kindness back at you, still talking of him, forsooth. Nay then, had he so treated me he would have been roundly cuffed, I tell thee; and so an end."

Broad-shouldered, easy-going Sancho laughed and gave a shrug.

"I am not fond of being ready with my fists, friend Pedro; my hands are large, and might hap to be over heavy; besides, I have a broken thumb. But you judge rightly; I have taken a fancy to that set-up, handsome-faced young beggar. And I have watched him, not only of an evening past these doors, but at other hours in the town; and although he rejects help for himself, many a time have I seen him give it to those weaker or more helpless than himself."

Meantime, while he was being thus discussed, that same "set-up, handsome-faced young beggar" was remonstrating with his mother against her oft-reiterated lectures to him on humility, and on a studied avoidance of everything that should draw observation upon them.

"I will not slink into corners like a thief, nor hide myself in holes like a rat," he exclaimed at last, with haughty indignation. "Hast thou not told me thyself, my mother, that I am an Aragonese?"

But Rachel Diego replied with a lip that trembled while it curled:

"In truth art thou, my son, a child of a barren land. The heir of territories so stricken from the Maker's hand with poverty, that perchance we waste life's breath in lamenting that treasures so miserable should be wrested from us."

But the mother's new line of argument, to soothe her son's dangerous agitation, was fruitless as the other. His eyes flashed still more brilliantly with his burning indignation, as he retorted again:

"You say right, my mother. The land of Aragon is so poor and barren, that perchance her sons and daughters might all long since have forsaken their churlish, niggard-handed mother, and finally renounced her, but that she gives them liberty. Even in our oath of allegiance we tender no slaves' submission to oppression."

The widowed mother turned her sad eyes upon her proud-spirited boy.

"My son, no oath of allegiance has as yet been called for from thy lips."

The flush deepened on the young Spaniard's face. He pressed his teeth into the crimson lower lip for some seconds to strangle back a groan that sought escape from his own over-burdened heart. He had heard of the tragedies of those months before his birth.

"No," he muttered at length bitterly. "No. It is true. I am esteemed too contemptible to have even vows wrung from me that are counted worthless. But the oath that my father spoke is registered in my heart; the oath due from us, whose proud heritage it is to call ourselves the nobles of Aragon. And such is the oath that I, in my turn, tender to my sovereign, Ferdinand of Aragon and Castile."

The lad paused a moment, and then, with folded arms, and in low, firm tones, repeated the proud words of the Aragonese oath of allegiance.

"We, who are each of us as good, and who are altogether more powerful than you, promise obedience to your government if you maintain our rights and liberties, but if not, not."

As he spoke Rachel Diego dropped her face into her hands, and as he ended she murmured in stifled tones:

"Your father pronounced that haughty vow, and what availed the boast?"

What indeed! The young Montoro gazed for a moment at his wan mother, at the bare room, and then, with all his haughtiness lost in a flood of sudden despair, he darted from the miserable apartment to wrestle with his agitation in the wild darkness of a stormy night.

That his heart should be torn with bitterness and grief was little wonder, for all too well he knew how it came to pass that his mother was fatherless and a widow, and how he himself had been robbed of his parent and his patrimony. Something of the dismal tale of Don Philip's tortured death, and of the base villain who had grasped at his daughter's fortune, had been told the boy from time to time by his mother. Something, also, of the avarice and barbarity that had wrested a few despairing words to the destruction of his own father, the noble Don Montoro de Diego.

But much fuller details of those dismal days of 1485 had been given to the disinherited son of a blameless father by the old priest Bartolo, who had secretly aided the outcast young widow and her infant when they were first driven from their home, and who had continued to give them all the assistance in his power until his death, some months ago; in that very month of December, in fact, of 1500, when the hearts of so many in Spain, and elsewhere, throbbed with indignation at the news that a vessel had arrived in the port of Cadiz with the great discoverer on board, in chains like a common malefactor.

While the young Montoro was mourning over the dying priest, however, he little heeded the gossip going on around him about one who, during the remaining five years of a well-worn life, was to have a far greater influence on the orphan lad's career than ever the good old priest would have had the power to exercise.

But the days of December passed on. The old priest was buried. Columbus was delivered from his chains by hasty order of the king and queen, and was further invited in flattering terms of kindness to join the royal Court at Granada; a thousand ducats to defray expenses, and a handsome retinue as escort on the journey, being sent in testimony that the friendliness of the invitation was sincere. And so the saddened heart of the glorious old Admiral was once more warmed with half-fallacious hope. Not so with poor Rachel Diego and her son.

Life had been hard enough while Father Bartolo lived, but after his death the struggle for existence became well-nigh desperate; and by the time the months had come round to this following December of 1501, more people, in the obscure little town of El Cuevo, than the worthy burgess Sancho, had come to the conclusion that the unknown young widow and her handsome son were dying of starvation.

But death was evidently preferable, in the minds of the helpless couple, to degradation. Work they could not obtain, and charity they would not accept.

"And small blame to them after all," muttered Master Sancho to himself, a few days after his vain effort to bestow a supper on the objects of his interest. "I don't believe that I, either, should relish the taste of other men's leavings. Thanks be to the virgin that I have never had to eat them. But yet—to starve? Umph! I know not whether I should like the flavour of starvation any better."

And he folded his arms across his portly person with a slightly mocking laugh of self-consciousness.

This short soliloquy had been occasioned by the sight of young Montoro Diego passing the end of the street. His reappearance now, in the street itself, with a large loaf of bread in his arms, brought the soliloquy to a sudden stop; and Sancho left his post of observation in his own doorway, and hurried as fast as his weighty figure would allow to the pedestrian, finding no very great difficulty in barring the lad's further progress along the narrow roadway with his broad form. Montoro threw back his head impatiently.

"What now?" he demanded, with flushed cheeks. "Have you some more dog's meat that you wish to be rid of?"

The burgess laughed.

"Verily, my son, there is a bold spirit hidden under those rags of thine. But a truce to laughter; for verily I feel angered with you now, and I have a right?"

"Because I would none of your mean gifts?" asked Montoro hotly.

"Nay, indeed; that was your affair. But I am angry, and have a right to be, that you should accept aid from others which you will not have from me."

"Accept aid!" repeated the lad wonderingly. "Of what are you speaking? What aid have we received since the only friend died of whom we would accept it?"

But even as he spoke he caught the eyes of his companion fixed upon the loaf by way of significant answer, and he added shortly:

"This I have earned. It is no gift."

Then slipping under his questioner's arm he thought to have escaped; but Master Sancho caught him by the shoulder and held him fast.

"Look here, my son, by your air and looks I judge you to have been born to a rank far above my own and so if it be your pleasure I will speak to you with uncovered head by way of deference. But speak to you I will, for I have taken a fancy to you; and if you are not as set against work as against alms I may help you."

There was a spasmodic twitch of the shoulder at those last words; and the boy's face was so turned away that his captor could not read it. But after a moment's silence the worthy-hearted man continued, with a different accent of somewhat impatient anger:

"Hark ye, lad, ye may be as indifferent about thyself as it may please thee; but I cry shame on thee to refuse aught that may provide needful nourishment for that sweet and gentle mother of thine. To nourish thy false pride—ay, I will even call it by a juster name, thy base pride—thy mother is offering herself a sacrifice."

There was a gulping sound in the boy's throat, and then with a choking gasp he muttered:

"She could not, she would not, live on charity."

"No," instantly agreed the burgess of El Cuevo; "that I begin to believe. But she could and would live on the honest earnings of your hands. And be you noble or no, you'll find ne'er a priest in Spain to dare tell you that it is more honourable to let a mother starve than to work for her."

For the first time Montoro Diego let his eyes fairly rest on his mentor's face. There was something so genuinely true in the ring of the voice that the boy's anger and indignation dwindled away he scarce knew how, and gave place to a growing trust. With an effort he crushed down his emotion as he replied in low tones:

"I have no coward scruples against work, believe me. But I am noble, as you say. The son of one who died wrongfully for the death of Arbues de Epila. It was at the peril of their lives that any helped my mother, even with work, at the time that my father was thus barbarously mur—"

Burgess Sancho sharply clapped his hand over the boy's mouth, muttering with half-angry solicitude:

"Knowest thou not, my son, that a still tongue is wisdom? Keep thy information of the past for those who ask for it, and to those who do so give it not. You, a starving boy in the streets of El Cuevo, I can help. You may have dropped from the clouds for aught I know. Dost thou not comprehend me?"

Montoro's dark eyes gleamed with a flitting smile. The Aragonese of those days were not wanting in intelligence. But at the same time his native pride, and even his nobility of character, forbade him to accept aught at the expense of his identity, and so he quickly let his new friend understand.

"I have no inheritance but my father's name and my father's unsullied memory," he declared firmly; "and I will bear that openly. I have earned this loaf to-day, and more, by grinding colours for the great painter staying yonder; but first I told him who I was."

"More foolish you," remarked Master Sancho, with a shrug. "But what said he to thy news?"

"Even as thou—that I had more truth than wit. But he gave me work all the same, for he said that he need have no fear. The king could replace heretic nobles with other nobles, but he could not replace a painter, and so he would be wise enough to keep the one he had."

"Ay, then," agreed Master Sancho, "the Señor is right; and if I were you I would turn painter also, for the royal ordinance of last September did not name that amongst the many things you may not be."

"No," returned Montoro with a bitter laugh; "that last ordinance of persecution only excludes me from such employments as would be possible, not from those needing gifts vouchsafed only to the few. But I must say adios, for my mother will already have feared some mischance has come to me."

"To our next meeting, then," said the worthy burgess. "And meantime I will cudgel my brains till I find some means to help you, for all you are so self-willed and impracticable, my son."

The friendly look and the confident nod that accompanied these gruffly good-humoured words were full of such pleasant encouragement that Montoro Diego flew home with a heart suddenly grown as light as though he had already regained the power to use the title of 'Don' before his name, and had already won back the heritage of his ancestors.

We say "already," for of course Montoro, like all brave-spirited, properly-constituted individuals, was perfectly convinced, even in the lowest stage of rags and hunger, that the day would most positively come when he should re-enter his fathers home as the publicly-acknowledged Don Montoro de Diego. Meantime there was good bread for his supper that night, and for his mother, together with a handful of roasted chestnuts and a bottle of thin wine, grateful in that warm climate from its very sourness.

"And to-morrow," he said cheerfully, "the great painter says, my mother, that I may work in his studio again. And, if only you would go with me, he would not again sigh that there were none beautiful and tender-faced enough in the land to sit to him for the Holy Mother."

Rachel Diego said hastily, "Hush, my son," and shook her head at him; but at the same time she smiled, and a delicate flush tinted the pale cheeks, for her boy's loving praises were so sweet in her ears that they turned the humble supper into a feast.

The mother and son were very happy together that night; but had those two who so greatly loved each other known that even then schemes were being revolved in a shrewd and busy brain that would result, within a few short months, in placing a wide and storm-tossed ocean between them, one at least of the couple would have found the bread given to her turned to ashes in her mouth, and would have changed her smiles to weeping.

Happily for them, however, no prevision marred the rare joyousness of those few hours, nor disturbed the sleep that followed, gladdened with bright dreams.

CHAPTER VII
CONSULTING A SWEET TOOTH

"Friend Pedro!"

"Ay, what now?"

And the spice-dealer looked up from a small pile of curiosities, lying on a tray on his knees, with a more than half-betrayed idea that nothing his neighbour had to say could be so important, as calculating how much he might hope to make by the sale of those uncommon wares.

But this belief was somewhat lessened when his eyes rested on his friend's countenance. "Hey, then!" he ejaculated; "our painter yonder saith that thou art never a true Spaniard, for thy face is too round, but were he to see thee now he would surely tell a different tale."

"It is but lengthened by the height of my considering-cap," was the answer, with a laugh that speedily restored his visage to its usual good-humoured breadth.

Master Pedro appeared greatly relieved by the change. To say truth, in that land of solemn faces and staid deportments, a cheerful neighbour was as refreshing as a sunlit breeze in the early days of spring; and the spice-dealer, although the solemnest of the solemn himself, duly appreciated the fact, not to mention that he had a true though hidden affection for this especial neighbour, and would have grieved greatly if sorrow had befallen him. But long faces only due to considering-caps—well, that was another thing, and really not worth wasting the minutes of a working-day upon. He bent his head once more over his tray of West Indian treasures, as he asked with diminished interest:

"And pray then what has led thee to the wearing of a cap so weighty? Have the good fathers of St. Jacomb refused the purchase of thy Venice lustres, or will not they give thee a fair price for them?"

Burgess Sancho laughed again. "Nay, neighbour, trouble not thyself to guess, for thy guess is wide of the mark. The good fathers closed eagerly with my offer of the lustres, and the maravedis I demanded in exchange are already in my pouch. But hark ye, friend Pedro!—with the lustres came to me also two Venice glasses of the most changeful pearly hue, tall and thin, and of a good capacity. And I have a mind to keep them to myself, and, moreover, to try to-night how the flavour of a good wine from Madeira goes with them. Come thou in, when the sun hath gone down, and help me with my judgment."

"And also with my judgment on a matter of far more moment," muttered the worthy trader to himself, with a shrewd twinkle in his eye at having thus cleverly angled for his neighbour's company.

For the spice-dealer was one difficult to entice farther than his own doorway; and nothing short of those promises of choice wine from the Portuguese island of Madeira, to be drunk out of yet choicer goblets, would have tempted him on the present occasion to break his rule. As it was, the last glimmer of daylight had disappeared more than an hour when a cloaked figure stepped from one door to the next, and gave a tap upon the nail-studded panels.

"Better late than never, friend; come thy ways in," said Master Sancho heartily, as he acted the part of his own door-porter, and ushered his neighbour into a room brightly lighted with fire and lamp; for even in that sunny land of Spain the cold, damp winds of December made the blaze of crackling logs pleasant after sundown. What would not have been so pleasant to English ideas, was the overpoweringly pervading odour of burning lavender, a bundle of which was slowly smouldering on the hearth, by way of giving the atmosphere of the apartment that special tone and perfume considered desirable by its occupants.

On a small table in front of the cheerful hearth stood the beautiful Venice glasses, tall and slender, shimmering with opal tints in the ruddy glow, which also shone through a flask of golden-tinted Madeira, and danced hither and thither over various dishes daintily set forth with sweet-meats. For, ascetic-looking as Master Pedro was in appearance, he had as sweet a tooth as any Roman, and Master Sancho was too anxious to gain his aid or counsel to neglect anything that might tend to put him in good humour.

But although Pedro's eyes gleamed with a certain satisfaction at sight of the festive preparations, he was shrewd enough to read between the lines; and as he stretched his feet comfortably towards the fire, and put back his delicate glass after a contented sip, he asked with grim humour:

"And now, friend Sancho, that you have baited your net and caught your fly, tell me, what wouldest thou seek from out it?"

The merchant's face flushed at the unexpected question, and he began hastily: "Now, by the Holy Virgin, I protest that good fellowship—"

"And some perplexity besides," interrupted Pedro with a knowing smile, "made you anxious for my company. But tell me without hesitation what you would have of me, for I would stretch many a point to serve so good a neighbour."

"Thou sayest so!" exclaimed worthy Sancho, as he rose hastily to his feet, and with hand resting on the table bent over his companion, eagerly scanning his countenance. "Thou sayest so, and would hold to that thou hast said?"

"Ay verily," was the calm answer. "Almost, maybe, to the extent of putting my limbs in danger of the rack, if they might save thine from the like peril thereby."

However, in spite of his declaration, Master Pedro was somewhat taken aback when his companion dropped again into his chair, muttering thoughtfully:

"Nay then, not quite so bad as that, I hope; not quite so bad as that; although—" and he raised his voice slightly once more, and raised his eyes to his friend again as he added—"although I certainly did think it were prudent to seek your advice in the privacy of my own home, rather than to proclaim my desires to the ears of the whole town. It is now three weeks since you accused me of taking an interest in a certain large-eyed vagrant boy—"

"Ay indeed," with fading interest, "of watching the bundle of rags as a dog might watch a rat."

"Even so. And when you have watched anything in that way for the space of months, you end by either loving it, or holding it in abhorrence. I have ended by loving it. And unfortunately I love where the law hates. Father and grandfather of that bundle of rags have perished at the mandate of the Holy Tribunal."

Master Sancho ceased, and bestowed a long, silent stare upon the glowing logs, while his companion took a long, slow sip of the rich wine. At last the spice-dealer put down his glass, placed his hands slowly, outspread, on his knees, and said in slow, muffled tones:

"Friend Sancho, I have some rules for life which I have found good. One of them is, 'Never give advice.' But this once I will depart from that rule, and advise thee to rid thy heart of this unlucky love, and for the future ever to wear thine eyes within thy cloak when yon lean-cheeks is within sight."

"Umph!" calmly ejaculated the host, still staring into the fire. "I knew that would be thy first well-meant advice; and, to tell thee the truth, I reckon that it may be as well for me not to be gazing at the lad quite so much as I have done of late. It is with that belief that I have turned to you to help me to get quit of the poor starveling."

At these last unexpected words the guest started, and cast a keen, swift glance of almost angry wonder upon his entertainer, as he said hastily:

"Nay, neighbour, what is that thou sayest? I advise thee to have nought to do with the lad, that is true; but canst thou think, even for thy safety, that I would aid thee to get rid of the poor fatherless one?"

A smile began to steal over the merchant's broad countenance, as he replied coolly:

"Ay, verily, and that is what I can and do expect. But not, as you seem to fear, to the lad's hurt. Here, in our Spain, it is not easy just now to set him on his feet. But if you will give him some commission to your son—nay, be calm and hear me out—if you will do that for the comfort of his mother, I will furnish him clothes and a fair purse, and trust me, I will also find means some way to smuggle him on board one of the ships, now fitting out in the southern port of Cadiz to carry the Commendador to Hispaniola. That is my scheme; many a good hour that I might have enjoyed in sleep have I bestowed upon it, and now you are going to aid me to carry it through."

"Never!" exclaimed Master Pedro, excitedly; "never, never! Not for all the maravedis that ever fell into the coffers of the Holy Office will I help thee to help one who inherits its suspicions. Dost hear me, neighbour Sancho?—I say, never!"

"Ay, ay, I hear thee," calmly replied the individual addressed. "I heard thee say that same 'never' in my dreams two days ago, and answered thee with 'ever.' Now I hear thee say it actually with thy lips, and still I answer it with 'ever.' But take another taste of the wine, friend Pedro; fill thy glass again, if but to see the mingling of the colours, and draw in thy chair closer to the warmth. No need to neglect the comforts of the body because thy mind is perturbed."

"Ah!" growled the other. "Thou hast well put into words the doctrine of thy life, I warrant me."

Master Sancho laughed.

"And if so, neither words nor doctrine, can any say, have served me shabbily. If it should so fall out in the future that even in this world I must suffer for my sins, or for other folks' caprices, nevertheless in the past my face hath had its share of rejoicing in the sunshine of its own smiles."

"It is in the sunshine of the smiles of others," retorted the spice-dealer, "that most men would fain be able to rejoice."

"Ay, even so, and that is where most men fall into error," was the calm reply. "Comfort from the smiles of others is like the fleeting comfort a sick beggar gets from the glow of another man's fire. A healthy man has the abiding glow in his own veins, and he carries it about with him where he goes. Thus is it when the spring of smiles is within thine own heart, man, and thou art led to accept gratefully blessings as they fall to thy hand."

The spice-merchant's eyes opened somewhat roundly as he heard this short philosophical-sounding speech, so very unlike his jovial neighbour's ordinary conversation, but before he could utter the sarcastic words of surprise hovering on his tongue, he was recalled to his recent anxieties by his friend continuing in a more earnest tone:

"And thus, as I like to grasp at the blessings as they come—the blessings of good fire, good friends, good food; good fun—so I can even open my hand wide enough to take hold of another sort of blessings, when they are thrust upon me so plainly that I can but see they are being offered. Do you mind the text upon which Father Ignatius preached to us on Christmas Day?"

Master Pedro considered a moment, and shook his head. To say truth, when that sermon began, his head was occupied with the doubt of whom he should trust to send with his next consignment of money, glass beads, and other things, to his son.

"It was appropriate to the occasion," he said at last with a clever evasion worthy of the Delphic oracle.

But his companion was too much in earnest now to smile. He replied quietly:

"The text was this: 'Inasmuch as ye did it not unto one of the least of these, my brethren, ye did it not to me. Depart from me, ye cursed, into everlasting fire.'"

So sternly solemn was his utterance of those two final words, that the other was thrilled with it, and moving uneasily on his seat, he muttered:

"One would think you were talking of the Holy Tribunal itself, to hear you."

"Only," ejaculated Sancho, "that I am talking of something infinitely more terrible. The one fire is for five minutes, the other—everlasting. I prefer the five minutes' one, if it must come to the choice. But, if you will help me, I think not we shall run much risk of either. Those who are in danger of their lives over here, and endanger those who aid them, are perfectly welcome, I have discovered, to imperil those same lives on their own account in the other hemisphere, for the glory of our country. And, on this I am resolved— yon black-eyed rascal shall have his chance with the rest."

CHAPTER VIII
A POWERFUL FRIEND

"Come with me, and ask no questions."

Such was the oracular order addressed by Master Pedro to his friend, Master Sancho, the morning after the conversation over that wonderful new wine of Madeira, and, with great alacrity, the merchant prepared to obey, exclaiming, with a joyous rub of his hands:

"Ah, neighbour, have your will in that matter of the questioning, for well I guess you would not think to fetch me from my business at this hour of a working-day but on account of our last night's confab."

However, for all so sure as he had felt on the matter, he began to be uncomfortably doubtful when his companion led him from his own door into the next, from which issued the mingled odours of every known spice under the sun, and none of them, to worthy Sancho's thinking, deserving to be compared with the sweet airs wafted over the fields of their own native lavender.

"Come in then," testily exclaimed Master Pedro, from the interior of a room just within the house, and at the entrance of which his friend had been arrested by the snarlings of two particularly vicious-looking pups. "Come in; they'll not hurt thee. They know better than to touch a Spaniard. They are to teach manners to the natives out yonder."

"Ah!" ejaculated Sancho, with an involuntary shudder, and a look expressive both of disgust and anger. But he quickly concealed these emotions. For the present he had one great object in view, and for its furtherance he must keep his companion in good humour, although his own was tested to the uttermost, not only by the dogs and their purpose, but by Master Pedro's employment for the next twenty minutes or so.

The trader with Venice well enough understood the merits and beauties of crystal-clear lustres, coloured vases, and golden goblets, and he had a fair taste in the velvets from Genoa and the fine straws from Tuscany, but of what use or value all those Moorish tags and rags could be, which the curiosity-dealer was turning over, save to patch the holes in the cloaks of the beggars who lay around the doors of the neighbouring church of San Salvador, he could not imagine.

"Nay, friend Pedro," he exclaimed at last, with an effort to show no temper, and to still speak pleasantly; "nay, friend Pedro, if thou hast brought me here to get a bid from me for yon small rubbish-heap, I tell thee frankly I value it at nought, seeing it will not even serve to feed a fire with. Nevertheless, I will even take it, to pleasure thee and to save mine own time, and at what price you list."

"Wilt thou then that?" said the other, with a grim smile, as he slowly lifted himself up from stooping over the pile of lumber, of all hues and textures, rich and sombre-coloured, thick and fragile. "Another time, neighbour Sancho, I would warn thee to be more chary of passing thy word to a blind bargain, lest one more cunning than thyself should hold thee to the promise. To purchase the rare wares of this small rubbish-heap would take many more than all the maravedis paid thee yester morn for thy lustres, by the fathers of San Jacomb. This veil alone hath been purchased of me for a fair round sum."

Master Sancho stared at the filmy texture, disfigured here and there with rents, and shrugged his shoulders.

"Thy wife, Doña Carlina, would not wear it."

"She will not have the chance. That veil, now many years since, shrouded the form of a Sultana—the ill-used queen of Aba-Abdalla, the last king of the Moors in Granada, thanks to the Virgin, our good knights, and Queen Isabella. And now Señor Antonio del Rincon hath hired it, and various others of these draperies, for the finishing of his great picture of the Life of the Blessed Virgin."

"And when he hath done with it?" inquired the good merchant, with something of growing reverence.

"Then it hath been purchased by a party of the ricos hombres,[1] who have vowed it to St. Jago, in memory of that grand day ten years ago, when our valiant Spanish knights adventured themselves, in the disguise of Turks, within the walls of Granada, as champions of their enemy's helpless queen. But come, friend, time passes, and Señor Antonio will be waiting for his stuffs."

As it was not good Sancho, but Master Pedro himself who had been delaying the expedition, the friends were soon enough on the road now that he was ready; and a hope began to dawn again in the mind of Montoro's new patron, that made amends to him for the loss of minutes from his daily toils.

"Señor Antonio del Rincon stands high in favour at the Court, neighbour," he observed at last, meditatively, as they walked along, side by side, to their destination; and Master Pedro answered shortly:

"Ay, neighbour; even so. He doth."

The reply was given in a tone not exactly inviting to further converse, but that zealous Sancho nevertheless continued, still thoughtfully:

"Ay, ay. And doubtless being a favourite he hath influence to obtain a favour if so be he could be influenced to ask one."

A shrewd, quick glance from his companion's eyes rewarded this conjecture; but they and the bundle of "properties" had now arrived at the temporary abiding-place of del Rincon, known to after-times as the father of the Spanish School. And Master Pedro's face assumed its usual solemn business aspect.

"Mind ye," he muttered hastily, as he paused outside the door of the studio for a moment, to pull and pat his great package into an orderliness somewhat destroyed by its carriage from his house—"mind ye, neighbour, I have brought thee hither, and the rest of the business ye must manage for yourself; for never another step in so craze-pate an affair, and one so near akin to rack and faggot, will you get me to stir, though you should promise me the free gift of your next freight of Venice glass entire."

"Nay then, friend Pedro, I'll do more," was the laughing whisper; "if my hopes succeed, I'll even 'you' thee in gratitude, as thou dost me for repression."

A little further compression of the wrinkled lips, a little further wrinkling of the furrowed forehead, gave the only sign of that mocking speech having been heard; and an instant later jovial Master Sancho appeared as sedately ceremonious as his companion, for they had entered the studio, and stood in the great man's presence, from whom both hoped great things; the spice-dealer for himself, the trader with Italy for another.

A man between fifty and sixty was the Señor Antonio del Rincon, the gravity of genius somewhat tempered in his countenance by the suavity learned from contact with that sweet woman, as she was noble Queen, Isabella of Castile.

At the artist's elbow stood the handsome young Montoro, who raised his great earnest eyes with a swift smile of recognition as Master Sancho entered, and then bent them once more over the colours he was grinding with most diligent care, for his employer. Never once again did he cease work during the animated discussion that ensued between the painter and the owner of the curiosities, although his friendly well-wisher marked the eager flush that crimsoned his whole face when a few words were spoken over the veil, of the splendid daring of Don Juan Chacon, Ponce de Leon, and their two companions, when they stood victors over the four false-hearted Zegries within the walls of Granada.

"Humph! He is worth better things than such a task as that," ejaculated the burgess, unconsciously uttering his thought aloud.

The painter turned to him surprised.

"Hey, master merchant, what is it thou sayest? That the veil is too honourable to take a subordinate place on my canvas, thou thinkest? Well, maybe thou art right," beginning to relapse into abstracted contemplation of his work; but with eager deference Master Sancho stepped forward, putting into words the first thoughts that occurred to him. Pointing a trembling finger towards a somewhat coarse dish holding gifts presented to the infant in the manger, he said hastily:

"It was not of the veil I was thinking. But if Señor Antonio would be pleased to accept of a dish of crystal, curiously chased, and worked with gold and gems, for use instead of yon, I would gladly bestow it for the grand picture's sake, and for the Virgin's honour."

And thus cleverly did Master Sancho, and with true unselfishness, slip his dexterous finger into the pie; and in the course of conferences that day, and a few succeeding days, over the costly dish and similar articles, he pulled out a goodly plum for Montoro Diego. The last use the dying Antonio del Rincon was ever to make of his Court influence was in the service of his young colour-grinder; and soon after the opening of the new year 1502, good Sancho treated himself to a holiday, and set out on a journey across Spain to the port of Cadiz accompanied by Montoro, and bearing a written recommendation of his *protégé* from the benevolent Queen to the great Admiral himself.

"I thought the Virgin had decreed, my son, that I should have to smuggle thee out of Spain in a cask of the Madeira wine, or in a Venice flask," said the generous-hearted burgess laughing, and rubbing his hands, as they proceeded on their first day's journey in fearlessness, and such comfort as even in those days a well-lined purse commanded.

The lad answered him with sparkling eyes. His emotions were as yet too strong for many words. Sorrow at parting with his beloved mother for the first time was somewhat soothed by having left her in the kind care and friendship of Doña Carlina; but wonder at his suddenly changed fortunes, and dazzling hopes of the future, filled his heart almost to suffocation.

CHAPTER IX
FROM THE NEW PRINTING PRESS

"And I am surety for you, my son; so if you owe me any thanks for my pains, be honest."

Such was the parting injunction of Master Sancho, as he bade his *protégé* farewell in the harbour of Cadiz on the morning of the 8th of May, 1502. And with a hot flush in his cheeks, and sparkling eyes, the youth replied quickly:

"Honest! Am I not noble? How should a noble of Aragon ever sully his name with dishonour?"

"How indeed?" replied Master Sancho as he laid his hand on the lad's shoulder and continued gravely: "One may well wonder that any bearing the name of man should sully his manhood by aught that is base; but you will henceforth be surrounded by many a companion who knows nought of honour but the honour of grasping more than his neighbour, who cares for no shame but the shame of being thought capable of virtue. See that you become not one of them."

"You have said that the great Admiral is far from being one of such blots on Spain," said the lad more humbly. "And as I am to be on his own ship, so I will trust to show myself deserving of the honour. And"—he added after a moment with a sudden burst of gratitude—"deserving of all your noble generosity towards me, and your most helpful trust. The memory of that will be a strong guard to me from temptation."

"May St. Jago grant it!" ejaculated the good-hearted man with affectionate fervour.

And then patron and *protégé* had to exchange hasty farewells, for Ferdinand Columbus, a boy a year or two younger than Montoro, came to summon him on board. Kind-hearted Queen Isabella, in her good-will towards the old and trouble-worn navigator, had given up the services of her young page that on this occasion he might accompany his father, and comfort him with his mingled love and enthusiasm.

To Montoro also it was some secret relief to see that there was one even younger than himself about to brave the very many known, and many unknown, perils of those far-sought adventures and discoveries; for more than his timid, grieving mother in El Cuevo had sought to persuade him that, in leaving that humdrum, safe little town for untried paths, he was foolishly relinquishing all chances of growing up to man's estate. That the Admiral was about to take one of his own two sons seemed a tolerable proof that matters could not be so altogether desperate as that.

Meantime, while these thoughts were flashing through Diego's brain, the merchant's eyes had been attracted by a great iron-bound, iron-clasped book under the boy Ferdinand's arm, and he at once remembered his friend Pedro.

Meantime, the merchant's eyes had been attracted by a great iron-bound, iron-clasped book under the boy Ferdinand's arm.

"My lad," he said, with one of his most winning smiles, "I have left a neighbour behind me in my own town who loves curiosities, and things from past times, not only for their value as articles of merchandise, but for their own sakes, and I would gladly pleasure him with some worthy gift, on my return, after his own heart. Thinkest thou that I could purchase yon great old tome of thee? Missal or Moorish prayers, songs or quaint sayings, I care not, so it be but rare and of a far-gone date."

He put out his hand as he spoke to examine his wished-for bargain; and as Ferdinand Columbus courteously yielded it for inspection he accompanied the civil act with a smiling:

"See for yourself, Señor, if it be old enough to suit an antiquary. Rare it is, certainly; but for the age—it cannot boast as many years as I. It is one of the Bibles printed, by the king's permission, in our own tongue, by Theodoric the German, at his printing presses in Valencia. This copy my father took with him on his first voyage, ten years ago, across the Atlantic, and he would not think of undertaking any great expedition without it."

"And doth he greatly study it, and do you?" inquired Master Sancho, as with mingled awe and wonder he turned the leaves of a book upon which his eyes had never before rested.

But its bearer appeared to think that it was being treated with too much freedom, and rather anxiously held out his hands to receive it back as he murmured in a shocked voice:

"*I* study it, Señor! The holy saints forbid. That is for the priests. It is taken with us that by its blessed power may be exorcised such spirits of evil, and baneful influences, as we may meet with in those unblessed regions of the West."

So saying, with a formal bow to the merchant, and a sign to Montoro to follow him, the son of the great discoverer of a new world, but not of a more enlightened faith, returned to the small boat that was to carry them on shipboard.

Master Sancho stood on the busy strand watching with many another, until they were drawn up the vessel's side, and then, with a tolerably deep sigh for the loss of his young companion, he wandered away into the streets of the bustling city, and soon became the owner of many curious treasures brought from all parts of the known world, and far safer possessions in that land of the Inquisition than the one he had made an attempt, in ignorance, to buy for his timidly cautious neighbour.

Indeed, with all his own honest courage shown on behalf of the orphaned and beggared young noble, the worthy merchant himself would not have cared to risk travelling with a copy of the Scriptures in his bales, unauthorized.

In those days the Bible was for the priests, as Ferdinand Columbus had said; and the priests took good care not to let the fountain of light out of their hidden keeping. They loved darkness to reign in the land rather than light, because their deeds were evil. But when the boy passed the book for a few minutes into Montoro's charge, as soon as they got on board, that he might the more readily go in search of his father, he was not again giving it into the hands of one so ignorant of its contents, nor to whom it was an affair of so much mystery.

One small, unsuspected portion of her inheritance had Rachel Philip saved from the rapacious grasp of the vile informer, Jerome Tivoli, the Italian. It consisted of three rolls of vellum closely written over in Hebrew characters, and when Don Philip's father became a Christian he did not declare his possession of these rolls; but, on the contrary, closely concealed them, lest he should be deprived of the pearl without price—the Word of God.

In a secresy that the more fully impressed the lessons upon his mind had Don Philip's father taught his son to read these rolls, and to write "in his mind and in his heart" God's law. In like manner had Don Philip, in his turn, taught his daughter; and in like manner had Rachel Diego taught her son to read those three rolls—the Pentateuch, the Psalms of David, and the book of the prophet Isaiah.

Through all her troubles of widowhood, wanderings, and poverty she had kept those books, and she still kept them, for she dared not risk her child's life with their transfer to him. But it mattered not, for their truths were imprinted in his soul, and his faith was a living faith, pure and free from superstition, being built upon the knowledge of God's own Word.

Many of those Jew converts who fell at the mandate of the Spanish Inquisition were the truest Christians, the most upright men, and the best citizens of their age, for they *knew* what they believed.

From his mother's secret teaching, and his own reading, the young Montoro had become wise unto salvation before the new career began that had been opened up for him by the merchant's benevolence; and when he stepped on board the world-renowned Admiral's ship it may be safely said that the young sweet-voiced, earnest-eyed lad was the mental superior of most of those with whom he was surrounded. He had now a great curiosity to see what might be the contents of the Christian parts of the Bible; and while he awaited his young companion's return, and was pushed with scant ceremony out of the way of the rough sailors, only to be hustled yet more imperiously aside by the penniless but haughty hidalgos who were setting out, as they fondly believed, on a royal road to fortune, he had the opportunity to gratify his desire.

Partly by others' driving, partly by his own good management, he at length got comfortably stowed away into a quiet corner, and there, dropping himself down on to a bale of goods, he carefully unclasped the great book, and turned towards the latter half.

He began to read at once the first words of the first page that opened beneath his eyes, for the disputes he had witnessed during the past few minutes between several of his self-asserting companions made them appear startlingly appropriate.

"And there was also a strife amongst them, which of them should be accounted the greatest."

Many a time did those words recur to his memory during the coming years, but just then, as he sat in his obscure corner in enforced quietude and inactivity, he read on and on with forgetfulness even of his novel position and commencing adventures, in his absorbing interest in a history then read and fully understood for the first time. We know the account of our Lord's agony, base betrayal, and awfully cruel death so well that we have not the faintest idea of how intensely it moved intelligent minds, who first quietly perused it for themselves in its own pathetic simplicity, unspoilt in its solemn appeal by any priestly shows or pageants.

Montoro Diego clenched his fists and his eyes flashed as he read of Peter's denial of his Lord and friend.

"Mean coward!" he muttered. And then his own eyes grew dim as he read how the slandered, insulted Son of man, the denied of his own chosen companion, "turned, and looked upon Peter." He seemed to feel his own being thrilled with the sad reproach, the tender compassion, and the full forgiveness of that look, and a smothered choking sob parted his own lips, as "Peter went out, and wept bitterly."

He read on undisturbed, until he suddenly, as it seemed to him, received an answer to many long-standing, half-formed questions in his mind, with the words:

"And beginning at Moses and all the prophets, He expounded unto them in all the Scriptures, the things concerning Himself."

That was the last of his reading for that day, and for many days to come.

Montoro's eyes were resting on the words—"And beginning at Moses," his lips were repeating a phrase that seemed for him to form the close connecting link between the religion given by God to his forefathers, and the crown of that religion as sealed by Jesus Christ, when energetic young Fernando found him out in his hiding-place. The younger boy pounced upon the volume instantly, with a half-indignant cry.

"Nay then, Diego, if that be thy name, I gave thee this volume of my father's to hold; there was no commission attached that thou shouldst read it, or even so much as venture to unclose the clasps. It is more than I have done, myself."

Montoro rose from his rough couch, and for all apology said with a long-drawn breath:

"I have found wonderful things therein."

Half-an-hour later it would have appeared that all memory of those wonderful things was lost. The anchors of the somewhat shabby little fleet of four vessels were being raised, and with flushed cheeks and eyes blazing with excitement Montoro Diego was making amends for ignorance by the most determined vigour and good-will. Such a little while ago he had been hustled on one side as a useless bit of goods, whose room was worth more than his company; but already his keen-sightedness and ready hands had reversed the judgments of those in his immediate neighbourhood in his favour.

The afternoon was wearing on, when a grave, kind voice addressed him:

"My son, I have been observing you. You have done well."

It was the Admiral himself who spoke, the grand old man who had attained to ever great heights of humility as he attained to greater fame, and who never held himself too high to see the worthy efforts of his humblest follower.

Montoro's handsome face grew brilliant with delight, and as he bent it gratefully in acknowledgment of the commendation, his heart seemed to rise to the possible achievement of deeds of hitherto unheard-of heroism. At that moment he little knew what those deeds would be; deeds not indeed wholly unmatched in the previous history of the world, but yet so rare that, not infidels, but, on the contrary, the most earnest believers in Christianity, are tempted sometimes to believe that their faith must be a fable, and those who proclaim its teachings must do so to tickle their hearers' ears, and as a pastime of the moment.

Having uttered his few words of encouraging praise, Columbus passed on, and Montoro, for whom there was no further employment for the moment, turned to lean over the side of the vessel, and watch the receding shores of his native land, the fast-diminishing lines of the harbour of Cadiz, and its throngs of traders from all nations. His mother was very present with him at that minute, and his mother's parting words:

"You, the unknown and disinherited noble of Aragon, son of a foully-slandered and slain father, are, in the world's eyes, nought. You, the boy Montoro de Diego, may be a hero, the winner of fresh glory for your name, the gainer of the highest honour from your fellow-men. The past is not your fault, the future may be your praise. Keep firm to God and the truth, and fear none."

That last injunction "to fear none" was indeed little needed in the sense in which the boy took it.

"I am not wont to fear," he said, with a touch of impatient pride, adding the next instant, as his eyes rested on his mother's gentle face, and with a mischievous smile, "I rather thought, my mother, that your counsels to me generally were against being overbold."

"That is true," was the reply, with a fleet answering smile. "But that is in matters concerning thyself, my son. Be ever backward in self-assertion, and ever fearless in the cause of justice, truth, and mercy. As thy father was, so I pray that his son may be."

"My father saith that he likes the look of thy face, and wills that we may be friends."

Such was the abrupt announcement of that courtly page and intrepid young adventurer, Fernando Columbus, breaking in upon Montoro's reverie, and joining him at his post by the vessel's side.

A third person stood there also for a minute, — a man with grey hair, and a form shrunken with old age, — and a tear rolled slowly down his furrowed cheek as he gazed for the last time at his country's strand.

Montoro's great eyes widened with questioning wonder at sight of the bowed old man, and when he withdrew he asked his companion, in low tones, what could have possibly induced one so infirm to set out upon such toilsome journeyings.

Ferdinand turned his head to look after the retreating figure, and shrugged his shoulders. "Well, I suppose his inducement would be thought by many people a more sensible one than those of the rest of us, although, if we have anything of a rough voyage, I doubt he will be proved to have set out too tardily."

"Still, I hope for my part we shall not always have these smooth waters," impulsively exclaimed the inexperienced young sailor. "I want to see what a storm on the ocean is like. But that by the by. Just now I wish to know what is the inducement of that old hidalgo for leaving his own home, and the comforts he seems to need. Why do you think it is a sensible one?"

"Because," answered the younger boy more gravely, "gold without life is useless, and even glory without it is not much worth. And various of our nobles at the Court have come to the belief that the fountain of youth wastes its precious waters in some hitherto undiscovered region of this New World. The brave knight, Ponce de Leon, hath determined on an expedition to go in search of it; meantime yon wealthy Señor hopes to bribe the Indians to bestow upon him a draught of the precious water before it be too late. And my father though something doubtful of this thing, hath consented that Don Aguilar should have passage with us for the chance. He, himself, would far rather find the Holy Garden of Eden, which he tells me most surely is out yonder."

"At any rate," said one of the knightly adventurers who had now stepped up beside the two lads; "at any rate, Ferdinand, whether thy father finds the Garden or no, I trust that no flaming firebrands of the Indians will hinder him from finding, and traversing, that strait leading from this ocean into the Indian Sea, of which he seems to be so well assured. The finding of that passage will be wealth for all of us."

Unfortunately for the hopes of those days, that expected passage proved to be a land one, and is now called the Isthmus of Darien, which art, not nature, promises soon to convert into the realization of Columbus's belief.

CHAPTER X
A JACK IN OFFICE

It was the 29th of June. There was a hush on board the Admiral's ship. Yonder were visible the white low houses of San Domingo on the island of Hispaniola. Around the ship the sea lay still and grey, and the sails hung limp in the hot, heavy air.

A knot of men gathered close around a cabin, listening with lowering brows and compressed lips to bitter groaning, and sobbing cries, that were being wrung from one within, by his wounded soul. Well might the old and way-worn discoverer of mighty continents feel tempted at that moment to cry: "Hath God forgotten to be gracious?"

A storm was coming on; one of his four poor, shabby vessels—that on which his beloved brother Bartholomew held command—was in a shattered condition, and he had asked leave to take shelter in the harbour of the small island he had himself given to Spain, and Spaniards had refused him! What wonder that the noble and generous heart of the old Admiral was wrung to its very depths! What wonder that, as Montoro leant with Fernando against the cabin-door, the lad clenched his fists until the nails almost cut his palms, and muttered fiercely to his boy friend:

"Fernando, ask thy father's leave. There is not a man on board will refuse to turn our guns against those miscreants, though they were twenty times our countrymen. Only let him give the word, and he shall be speedily avenged."

"Ay, speedily," echoed two or three hoarse voices in the group, from those who had caught the tenor of Montoro's passionate request, and the Admiral's young son raised his eyes gratefully. His steadfast face was pale with emotion, his lips trembled. Even this weak testimony to his father was some comfort.

"I only wish," he exclaimed, struggling to speak with manly calm; "I only wish that, as you say, the Admiral would give the word that we should let our guns loose against the dastard hounds. We would soon teach them a lesson they should not easily forget."

"Nay then, young Señor, how about yon fleet?" asked one of the sailors significantly, pointing to a number of gay and gallant-looking ships at a short distance within the harbour. "Think you, Señor Ferdinand, that yon fleet would leave us alone if we took to avenging our insults by bombarding the town? And they are close upon twenty to one!"

"What of that?" hastily ejaculated Montoro, his cheeks still crimson with excitement. "God fights on the side of right and just—"

He stopped abruptly. The sounds of grief within the cabin had ceased during this short discussion, and at this instant the door opened, and a hand was laid on Montoro's shoulder, while the well-known slow, distinct voice said with grave earnestness:

"That is true, my son. The great Father fights on the side of right and justice. But He still better loves to espouse the cause of the merciful. Instead of seeking to destroy life let us rather try to save it, that with the measure we mete it may be measured to us again."

"That comes out of the great book I gave thee to hold the day we started," whispered Fernando to his companion, who nodded. It had been a favourite quotation of the benevolent old priest, Bartolo. Meantime Christopher Columbus proceeded to give proof that he spoke not with his lips only but from his heart.

The great fleet in the harbour of San Domingo was that which had brought out his superseder, Ovando, a few weeks since, and it was now in all the bustle of preparation for a speedy return to Spain with crowds of home-going adventurers, many ill-wishers to the just and virtuous discoverer, numbers of prisoners Spanish and native, and an immense amount of gold, pearls, and other treasures, well-nigh every ounce of which had cost a life.

On board this fleet were the Admiral's most bitter enemies; on board its grandest vessel was the narrow-minded, mean-spirited upstart, Bobadilla, who, to the ever-enduring disgrace of his own name and of his country, had dared to send the great seaman, the great thinker, the man of unbounded hopes, enthusiasm, courage, endurance, and magnanimity—the man who to Bobadilla was as a lion to a rat—had dared to send this giant hero home in chains like a vile malefactor but two years before, and had covetously grasped at his possessions, impudently installing himself in the house of his patient victim, and laying greedy hands upon his arms, gold, plate, jewels, horses, books, and even his letters and precious manuscripts.

Against that fleet, with all its proud sumptuousness contrasted with the miserable little squadron granted to Columbus, and against his base enemies on board, the company on board his own ship considered that he had a full right to feel the most vengeful wrath. It was not Montoro only who could scarcely believe his ears when, after the pause of a few moments following his sacred quotation—moments devoted to further keen, close scrutiny of those weather signs in which he was so deeply skilled—the Admiral summoned forward the crew of the boat that had just returned, and despatched them with a second message to the new governor Ovando, to entreat him to save the fleet from the certainly approaching storm, by a few days' delay of their departure.

"Better to leave them to meet their fate as they leave us," muttered Montoro, with the yet unconquered passion of his nature. But once again that firm touch came upon his shoulder. The Admiral's quick ears had caught the growl, low as it was.

"My son," he said quietly, "you shall go with my messengers. That will be a fitting rebuke for you, will it not," he added with a grave smile, "for uttering opinions contrary to those of your commander, and contrary to those of the Divine Ruler of the universe?"

Obeying a sudden impulse of veneration, Diego snatched the aged hand in his own, and pressed it to his lips. "I can never attain to your generosity, Señor," he murmured, "nor be thus forgiving to those wrongfully my enemies."

Just as the boat was starting, Ferdinand Columbus bent over the ship's side, and called mischievously:

"Diego, there, hark ye!"

"Ay, what is it then?" asked Montoro, as he lifted his head, resting on his oar the while. "What news hast thou since I left thee and the caravel?"

"Great news," was the mischievous answer. "My father gives me leave to tell thee that, since thou art doubtless feared by reason of the coming storm, he will obtain permission at least for such a whipper-snap as thou to abide on shore."

That quick, unmanageable spirit of Montoro's was set all ablaze for a moment at the supposed imputation of cowardice; and he was about to shout back an answer little in accordance with his late act of reverence, but Diego Mendez, the officer in command of the little embassy, hastily clapped his hand over the lad's mouth, as he said with a short laugh:

"Nay now, art thou not a very fool to be so taken in? Dost thou not see by thy tormentor's face that the brain of no Columbus but himself made up that message for thee?"

The friendly intervention was timely. When Fernando called down again—"Say then, dost accept the offer?"—his companion's face was brimming over with merriment like his own, as the retort was shouted up:

"Ha, Fernando, my good Señor, thou art but a sorry messenger. My absent ears have caught the purport of thy father's words better than thy present ones. The Admiral's message to me is, that since thou art feared, I must obtain a leave to land for thee. I bid thee, then, calm thy quaking heart, since I will not fail. Adios."

"And a slap o' the ear for thee when thou returnest," was the answering shout; and then the boat cast off, and was rowed with vigorous strokes to that once fertile, but already so dismal and desolated island of Hispaniola, the head-quarters of cruelty, lawlessness, suffering, and rapacity.

Montoro was very quickly to have a specimen of the deeds that had brought the island to its present wretched condition.

As the boat approached the strand, crowds of idlers gathered about, some to give the new-comers welcome, more to express their contemptuous dislike of the Admiral by covert sneers or openly-expressed scorn bestowed upon his followers.

There, flaunting in silks and brocades, which not even the proudest hidalgos dared any longer wear in Spain, stood half-a-dozen men, who had been loosed from richly-deserved felons' dungeons at home, to serve as colonists for the New World. Near them, reclining in a sumptuous litter, borne upon the bleeding shoulders of four of the meek-spirited and unhappy natives, was an ignorant, cunning rascal, whom Montoro had himself seen carried off to prison for theft in El Cuevo. Now he lay there in all the insolent dignity of riches, with a palm-leaf umbrella borne over his head by one slave, whilst another sickly-looking creature fanned him.

Closer to the edge of the soft-lapping waters was a real Spanish Don, whose poverty-stricken estate had driven him to hide his thread-bare pride in exile. To indemnify himself for leaving his beloved Castile, he spent his whole time and thoughts on the island in squeezing wealth, almost, as it seemed, even out of its very stones. His slaves died off day by day, very nearly as soon as they were allotted to him; but that was nought to their owner, so long as with the remnants of their dying strength they reaped his harvests, and brought up gold for him from the mines. They were to him as machines for making riches; and when one of the machines wore out, it must be tossed aside to make room for another.

But with all Don Alfonzo's heartless barbarities to his miserable victims, he had a warm corner in his callous heart for his own countrymen, whoever they might be. All Spaniards were friends to Don Alfonzo, while the ocean lay between him and his home. He watched the progress of the incoming boat with eyes almost as eager as those with which, week by week, he counted his golden gains; and when, from the shallowness of the water, the rowers had to stop some way short of dry ground, he looked round hastily for some one whom he could order off for their assistance. None of his own people were in sight, but a weak, wan-faced Indian lay beside him, and him the nobleman immediately commanded to rise, and go into the water to help drag up the boat.

With a moan the poor creature began to obey, but too slowly to suit the despotic impatience of the Spaniard.

"Hurry thy lazy carcase, then, thou black-skinned dog," he exclaimed imperiously; and to enforce his words he raised a bamboo cane he held, and brought it down with a fierce swish through the air, which told its own tale of what its effect should be if it came in contact with the native's tender flesh. As the cane rose the Indian crouched with a low, pitiful cry, which was echoed with an added note of indignation by Montoro from the boat.

The next moment Montoro sprang to his feet with a second cry of impulsive admiration. The stinging slash of that bamboo cane had come down upon the arm of a young Spaniard, who had stretched it out as a cover for the helpless Indian; and then, when the arm had performed its allotted task, it was quietly withdrawn, terribly cut as it must have been, and folded over its owner's chest, who as quietly turned and confronted Don Alfonzo.

"It is the command of our Sovereign, Queen Isabella," he said firmly, "that the Indians be treated with humanity, and according to law."

"Who is that?" asked Montoro, as he sprang on to the sandy shore, and pointed out the young man who had made his arm serve so readily for another man's shield.

Shyness was never one of Montoro Diego's failings; and now curiosity and a generous admiration made him put his question eagerly to the first person he came up to. All he got at first was a return question to match his own, a good-humoured:

"And pray, then, who are you? If you're come to work you are welcome; if you have come to make others work, you may as well be off again, for there are more than enough of that sort here already."

"I am going off again," replied Diego laughing. "I have not come to stay; not just yet, at least. But do tell me who that young Señor is."

"Well, he's a crack-brained young Señor, to begin with," was the reply, with a shrug of the shoulders. "His name is Bartholomew Las Casas, and he's only been out here a few weeks. He came out with Ovando. His father came out here before, with the Admiral himself."

Montoro grew still more interested.

"But why do you call him crack-brained?"

"Because he is crack-brained. Crazy as he can be about what he calls the wrongs of the black rascals out here. His father took one over for him to have as his own in Spain, five or six years ago, and comfortable enough the fellow was with such a soft-hearted master. Then comes the royal order that there are to be no more of these Indian slaves in Spain; that they are not cruelly to be kept from their own country, and they are forthwith all packed back again, to be grabbed at as fast as they arrive, and worked to quick deaths in the mines. Meantime, our young Señor Las Casas has been taught to think a whole host of nonsense about their miseries, and his duties of relieving them. If he uses his arms as their covers in his fashion just now he'll pretty soon need some one to relieve him."

"Ay, verily," murmured Montoro musingly as he turned away from his informant and rejoined his companions. The history of his own family's wrongs had made him more keenly alive to the wrongs of others. He had a generous feeling of envy that it had been the arm of the young Las Casas, and not his own, that had taken the blow for the Indian. But, as the great American poet says,

"A boy's will is the wind's will."

Before half-an-hour had passed Montoro's will had veered round once more — from a desire to relieve injuries to a desire to inflict them. For humanity's sake Columbus had sent urgent warnings and entreaties that the departure of the fleet might be delayed a few days, to avoid the coming storm. And for his charity he received contempt. The Governor and his counsellors looked at the quiet sky, the calm sea, they felt the soft breeze on their cheeks, and the contemptuous answer was sent back:

"In this year of grace dreamers of dreams are out of fashion."

"When I see the Admiral's letters patent as the authorized reader of the heavens, and the interpreter of its signs," said the Governor haughtily, "doubtless he will find me an obedient pupil. Meantime I prefer instruction when I ask for it."

"He and all the rest of them deserve to be drowned if they are not," said Diego Mendez indignantly, as he returned with his party to the boat, and put back to the ship.

Montoro's thoughts flew back to the cannon on board. He felt just then as if nothing on earth would so well satisfy him as to see them pointed at the Governor's house, to see their flash, to hear their roar, and to witness the wholesale destruction they could cause.

"Why was there no young Las Casas to avenge this insult to the Admiral?"

But there was One mightier than Las Casas to do that, One whose artillery was mightier than the cannon in which Montoro put such confidence. Two days passed, and then the tropical storm burst in all its fury. To such poor, unforbidden shelter as he could find the Admiral had guided his battered little squadron, and there he and his followers waited, and watched the gathering gloom of earth and sea and air and sky; and well it might seem to some of those watchers that a spirit of retributive wrath was brooding over the scene of cruelty, treachery, and insolence.

"It will require all their seamanship to ride out the coming hurricane," said the pilot, Antonio de Alaminos, on the second day, as he regarded somewhat dubiously their own quarters.

And Diego Mendez answered moodily:

"I should heave no sigh if they and their ill-gotten wealth went to the bottom of the deep before mine eyes; but I do grieve to have heard that on the craziest of their barques they are carrying home the Admiral's gold, the poor remnant of his rents they have permitted him."

"Never have care for that, Señor," said the young Fernando earnestly. "It is my father's, and it will be kept safe for him."

"It is as well that thou canst console thyself with that belief, any way," muttered the man, as the boy went off to where Columbus was already issuing orders, needed by the sudden wild gusts of wind that came as forerunners of the tempest.

Then came the wild roar and whirl, and darkness made more awful by the fiery flashes that momentarily illumined the terrors of the scene. On land trees uprooted, houses flung into ruins as though made by children's hands of cards, the fields of maize changed as in an instant from fields of gold to grey, scorched deserts. Living beings struck at a breath into corpses; others crushed in the downfall of their homes. And at sea those four poor cranky vessels, which were all a great country could afford its great benefactor, tossing and toiling in the boiling sea.

Now the waters would seethe as though some hideous cauldron, prepared by evil spirits for some demon feast, and the doomed vessels shook through every plank and spar as though with living horror. And then, with a sudden shock the waters would rush together, and mount wildly into mountain waves crowned with crests of foam.

The ships lost sight of each other. Sailors and adventurers all gave themselves up for death. In a delirium of fear they confessed their sins to whoever would heed the dismal catalogue. Ave Marias, invocations of the saints, and such fragments of Scripture as they knew, were groaned forth on all sides, rather as invocations than prayers, as the days went by, and still the furious battle of nature raged.

The fellow to that storm not even the veteran navigator of all seas had experienced before. At times during the blackness of the night it would seem to the affrighted mariners as though hell itself had opened its jaws to swallow them. Making a pathway for themselves through the darkness, the raging billows would suddenly rush onwards brilliant with light, and surround the ship and its awe-struck occupants with a sea of flame. For a day and night the heavens glowed as a furnace; and the reverberating peals of thunder sounded to the distracted sailors as the last despairing cries from the other ships of their sinking comrades. What was becoming of the wretched, foolhardy creatures on board Ovando's proud fleet they had no longer care to think. Drenched with the ceaseless sheet of rain, which poured down day and night throughout that long week of storm continually, exhausted with toil, worn with fears, Columbus and his company were to be still further tried by the majestic terrors of those southern seas.

Wildly tossed as was the whole ocean, it suddenly became observed, with deepening dread, that in one spot the agitation was still redoubled. Even as they looked the waters reared themselves higher and yet higher, grim and terrible as a giant pillar of molten lead; while a livid cloud bent down from the heavens to meet it. Thus joining, and ever gathering fresh size and force as it sucked up the waves in its headlong course, the dreadful column rushed on towards the ships.

The Admiral came forth from his cabin with the iron-clasped Bible open in his hands, to exorcise the evil spirit abroad for their destruction. Men hardened in callousness fell on their knees in silent prayer. Antonio de Alaminos stood gazing with fixed eyes at the invincible enemy. His skill and knowledge were powerless in the presence of that foe. As he stood there waiting for the end he was startled by a voice beside him so clear, so calm, that it was distinct even in the midst of that wild tumult.

"Alaminos, thinkest thou that we shall live through the storm?"

Starting, the pilot turned his gaze for a moment from the advancing column, and exclaimed:

"Montoro! boy, hast thou no fears?"

"None," was the low, soft answer of his lips. "None," was the answer of his rapt, earnest eyes, full of a beautiful awe and reverence. "He holds the storm in His hand, and us."

Even as the boy spoke the vessel swerved, the waterspout passed on beside it, and they were safe.

"The Admiral's Bible has saved us," exclaimed the mariners, as wild with joy as they had been with fear.

Alaminos, the pilot, looked at Montoro de Diego, and said nothing. For the first time in his life the thought had stolen into his mind whether the faith to be learnt from the teaching of the Bible might not be a more precious thing than even its print and paper.

The force of the long-protracted tempest was at length spent; the sea subsided, and Columbus's scattered caravals, none of them lost, gathered together again to offer thanks to God for their preservation, and to seek the shelter and refreshment no longer denied them, in the ports of Hispaniola.

The storm had passed, but it had left behind it sorrow and shame and gloom on the countenances of Ovando the Governor, and those about him. The gay, grand fleet, despatched against the Admiral's advice, was lost, with all those many hundreds of souls on board, and all that wealth. The Admiral's enemies had perished; Bobadilla, the mutinous Roldan, and many another. Those gallant ships were gone. Only that poor, mean, weak little barque, inferior to all its consorts, that had been thought good enough to carry the Admiral's grudged revenue, that lived through the storm, and took its little treasure safe into the Spanish port.

"It is my father's; I told you that God would guard it," said Fernando Colon, some months later, when the strange, good news of that survivor reached his ears.

CHAPTER XI
THE FIRST FIND

Great storms are very terrible, and weeks of drenching rains, Montoro de Diego, and his friend Ferdinand Columbus, had time to discover, were most disagreeable accompaniments to travels whether by water or land. As for poor Don Aguilar, the hardships of the way killed him, as Fernando Colon had foreseen, before he had a chance to purchase a draught from that dreamt-of fountain of youth. And long-continued dismal weather very nearly also killed the courage at least of most of the old hidalgo's companions.

After that first great storm, a few days were passed at Port Hermosa, to refresh the crews, and repair the caravels, and then Columbus started forth again to find the wished-for, but non-existent, strait through the Isthmus of Darien. Having spent about five months in this fruitless search he gave it up, greatly to the delight of the whole of his companions. They were much more anxious after what they considered the infinitely superior quest for the gold mines of Veragua, distant about thirty leagues from Porto Bello.

What with cross currents, however, contrary winds, and bad weather, those thirty leagues took nearly a month in the traversing, and it was not until the day of the Epiphany, 1503, that the Admiral reached the mouth of a river, to which he gave the name of Belen, or Bethlehem. In the immediate neighbourhood of this river was the country said to be so rich in the precious mineral that Columbus felt convinced that, as further discoveries would find the Garden of Paradise in the new-found world, so also he was on the borders of that land of Ophir whence king Solomon had drawn his stores of the valued treasure. Meanwhile, every one but himself, and his son Ferdinand, was very eager to get similar treasure for his own purse, and so soundings somewhat less cautious than usual were taken, the four caravels crossed the bar at the mouth of the river Belen, now swollen by past months of rain, sailed some little distance up it, and there cast anchor for a season of exploration.

Montoro was as wild with eager excitement and delight as any one, when he obtained leave to go with the first boats sent on shore.

"Do you then, too, care so much for gold?" asked his friend Fernando, in a disappointed tone, as he saw his companion's glowing face. "I had not thought it of thee."

"Nor need now," was the quick answer. "I go not to hunt for gold, but glory. My father's wealth they robbed him of. The glory he won on the walls of Alhama will cling as long as time shall last to the name of Don Montoro de Diego. Such glory, and not gold, would I win also."

"Nobly spoken, my lad of the quick temper," said Señor Diego Mendez, in smiling allusion to the time when he had hindered hasty words by putting his hand over the boy's mouth. Since that day Diego Mendez had many times taken note of his young companion. Neither Montoro's ability, courage, wit, nor readiness were lost upon him, and the occasion was soon to come now when he was to show his appreciation of them.

As the boats' crews stepped on shore, one or two of the eager seekers after fortune gathered up handfuls of the glistening sand, eyeing it sharply, as they did so, in such a way that Diego Mendez exclaimed with a laugh:

"Why now, comrades, would it not be well, think you, just to set to work, and shovel the shore pell-mell into the boats, and carry it off at once to Spain? Of course you'd be rich then, no doubt, without further trouble."

"Well, we've had enough of that, at any rate, already, to deserve some pay," grumbled one, while a couple of others sulkily enough dropped their glittering burden to avoid further ridicule.

"How pretty it is though," exclaimed Montoro, who stood watching the wet grains as they fell shining in the sunlight. "And here is some more up here!" he cried in astonishment half-an-hour later, suddenly stopping short from his companions, in their progress through the forest, and dropping on his knees beneath a tree.

"Some more what?" asked half-a-dozen voices at once, as their owners crowded round in amazed watching of their young comrade, who was most busily grubbing away at the tree's roots.

"Ay, indeed, some more what?" repeated the Adelantado, in equal surprise. "What is it that you have found?"

"Why some more of that shining sand," was the ready reply. "And of course it is nothing worth really, only that it is somewhat strange, methinks, to find it up here so far from the sea wet and shining."

"Strange! ay, strange indeed," echoed Diego Mendez, now quickly pressing through to his namesake's side. "Passing strange, my lad, if it be indeed, as you say, shining because, this dry, hot day, it lies there wet. But— is it so?"

Just as that question was put Montoro raised his stooping face with almost a startled glance at the questioner. He had told Fernando, and told him truly, that it was glory, not gold, that he desired. Still treasure meant power to return to his mother, power to give her comfort, power perhaps to win back his ancestral home. And he knew now that his hand was full, not of grains of sand, shining because they were wet; but of grains of gold, shining with their own lustre.

"No," he breathed, for a moment awed by his discovery. "No, my Señor, this is no sand heavy with the spray of sea waves. This is the treasure you are seeking."

Montoro's find put a stop to all further explorations for that day, excepting explorations about those roots. The entire party fell into a state that might, far more literally than usual, be termed one of 'money-grubbing' excitement. More diligently than the greediest pigs ever grubbed for a feast round about oak trees or beeches, or Spanish pigs grub for truffles, did those Spanish gentlemen grub with fingers and nails round about the trees of that wild American forest.

Montoro put a crown to the triumphs of his keen-sighted eyes by finding quite a fair-sized little lump of gold at the edge of a streamlet, which he put by carefully for Fernando; and then he employed himself in gathering a supply of the abundant fruits to carry back to the ship for the general benefit.

"Nay then," said Antonio de Alaminos, gratefully accepting a bunch of bananas, "but these are worth all the gold that was ever found or fought over, my lad. Our God gives us these as loving gifts. I sometimes think that He has given us gold as He gave the forbidden fruit—to try us."

Montoro raised his eyes for an instant and then lowered them again, as he murmured:

"Often hath my mother said that there are many things more worth."

"Truly are there," was the assent. "But hark!" he added in a louder tone and more quickly, "here is the Admiral. He is calling for us."

The summons was an important one. So satisfactory were the accounts brought back of the country, not only as regarded the promise of gold, but as to its general appearance of fertility and beauty, that the Admiral forthwith resolved upon the establishment of a colony.

"You think not," he demanded as Montoro and the pilot drew near; "you think not, Mendez, that it is the finding of this glittering dust only, that hath dazzled your eyes with respect to the virtues of the land?"

Mendez was about to reply with due gravity when his friend, Rodrigo de Escobar, broke in boldly, exclaiming:

"Nay then, as the Jewish spies said of old so can we say now, that it is a goodly land and a pleasant; and if it overfloweth not with milk and honey, neither is it inhabited with a people akin to the Anakim; and it has at least the grapes of Eshcol, and many a pleasant thing besides."

The Admiral smiled gravely.

"All which meaneth, I take it, Señor Rodrigo, that whosoever else believeth thy report, thou believest it thyself."

De Escobar bowed, while one beside Montoro muttered with a low laugh:

"Most assuredly friend Rodrigo would believe everything favourable of a land that flowed with that best of all sweet golden honey, the real gold itself, even though all else were desert."

"And small blame to him," retorted Tristan, captain of one of the other caravels, who had just come on board to hear the news. "Señor de Escobar is much of my own way of thinking—that life united with poverty is but a poor sort of an affair, not worth the trouble of the guardianship."

This being the general opinion, and a very slight amount of questioning eliciting the universal adhesion to Rodrigo's proposition, that a land where gold was to be gathered, even about the roots of the trees, was a good land to stay in, it was not difficult to obtain volunteers for the new colony.

Besides, even for those who were not so madly eager for gold Veragua had many attractions, seeing that the land abounded in rich fruits, the water in fish, the soil was fertile, and the Cacique and his people friendly.

"And what more can you want?" said Amerigo Vespucci decisively.

"What more can any men want?" said another, with a shrug of the shoulders. "Especially men like us, who have had for these weeks past to munch our biscuit in the dark, lest our stomachs should turn at seeing how many and how fat were the other eaters we were obliged also to devour."

"Bah!" ejaculated De Escobar, as he flung over a morsel of the said biscuit at the same time into the water. "It is too abominable of thee, Tristan, thus to remind a hungry wretch of the foul nature of his food. For thy barbarity thou shalt owe me thy first—"

"Nay, Señor," interposed Montoro Diego out of the dusk; "here is somewhat to make amends for thy lost supper. These great nuts have hard outsides; but within they are better than our little ones of Spain."

CHAPTER XII
SURGEON TO THE REDSKINS

Colonists for the proposed new settlement having proved so easily forthcoming, the next step in the business was to provide them habitations, and shelter of some sort for the needful stores. Accordingly the next morning, almost as soon as it was light, a number of men were sent on shore, as builders of the first European town to be founded on the mainland of America. Bartholomew Columbus went with them to choose a site for the place of which he was to be the Governor; and amongst the number of his companions were Diego Mendez, Diego's special comrade Rodrigo de Escobar, and of course Montoro.

"I cannot get on at all without my sharp-eyed namesake," said the notary good-naturedly, when he pleaded with the Admiral for Montoro's company. And thus, some little it must be confessed to Ferdinand's vexation, Montoro was once more of the land-going party, proving of as much service on this occasion as on the last, although the results were not so immediately apparent.

Cutting timber, clearing ground of a troublesomely-luxuriant vegetation, and driving stakes, had progressed for some time merrily enough, to the evident wonder and interest of an ever-increasing crowd of natives, men, women, and children, when Diego Mendez, looking about him for a help in a hard piece of work, discovered Montoro some couple of hundred yards or so distant from the building-ground, and apparently engaged in a very private and earnest conversation with a couple of native women, and three or four children.

"What, in the name of St. Jago, is the lad after now?" he exclaimed rather irritably, for he had got his fingers pinched in a split bamboo he had wanted his *protégé* to help him in sundering, and small annoyances were more trying to these brave Spaniards than great disasters. "Montoro," he shouted, "Montoro, you come here, can't you!"

Montoro was back like an arrow.

"Ay, Señor Mendez; what would you with me?"

"What would I?" was the hasty answer. "Why everything; all manner of things. But thou'rt such a fellow! Thou'rt never at hand when needed. At least," —still growling, but with a grim dawning accent of compunction for injustice,—"at least not always. Here thou'st left me to well-nigh lose the half of my hand, while thou'st been trying to wheedle gold mine secrets out of those poor fools yonder, with that soft tongue of thine."

"No such thing," exclaimed Rodrigo de Escobar with his usual volubility, before Montoro could answer for himself. "You are mistaken, Mendez. Had the lad been using a soft tongue so usefully his absence might be the more readily forgiven him. But it is a stupid soft heart that deserves the blame this time. Because gold-seeker, discoverer, navigator, builder, and half-a-dozen other things are not trades enough for the young jackanapes to take to at once, he must needs be taking a turn now at surgery."

"Nay then, Rodrigo," said his friend incredulously, and looking alternately from the laughing accuser to the half-troubled accused. The face of neither tended in any way to relieve the notary's curiosity. "Speak out, man," he said at last. "With what is it that you charge the lad?"

"With what I say," replied de Escobar with another laugh. "With playing the surgeon unauthorized, Children and monkeys are all alike— they must needs imitate what they see others doing; and consequently, one of those monkey-children yonder got hold of my hammer awhile since, and of course contrived to hammer its own fingers pretty sharply."

"Terribly!" broke in Montoro impulsively, forgetting his temporary shyness in the recollection of his pity. "The poor little creature, my señor, has hammered his fingers perfectly black, and the poor ignorant mother could only cry over it, and do nothing; and so—and so—"

And so, and so Montoro Diego once more grew shy as his own part in the business drew to the fore, and came to a stammering conclusion, and Diego Mendez with a smile took up the tale.

"And so, and so then, my friend, I suppose you do really confess that Don Rodrigo de Escobar has laid only true things to your charge, and that you have thought, by adding your ignorance to the woman's ignorance, to make one wisdom. Hey, my modest young friend, then is it so?"

Montoro looked up now, with flushed cheeks it is true, but with some returning boldness also, as he replied sturdily—

"My ignorance, at any rate, my señor, has had this good result—that the child no longer cries. But if you would spare me yet another five minutes, I would fain return to him, just to make my bandages more secure than I left them in my haste upon your call."

"Come then, have your way," said his new patron good-humouredly. "I confess I am not a little curious to see what sort of surgery you have evolved from that daring head of yours, and whether it be not a gag in the squaller's mouth that has produced this peacefulness."

But there was no gag in the small redskin's smiling mouth, neither, assuredly, was there one in the mouth of the small redskin's mother, who poured forth a perfect torrent of incomprehensible words as she alternately kissed Montoro's feet and her child's injured hand, or rather the great bundle of wet leaf-poultice in which it was most scientifically enveloped.

"Umph!" muttered Diego Mendez, as he looked at the bound-up limb and the grateful mother. "And pray how hast thou come by thy skill, my friend? Is St. Luke thy patron saint, and has he instructed thee?"

"My mother has been my teacher," was the quiet answer. "And she had much learning of many various uses to mankind, from her father."

The notary cast a keen glance of sudden intelligence at his companion, and then said slowly—

"Ah, now thou hast let me into a secret as to thy birth that I had partly guessed at before. Now I know from what race thou hast drawn much of thine intelligence, and the bookishness that hath ofttimes surprised me. But hark ye, lad, for I have a kindness for thee. Tell to none others of our companions what thou hast thus told to me; for remember, Spain has decreed just now that she will have no dealings, save those of the fire and the rack, with the great race that is too wise for bigotry to let it live. And the favour thou art sure to win, and the good fortune, will make men but too ready to use ill tales against thee. But now—leave thy patient, and let us back to our building again, for the day wears fast."

So saying, he turned his steps back towards the rising settlement; and when Montoro had managed with some difficulty to disengage himself from the thankful woman, he followed his patron, the native child clinging to him with his sound hand, and contriving to make his short legs keep up with his companion's long ones.

A general laugh greeted the truant when he returned thus accompanied; but Montoro tossed up his handsome young head very independently as he shouted—

"Laugh as you may please, my señors; but when you desire a guide and an interpreter, do not then think to borrow mine."

"Ah! ha!" exclaimed Diego Mendez, not at all displeased at his *protégé's* readiness. "My friends, methinks the lad hath had the best of it; and we were wise not to provoke him to register a vow to keep his useful new acquaintances to himself."

"If he did," muttered Rodrigo, "there would but need to draw a long and doleful face to make him break it. For no oath's sake would he ever be got to cut off a John Baptist's head."

"I'll cut off thine, though," grumbled Juan de Alba, "if thou keepest not those bamboo points to thyself, instead of using them to pierce mine eyes. Thou art a clumsy carpenter, in very deed, as ever I saw."

"And I rejoice that thou shouldst have to say so," retorted the other. "The fingers of Rodrigo de Escobar scorn this servile work."

"Do they also scorn to peel bananas?" asked the Adelantado, coming up with a great ripe bunch at an opportune moment to stop a squabble from growing into a quarrel. He had enough to do to keep the peace among his gang of noble workmen.

CHAPTER XIII
FOR LIFE OR DEATH

For some few days the work of building progressed merrily enough. The seemingly ubiquitous Montoro Diego, with his beautiful voice, his bright eyes, and his untiring activity, inspired the whole party with a portion of his own spirit; and his grateful native friend, the mother of his small patient, proved of the greatest comfort to the new colonists by keeping them plentifully supplied with fruit, fish, birds, and food cooked after the native fashion, but very acceptable to men who had lived hardly too long to be fastidious. Besides, they were very desirous of sparing as much as possible their own small remaining stores of biscuit, cheese, wine, oil, and vinegar, of which the Admiral could only leave so small a quantity for the civilized provision of the colony.

At the outset of the new undertaking, others besides the mother of the child had shown most hospitable alacrity in bringing gifts for the white strangers' larder; but by degrees these gifts ceased, and at last, whilst all the others of the Spaniards still looked gay enough, Montoro's face began to grow very grave. He still had many good things brought to him, but he noticed that they began to be brought with an air of secrecy, and at last the poor creature proved her gratitude by giving him signs as plainly as she dared, that Quibian, the Cacique of Veragua, was not altogether so friendly as he seemed.

"It was not his own gold mines, but those of a dreaded neighbour chief, that he had pointed out to the Spaniards on their first arrival," she declared; "and now he was noting with jealous eyes, and an angry heart, the preparations of the white strangers for taking up their abode on his territories."

Poor Cacique! Had he known the dismal fate that was so speedily to overwhelm him and all he cherished, his jealousy and wrath must have burnt with a fierceness to consume his heart. But for the moment the Spaniards were but a handful of men in an unknown and populous country; moreover, the water in the river had fallen, dry weather had set in, and threatened to continue, the bar at the river's mouth was visible at low tide, and the ships were shut in beyond the possibility of present escape. It behoved the Admiral and his band of followers to be careful, and each individual felt it incumbent on him personally to watch for the safety of all; even to sleep, as the saying is, like a dog with one eye open.

Under these circumstances it is little wonder that Mendez noticed with some uneasiness the unusual gravity of Montoro's face one morning, after a short interview with his Indian patient, and the child's mother.

"Hey, then, master Long-face" he exclaimed, with half-affected gaiety, "say, what treason is it thou hast been concocting with thy dark friend yonder? Hath she been offering thee the kingdom of the Cacique Quibian, if thou wilt engage to share the throne with her?"

Montoro threw back his head for an instant haughtily. Boy as he was, he did not like such jests. But he too much admired Diego Mendez for his anger against him to be long-lived. Besides, he had a weight upon his mind of which he desired to unburden himself. After the momentary pause, he said hastily—

"The woman's communication, Señor Mendez, had no reference to me further than as I am one of us. But if I at all rightly comprehend her signs, this Quibian, the Cacique of Veragua, under his smoothness to us has designs of the deepest treachery. Even now I believe that we are being surrounded on all sides by his warriors."

Señor Mendez stroked his chin thoughtfully. To say truth, he was deeply startled by the suspicion thus presented to him; but he was a Spaniard, and therefore chary of displays of any other emotion than that of pride. Moreover, he was a notary by profession, and had thus learnt caution: to hear all he could, to see all he could, to think much, and to say little.

His meditations were undisturbed by Montoro. At last he took the boy by the arm, leading him farther away from their companions before he said quietly—

"You have done well, my namesake, in bringing your tale to me. Let it rest there for the present, and see that you show the woman no great belief of her news, and no shadow even of a fear."

"But—" began Montoro eagerly, and then he stopped as suddenly as he had begun.

His companion looked at him doubtfully.

"Well, Diego, 'but' what? Wouldst say thy fears are too strong to be dissembled?"

"Even so," was the startling answer, with flushed cheeks, but with such a bold, brave look in the uplifted eyes that the unexpected reply was still more bewildering.

"Nay, then; thou art audacious enough in confessing cowardice," ejaculated the notary, with eyes so widening with wonder that they seemed to monopolize his face.

Just a flash of a smile shot across Montoro's face at having for once thus overbalanced the self-possession of the shrewd man of business. But he replied almost in the same moment—

"In truth, Señor, I can afford to be bold in confessing to these fears, seeing that they are not for myself, but for others, and for the honour of our expedition. Verily I think that it would break our great Admiral's heart, should terrible mischance happen to us who are with him now in his neglected, sorely-tried old age. And that must not be."

"And how then do you purpose to prevent it?" asked Mendez, once more the cool, self-contained notary. "Do you propose to call out the Cacique to prove his honourable intentions by single combat, after our own Spain's knightly fashion?"

"Would that it were possible!" was the reply with kindling eyes. "But no, Señor, my meaning is more simple. I have told you my fears. But if you mean to treat them as idle fancies, or to stand by to see what comes of them, I shall forthwith carry them to the Admiral himself."

"Umph!" said Diego Mendez deliberately, "you would so, would you? And you would do well. But hark ye, youngster—I neither intend to treat you nor your tale as nought, so with that assurance rest thee satisfied a while. I too have noted somewhat of late, upon which your news throws fresh light. But be wary. Tell no one what you have told to me, and show no sign of trouble."

Convinced at last that his warning was received as seriously as he desired, Montoro returned to his task amongst the amateur house-builders, and displayed considerable ingenuity as a constructor of neat roofs out of palm leaves. His alacrity at his work was the more cheerful when, from his position on the hill above the mouth of the river, he saw the accountant for the new settlement put off in one of the boats to return to the Admiral's ship. This happened within half-an-hour of their conversation on the native woman's intelligence, and increased Montoro's good opinion of his own wisdom in choosing Señor Mendez as the recipient of his confidence. Cautious as he was, he could evidently act quickly enough in an emergency.

In a short time he was rowing rapidly back to the building-ground, bringing half-a-dozen fully-armed men with him, and making signs to Montoro to meet him on the shore.

Down went tools and palm leaves, down from the roof with a bound sprang the tiler, and a minute later a second flying leap had carried him into the boat beside Diego Mendez. A few rapid words were exchanged between the two, and then the notary said gravely —

"Well, I have made you the offer of coming with me by the Admiral's consent; but remember, our undertaking is one of life and death."

"I understand," was the quiet answer. "But if we die, our deaths will be a sign to all these others to prepare for defence; if we live we shall at any rate have discovered the nature of our danger. I go with you gladly."

And of that latter fact his earnest, animated countenance gave abundant evidence as they proceeded on their perilous enterprise. Passing from the river Belen, they rowed along the sea-coast until they reached the Veragua, at which point the real peril of their enterprise began, and the first proof was obtained of the woman's veracity.

There upon the shore, within a few yards of them, was a great encampment of the Indians, the warriors of their tribe, and fully armed. The number of the Spaniards was eight, the number of the Indians more than as many hundreds. For one moment the Europeans rested on their oars in silence. It was no preconcerted act, but one of involuntary homage paid by all things living, however daring, when brought face to face with imminent death.

The half-whimsical, unbidden thought darted through Montoro's brain that his mother had declared she should never see him again on earth, and so she could not reasonably feel hurt if her words came true. What unconnected thoughts flashed for that same supreme instant through the mind of Diego Mendez none can say. It had scarcely passed when he sprang into the shallow water, walked on shore, and with an air of the most dignified composure advanced alone into the very midst of the great fierce gathering.

Utterly overawed by the white man's astounding temerity, the Indians fell back, with wonder and irresolution depicted on their countenances. They answered questions with trepidation.

"Yes; they were on the war-path. Their Cacique had enemies in the neighbourhood."

"Ah!" replied Diego Mendez with cool courtesy, "then our coming is well-timed. In return for your Cacique's attentions to us we will now aid his arms against his foes. We will accompany you on your expedition."

"Not so," was the Indian chiefs angry reply. "We are strong enough to fight our own battles; we seek no help. Only leave us: that is all we desire."

By manifold signs his followers equally betrayed their impatience to be rid of the new-comers, and strenuously declined to have anything to do with the boat, or its crew. Seating himself in the small barque with his face toward the Indian camp, and closely wrapped in his cloak, Diego Mendez calmly sat, hour after hour, and watched the dusky warriors.

The day waned; the short twilight drew on. One of the occupants of the boat began to feel his courage cooling under this tedious inaction, and he ventured to mutter somewhat anxiously—

"The night is coming, Señor Mendez. We shall be wholly at their mercy in the darkness."

"Even so, Juan," was the calm answer; "and yet we must remain. We set out with no thought of going in search of child's play. It is our lives or the expedition."

And so they sat on in that boat, watching and watched, and the night fell. Easily could the Indians have slain them all, but they were afraid. The spirits of a thousand warriors were quelled by one man's fearlessness. And as the blackness of night began to fade away into pale dawn, the chief and his army faded from the scene—stole back to Veragua stupefied and conquered. Moral power had won its strange, bloodless victory. Then the watchers in the boat roused up, took their oars again, and returned with their news to the ships.

"And thus the woman's truth is proved," said Montoro eagerly.

But his convictions were something lessened when the Admiral said slowly—

"You are more sure than I, my son. That you saw an army of the natives I fully believe. But that they had any purpose to attack us I strongly doubt. Quibian has given many proofs of his friendly feelings towards us. And even to-day he has sent us a plentiful supply of fish, and game, and cocoa-nuts, maize, bananas, and pine-apples."

"And even to-day," interrupted Mendez with unusual heat, "even to-day, Señor, the Cacique Quibian is meditating our massacre. Give me but this cool-headed boy to go with me, and we will penetrate to the very head-quarters of his people, to his very residence itself, and learn the truth so fully that you shall no longer be able to doubt our testimony."

There was a pause. The veteran navigator gazed with keen eyes at his two excited companions, and at length said slowly—

"I send you not on so perilous a quest, but you may go."

The faces of his hearers lighted up as though he had endowed them with some new-found gold mines, and with a hasty farewell from Montoro to his half-jealous friend Fernando, the two companions were rowed back again to land, and at once set out alone on their desperate expedition.

For nearly an hour they walked on rapidly side by side in silence. At last Montoro asked doubtfully, —

"Why keep we thus to the seaboard, Señor? Surely we have learnt that the residence of the Cacique is far away up yonder, beyond the forest. We should be turning inland if we wish to reach it."

Mendez turned his shrewd face towards his questioner with a slight smile.

"Ah, my friend, thou art bold and brave beyond thy years, and ready, to boot; but thou hast not yet quite an old head on thy shoulders, I perceive. If our foes are watching for our destruction as we suppose, how long thinkest thou, I and thou should live, bewildered, trapped, and helpless, in yonder jungle? No, we will keep to the shore till we reach the Veragua, and then we will follow the Veragua till it leads us to this Cacique's village, and his own abode. Light, and a clear space, are valuable to us just now."

Diego Mendez was willing to sacrifice his life freely for the general good, but he had no idea of wasting it. Montoro did not wish to waste his either, but to his impetuous nature this winding round, instead of making a straight dash, was becoming very tedious, when they at length reached the river's mouth, and at the same time came upon two canoes and a party of native fishermen. Whether subjects of Quibian or of his rival, the Spaniards could not ascertain, but whoever they were, they showed themselves so kind and hospitable that the tired and footsore pedestrians made signs to be taken into the canoes, when they were about to set out on their return voyage up the river.

Making sure of consent, the notary went so far as to put his foot on to the end of the canoe ready for stepping in. But the owners sprang forward to push him back, with most vigorous shakings of the head, and still more significant pointings towards the village, and the bundles of arrows in their own canoes.

Mendez and Montoro exchanged glances. There was no longer, then, much doubt of the fate intended them, and ere many minutes had passed they had learnt that the disconcerted warriors of last night were only waiting for the next day, before making a fresh descent upon the white intruders, shooting them, and burning the new settlement.

"Even so," said Diego Mendez at last. "We have but learnt afresh what we were well assured of before. But we will not wait for the doom intended us. It better beseems Spaniards to be the first aggressors."

As to the general humanity or morality of that sentiment young Montoro might have taken exception at a quieter moment; but just now he was infinitely too excited for tranquil thought, and eagerly seconded his older companion in so urging to be taken up the river, that at length the kind, simple-hearted fishermen consented, although with great reluctance.

The poor people's astonishment was still greater when, on reaching the village, picturesquely situated on the banks of the river, and now in all the bustle of warlike preparations, their two passengers insisted on landing, and putting themselves into the power of their enemies.

Still Diego Mendez preserved his cool presence of mind. Having learnt that Quibian had been wounded by an arrow, he gave out that he was a surgeon come to heal the injured leg; and demanding immediate admission to the Cacique, he mounted the hill to the very walls of the royal residence.

Arrived at the summit of the eminence, he and his companion paused a moment to take breath, and Montoro, for all his courage, could not wholly suppress a shudder at the hideous ornamentation of the royal domain. Three hundred human heads, recently torn from their trunks, were arranged in circles, in all their grim horribleness, before the Cacique's abode, the trophies of his valour, and significant warnings to his adversaries.

Mendez also glanced at these heads, and from them to the handsome lad beside him, so rich with the blessings of vigorous youth and health, and a shade of regret passed over his face.

But it was too late for such reflections now. The die was cast, and they must advance, and resolutely. The slightest token of hesitation or fear would most assuredly be fatal.

But however brave they might be, others were cowardly enough. They had scarcely moved forward a dozen steps on the plateau of the hill when a crowd of women and children caught sight of the strange new beings, and throwing their arms wildly above their heads in a very abandonment of terror, they fled in all directions, startling the echoes with their shrieks.

It soon became evident that they had startled more than the echoes, for a son of the Cacique, a tall, powerfully-built man, rushed out to ascertain the cause of the commotion, and looked ready enough to add the Spaniards' heads to his father's collection when he perceived them thus braving him, as it were, on his own ground.

Not being versed in the laws of chivalry, he took the notary at unawares with a blow which nearly sent him headlong down the hill, and Montoro almost as suddenly dashed forward with doubled fists to revenge his companion; but Mendez was far from desiring to be so championed. Recovering his footing, he grasped the boy by the shoulder and pulled him back, saying hastily,—

"My friend! patience is a virtue—when it is expedient."

Thus pocketing the affront for the present in a way that was very astonishing to Montoro, the notary by signs complimented his antagonist on his vigour, and ended by winning the powerful young savage over to the side of peace and good-will by presenting him with a comb, a pair of scissors, and a looking-glass, and giving him a lesson in hair-dressing. So delighted was the great Quibian's heir with that new accomplishment, that he fairly hugged his instructor, and although he could not obtain the bold Spaniards an interview with the angry, invalid monarch, he sufficiently showed his gratitude by despatching them safe back again to the waiting Admiral, and their anxious comrades.

He ended by winning the powerful young savage over to the
side of peace and good-will by presenting him with

Thus began and ended Montoro de Diego's first great adventure in the New World, and from henceforth he was marked out as one of those for whom the new scenes were to be scenes of renown. With the bitter termination, for others, of that exploit he had no concern. He was lying in his berth in the unconsciousness of fever when, a few days later, the Adelantado and eighty men, guided by Diego Mendez, seized the unfortunate Cacique, and carried off his wives, children, and chief friends to die miserable deaths of despair and broken-heartedness. Well might the poor creatures long to prevent even the least cruel of the white invaders from landing on their shores.

Even in the present day it is hard to teach civilized people that the uncivilized have rights equal with their own, and as sacred. In those days it was impossible.

CHAPTER XIV
MASTER PEDRO'S DOGS IN DANGER

It was still high day when Mendez the notary, and Montoro de Diego, returned from their expedition to the heart of the Cacique's territory, and reported themselves once more on board the Admiral's ship; but by the time the history of their doings and discoveries was ended, it was too late for any further undertakings in the building line that afternoon. Fernando got hold of his chosen friend and comrade as the interview with the Admiral came to an end, and said resolutely—

"Come now, Diego, I take upon myself to say that thou hast earned a holiday for the next twelve hours, and those not given to sleep I intend shall be devoted to me; or, if it please you better, to me and those dogs of thine."

"My dogs, indeed!" laughed Montoro. "I have told thee before, and I tell thee again, that they are no more mine than thine. Had I but known in time that I was to go ashore at Hispaniola, they should have been landed there for their rightful owner, I can tell thee, and I had been quit of their care once for all."

"Ay, and of their love too," retorted Fernando slyly.

Montoro shrugged his shoulders; but his affectation of indifference went for nought. The mutual affection existing between the couple of young bloodhounds, and their young keeper, was too well known by every one on board for his occasional pretence of carelessness about them to go for anything. His companion soon proved its present shallowness.

"Oh, well," he said, in his turn shrugging his shoulders, "if you have left off caring about them it's all right. But I do pity the poor brutes a little myself, having nothing to eat for the past—well, there's no saying how many hours. But you know you didn't feed them before you went off yesterday."

"Of course I did not," returned Montoro angrily, all his coolness utterly vanished. "It was much too early then to feed them; but I did not suppose I left behind me a set of heartless wretches, who would let poor dumb animals suffer."

Fernando Colon's lip twitched with something uncommonly like a smile as he expostulated —

"Nay then, you know perfectly that you choose always to feed them yourself. You have ever given small thanks to those who have dared to do so in your place."

"Ah!" exclaimed Montoro with rising passion. "And so because, forsooth, I choose to attend to the dogs myself, when I am on board, if I were dead you would let them starve?"

"Nay, for I should not then have to fear your scowl," was the answer ending with a laugh. But Nando added the next moment with a good-natured smile —

"Even the Admiral himself was not afraid of your wrath anent those doggies, when you were safe out of the way, for he fed them with his own hands."

As those last words were uttered Montoro turned sharply away and brushed his sleeve across his eyes. He turned back again almost as quickly, and laid a tolerably hard grip of his strong fingers on his companion's arm as he muttered huskily —

"You'll never let me get a hold over my temper, Nando, if you torment me thus. But did — did thy noble father in very truth think upon the wants of the poor doggies?"

Ferdinand's eyes were glistening too as he replied —

"Ay, that he did indeed. And know'st thou, Toro, half I feel jealous of thee, for verily I believe that it was as much on thy account as for the dogs' sake that my father did them so much honour. But hark to the storm they are making. They have found out thou art on board. Come away, and let them loose."

The next minute the two dogs of Master Pedro, the spice and curiosity dealer of El Cuevo, were bounding up on deck, giving vent to a succession of excited hurrahs in their own especial tongue.

Those half-unconscious caresses bestowed upon the hounds by Doña Rachel Diego at the hour of parting, those tears with which, in trying to conceal them, she had bedewed the dogs' heads, had so endeared the animals to her son, that from the outset of his long journeyings he ever considered their comfort before his own, and reaped the just reward in their fidelity and strong attachment to himself. But that evening he was destined to pay a somewhat heavy penalty for the friendship.

"Toro, you never give the dogs a swim," said Ferdinand suddenly, when, after a regular romping match, boys and animals had tumbled themselves down together in a promiscuous heap, to get back breath and energy for further proceedings. The dogs were so enormously strong that playing with them was not easy work like playing with kittens.

"I feel as if I had been engaged in a pretty stiff wrestling match," said Montoro, laughing, and stretching his arms, "and oh! how warm it's become, or I."

"You may as well add that 'or I,'" laughed back the other; "for I suspect, as the sun is going down, that the air must be somewhat cooler than when you came on board. But the hounds really do look hot, poor creatures, and they could get such a splendid bathe here in the river—and so could we."

"Umph!" growled that rather tired-out young Don Diego. "I think it would have been a much more sensible suggestion that we could have a splendid turn-in to our berths. But you are such a horrible fellow. I don't believe you ever know what it is to feel done up."

"Nor you either, generally," said Ferdinand with another laugh.

But his companion was not going to be weak enough to echo it, not he.

"'Generally' isn't 'never,'" he returned. "But here goes, you energetic plague. In with you as hard as you like, I'll follow."

And so saying he rolled himself over with a very good imitation of used-up laziness, and got himself slowly up from his hands and knees on to his feet, with the wind-up of a solemn, self-satisfied "Oh!"

"Oh, indeed!" came the mocking echo from half-a-dozen deep throats, followed by shouts of laughter.

Montoro was just a trifle disconcerted. He had not known of these extra witnesses of his performance.

"Pity but thy mother were here," said Diego Mendez, one of the group. "Then wouldst thou have surely had such another lollipop as must have rewarded thy first triumph in this exhibition."

"Nay then," came the reply, for the performer had not taken long to recover his self-possession; "nay then, Señor, if you are pleased to bestow that lollipop for the show it will be the first, seeing that on that other past occasion of which you speak I returned myself to the floor with a suddenness that bumped my forehead, and my reward, therefore, was a plaster."

"Thy impudent mouth deserves a hot plaster now, methinks," muttered a surly hidalgo in the background.

But fortunately hot-tempered Montoro did not hear the mutter, and no one else heeded it. The group of men moved off, and left the lads once more to their own devices. Montoro stepped up to the side of the vessel and looked over at the clear, bright waters of the river. The dogs shook themselves and followed him, Don rearing himself up on his hind legs on the right hand to look over, and Señor resolutely pushing himself in between the two boys, and rearing himself up on Montoro's left hand, with forepaws resting on the vessel's edge.

"How different the river looks now to the dingy-coloured, troubled stream we sailed up such a short time ago," said Montoro.

"Yes," answered Ferdinand; "the fair weather has given the mud and sand time to settle. That is why I think it looks so tempting for a bathe."

The dogs gave their answers also in an expressive fashion of their own, like the hurrah business, hunching up their shoulders, and settling their heads down between them with noses pushed forward, and intent eyes that meant anything you like to imagine, except disagreement with their friend. Still that same friend hesitated. His human companion glanced at him with some wonder.

"Toro—"

"Ay, Nando, what now?"

"Only—the banks are very nigh on either hand, and thou canst swim now, I take it, as well as any one on board these caravels?"

"Hey, what sayest thou?" said Montoro, with a bewildered stare in his eyes, which was very nearly reproduced in the other pair when he suddenly recollected himself, and exclaimed with a short laugh—"Why now, Nando, you may fairly think that I have lost my wits; but in truth they had but gone travelling on their own account hence to El Cuevo, and—Come. I can swim, saidst thou? Truly can I then, and I'll prove it by beating you and the dogs in a match from here to the shore yonder, and back again."

"Done with you," exclaimed the sailor's son, beginning his disrobing with eager haste as he spoke. "Antonio," he shouted to the pilot, "Antonio! be good-natured; drop us over a rope, and bide here to summon us back if we are wanted."

"A crocodile, maybe, will have you first," answered Alaminos as he sauntered up.

"In saying so you belie your own boasted knowledge that these ugly brutes will not, unprovoked, attack a human being," was the quick retort.

"Even so," was the calm reply; "neither will they. But I said not they would hesitate to make a snap at imps."

However, there were no crocodiles—to give the alligators the name given to them at that time—to be seen, neither were other more dangerous enemies to be seen, when the two boys and the two dogs took their simultaneous plunge, with a splutter and dash and commotion that drew two or three of the crew to keep watch beside the pilot.

Once in the water, Montoro quite forgot that he was tired, and struck out vigorously for the shore. Unfortunately, however, for the fulfilment of his boast, his four-footed admirers would insist upon trying to help him, first to get back to the caravel, which they appeared to consider the wisest proceeding; and when he had at last thoroughly convinced them that he intended to keep his face for the present turned the other way, their attentions were little less retarding. One would get a whole bunch of the curly black locks between his teeth firmly, if not exactly comfortably to their owner, while the other made perpetual lip-nibbles at his ears and shoulders. Montoro was not at all sorry at last to join the laughing and exultant Ferdinand on the river bank.

"Don and Señor shall go back first when we return," he said with a reproachful shake of his head at the four-footed individuals in question. "I should have beaten you easily but for them."

"Poor old doggies!" said Ferdinand, stroking the great head nearest to him as he spoke. "Good old fellows; you'd better far make friends with me, as he is so ungrateful to you."

As though the dogs understood the address made to them, when Nando took his hand from Señor's head, and rolled himself down the bank back into the water again, with a great souse, and forthwith set to work floundering and swimming and diving and jumping, Señor jumped up, gave a hasty lick to Diego's hand, and then followed the other boy into the water, and the two together began to hurry back to the ship, actuated at first by a spirit of mischief, and then, by the sharply-uttered orders of the Admiral.

And while Columbus shouted his commands to his young son to return to him, others were trying to obey the orders to man a boat instantly, and put off from the ship for the shore Fernando and Señor had just left.

"But there is no boat! they are all yonder!" groaned Antonio de Alaminos as he wrung his hands. "And the bravest and brightest spirit of us all will die unrevenged."

CHAPTER XV
NOISE TO THE RESCUE

That Montoro Diego should die 'unrevenged' was Antonio the pilot's only moan. To wish for his life might well seem useless. How should he live without aid, and how should aid be got to him in time, even should there be a dozen boats available! Arrows were flying around him, and arrows fly faster than any rowers yet heard of can ply their oars.

The fact of the matter was this. Very few people care now-a-days, nor ever have cared, for uninvited guests; and the Cacique of Veragua and his people were no exceptions to the general rule. When Columbus and his four caravels appeared off their coasts, they were as pleased with the novel exhibition as we are with a sight of the Persian Shah, an elephant called Jumbo, or a king of the Cannibal Islands. And they treated the exhibitors very well, giving them much more than enough for one feast; and then, when they were satisfied with the sight, and had found that enough of that was certainly, so far as they were concerned, as good as a feast, they gave their visitors some very valuable little presents, and courteously hinted — "Now you may go."

But, instead of taking the unacceptable hint, they didn't go. On the contrary, they coolly took possession of other people's land, built a considerable number of houses upon it, and showed plainly enough that they meant to take up their abode there without an invitation. These Spaniards would never have dreamt of trying to treat their home neighbours, the Portuguese or the French, with such scant ceremony. But these Veraguans were "only savages, heathen, miserable dark-skinned creatures, with no rights at all." No claims to halfpence, only to kicks.

Unfortunately, these poor heathen savages thought differently. Quibian, with his bad leg laid up in his uncivilized palace, growled forth his orders to his painted warriors to expel the impudent intruders; and all his able-bodied subjects turned themselves into volunteers for the furtherance of the same purpose. Here, there, and everywhere around that bit of coast, and between the two rivers, lurked the Spaniards' foes, and half-a-dozen particularly malicious ones were concealed just within the borders of the forest, facing the Admiral's ship, when Montoro and Ferdinand forsook its safety for their ill-advised bathe. The spies grinned at each other with silent delight when they saw the boys swim straight for the bank, mount it, and actually place themselves in the full power of the enemy. The arrows would have left the bows at once, and both the lads might have suffered but for the dogs.

The Veraguans, like their neighbours on the great new continent, had no domestic animals, and the gambols and tricks of Don and Señor were most fascinatingly wonderful to those hidden spectators, who almost forgot their desire to kill the dogs' companions in delighted attention to the dogs themselves. But suddenly Fernando, in that very unexpected way, rolled himself down the bank and disappeared,—he and one of the four-footed friends,—only to reappear to their eyes half-way back to the ship. The Indians were furious at his escape and their own stupidity, and, darting out of their hiding-place, shot off all six arrows simultaneously at the two hoped-for victims still remaining in their power.

Rather, it should be said, the one hoped-for victim, for the Indians would have rather preferred to spare Don had it been possible. But the animal, obeying its instincts, sprang forward on seeing the strangers, and received three out of the six arrows in its own body. The others fell harmless, for Montoro, on seeing the unexpected adversaries, had obeyed his natural human instincts, and sprung on one side.

In so springing he involuntarily followed Fernando's example, and rolled down the bank. Had he then and there set off swimming back to his friends, he would in all probability have got off uninjured; but the help Master Sancho, the merchant, had many a time in El Cuevo seen him render to those more helpless than himself he was ready with now, almost as much as a matter of instinct as the actions that preceded the unselfish act.

As he disappeared down the bank the Veraguans uttered yells of disappointed rage; but through those sounds there fell upon his ears, with an accent of bitter disappointment, a most piteous moan. Poor Don had given his body as a shield for his companion, and now that he lay suffering, perhaps dying, his companion was forsaking him. Don felt that to be very hard lines, and so he howled out his sorrow. He certainly would not have treated his friend so, and though his friend was only a human being, and not a faithful dog, he had imagined this especial human being to be different to most. It seemed he was mistaken, and so he howled for his disappointment. And Montoro heard the mournful howl, and understood all it said as well as if it had been the very longest and most comprehensive German word that even Bret Harte ever got hold of.

Ten seconds later the spectators on board the ship saw the lad remounting the bank with a wild bound, actually returning towards his enemies—one unarmed, defenceless boy against half-a-dozen fierce warriors.

"And all for the sake of a dog," said Alaminos to him some time later with a touch of anger.

"All for the sake of a creature that cried to me for aid," was the reply. "And ere I cease to care for such, I trust that I may no longer cumber the earth."

But during those present moments, while Montoro was climbing the bank, the pilot was standing with wide eyes gazing across at him, and wondering greatly as to the motives for his strange proceeding. He had forgotten about the dog, or thought it was dead and done for.

Poor old Don himself knew better. He was lying there helpless, with three arrows in his faithful side; but he was not yet too dead or done for to be able to give vent to an ecstatic weak squeak of a bark when he caught sight again of his beloved master.

So astounded were the Indians that they beat a momentary retreat into the forest, while Montoro knelt down and pulled the arrows out of the dog's wounds, Don the while alternately licking his hands and moaning. But it was no time just then for delicate handling. The three arrows were out in little more than as many seconds, and then with an inspiriting "Hi, good dog," Diego roused up the poor animal and pulled it down the bank with him once more, just as a second flight of arrows sped more truly to their intended mark. This time Diego quivered, and uttered one sharp, irrepressible cry as four of the darts struck and pierced his unprotected flesh. Pulling out the one most accessible, he plunged into the water, the dog with him. The Indians rushed forward. For those past few seconds they had imagined he must have some means of defence at hand to make him so daring, but now they were undeceived, and proportionably brave, themselves. Another flight of arrows was launched, this time happily with such eager, excited haste as to be harmless. But what advantage was that? The foe had plenty more arrows, and would apparently have plenty more time to shoot them at their wished-for target, for both the lad and the dog were evidently much hurt, and were swimming very slowly and feebly.

Then it was that Antonio de Alaminos wrung his hands and groaned over his favourite's impending fate. But the Admiral did something better than groan. There was no possibility of getting a boat across from the building-ground in time to be of any use, and the position was imminent.

One more glance was cast by the father at his young son rapidly nearing the vessel, and still unconscious of his friend's danger, and then the order was shouted forth—"Fire off the guns—wait not to take aim."

Answering shouts of comprehension greeted the order, and as the guns were now always in a state of readiness for immediate use, it was obeyed with almost incredible speed, so great was the eagerness to save the young life now in jeopardy. Even while the exhausted Montoro was plunging himself and Don under water to escape another shower of arrows, there came the flash, the roar of the four falconets, followed by peal upon peal of the most frantic screechings from the Indians. Whether they were hurt was very doubtful, but it was evident enough that they were madly terrified. Flinging away their weapons, they decamped into the shelter of the forest again, and it was only by the fading sound of the continued shrieks that the direction of their retreat towards the village could be learnt.

"That was a lucky thought—to fight by fear," said Diego Mendez with a sigh of relief, as he prepared to spring into the river to the further aid of the rescued Montoro; but the Admiral checked him one moment, saying reverently—

"It was a blessed thought, my friend, for it was inspired by God."

Twenty minutes later Montoro was safe in his berth; the arrows had been extracted, and the wounds dressed, and poor Don lay dozing uneasily at his feet. It had just been suggested that the dog should be put out of its sufferings forthwith by a blow on the head. But Columbus would not have it done. The lad had nearly lost his life to save the animal's, and it should not prove such a useless service.

"You will at any rate, my father, allow me a little time to try to get him well?" said Ferdinand eagerly.

"Most assuredly, my son," answered the Admiral. "For thy friend's sake, and for the dog's, it shall be so."

And thus it came to pass that while Montoro lay ill of fever from his torn wounds and over-fatigue, many weighty things befell his companions and the Indians of Veragua, and faithful Don lay at his master's feet and licked himself back into wholeness. In fact, Don's surgical appliances did him good far more speedily than those made use of on behalf of Montoro. And when his comrade Señor's bones lay bleaching in the American forest some few weeks later, he was bounding about the deck in full strength and health, and utter disregard of the calamities that had befallen nearly every other living creature any way connected with him.

When Montoro again recovered consciousness the Admiral's caravel was once more on the way to Hispaniola. The settlement at Veragua had been half destroyed, wholly abandoned; the poor Cacique of Veragua and his people were slain, dead or dispersed; and once more Montoro de Diego, and many of his companions, had to turn their hopes of fortune to the island colony that had already, in the short space of eight years, been so frequently the hotbed of envy, hatred, malice, and all uncharitableness.

CHAPTER XVI
I AM 'DON ALONZO.'

It was a splendid evening one day towards the end of the year 1503, when a tall, plainly-attired, handsome youth drew near the home of a Spanish colonist to whom he had notes of introduction. He had walked out to it from San Domingo, a distance of some five miles, and now stood still to survey the scene, his hand resting on a dog's head the while that had accompanied him.

"It is a glorious place, old Don," he muttered in a tone of considerable satisfaction, although it betokened great surprise as well.

And a glorious place it was, and most especially beautiful now that the long, low houses of stone and earth, the waving palms, and all the other luxuriance of that southern clime, were bathed in the golden glory of a southern sunset. In a cushioned reclining chair, placed in a shady spot of the broad verandah, lounged a young man, handsome, but for a Spaniard coarse-featured and rather thick-set. However, all defects of person were thrown into the background by a sumptuousness of attire that fairly startled the youth as he at length approached, and delivered his letters.

"And you are the son of Master Pedro, the spice-dealer of El Cuevo!" he breathed forth at last.

The words of that ejaculation were common-place enough, but the tone in which they were uttered, and the look with which they were accompanied, made them so inexpressibly gratifying, and at the same time comical, to the man to whom they were addressed, that he burst into a loud, long laugh before vouchsafing them any other answer.

"Yes, yes," he said at last, recovering himself with an easy nonchalance. "Yes, yes, youngster, I do not mind confessing to you, since you know the fact before my confession, that the worthy old gentleman yonder, with his frugal fare, and his better stuff cloak for holidays, is my father, and a rare good old miser he is, to save the maravedis for my spending. But mind ye, that is between you and me and Saint Peter."

A wondering gaze from a great pair of thoughtful, brilliant eyes was the questioning reply to this intimation. "And for the rest of the world," asked the owner of the eyes after a short pause, "who is your father for the rest of the world?"

Another laugh greeted this query.

"Why, for the rest of the world, being what you have found me, Don Alonzo de Loyala, my father is, like thine own, some long-deceased grandee of Spain, who neglected his duty towards his son as regarded the due endowment of riches to maintain my rank in mine own land."

As this mocking speech ended, Montoro de Diego's cheeks flushed angrily, and he exclaimed—

"Do you then imply that my claims to noble birth are thus also assumed? By St.—"

"Nay then, nay," good-humouredly interrupted the other. "In these latitudes it is not well for health to heat thyself for nought. Keep thy passion for the red rascals, who are so lazy that they'll die rather than live and work. I imply nothing to thy detriment. Wert thou placed as I am, then wouldst thou also have a wealthy father at thy back, to help thee to maintain that rank out here it should pleasure thee to claim. Meantime, I do no more than half of those around me, and with better right; for I am no released felon, and I deal honestly by those I trade with. I will deal honestly with you. Twice have I had advices from my father, and from good master Sancho, that I should try to secure you for a companion and aid, should you elect to remain here on the Admiral's return to Spain. And I like you at first sight well enough to be willing to take their advice. Will you stay with me then, or shall I help you to find friends elsewhere?"

Montoro looked at the man from head to foot slowly and earnestly, as he lounged there before him, so great a contrast to himself, and then as slowly and earnestly said—

"I agree to stay—for a time."

"Umph!" muttered the self-styled Don Alonzo, somewhat taken aback in his turn. "Umph! my noble youngster, methinks from your air you suppose the obligation to be rather more mutual than I esteem it. You are a beggar and friendless, and I—am not."

However, Montoro was not now so friendless as his new colleague assumed. Had he returned to Spain, even there he might now have been found some sort of employment, and out in the Colony the spirited young adventurer, with a pair of hands both able and willing to work, could have easily found some more indolent seeker after wealth willing to go into partnership with him. But Rachel de Diego was sheltered under the roof of the spice-merchant, and her son had a hidden eagerness that he might be able to find shelter under the roof of the spice-merchant's son. It was to that motive that 'Don Alonzo' owed the easy settlement of his agreement with his new young partner, and not, as he imagined, to the promising air of luxurious comfort in his surroundings. That offered more allurements to a third party to the affair.

Don threatened for a few minutes to upset the amiable arrangements between his real owner and his self-adopted master, for poor Don had very faint notions of the rights of property and ownership, and Don was thirsty and Don was hungry, and, moreover, Don was as fond of grapes as any Christian Don, real or pretended, to be found in or out of Spain. All of a sudden, while Montoro was gazing thoughtfully out at the silver line of distant sea, and Don Alonzo was muttering to himself the remark mentioned above, tired Don caught sight of a piled-up dish of grapes on a table in the verandah. He licked his dry lips, and went on eyeing them. Then he licked his dry lips again, and ventured upon a small whine. That sound recalled Montoro's wandering wits so far that he turned round and nodded to his four-footed friend, and said dreamily—

"Yes, yes. All right, good old Don."

That was enough. Don was in that state of longing that a very small amount of encouragement was enough to induce him to help himself to the desired feast, and before either of his companions knew well what he was about, he had bounded up to the table, scrunched up one juicy, deliciously refreshing bunch of grapes, and had a second in his mouth about to be treated in the same way. But "there's many a slip 'twixt the cup and the lip," and in this instance there proved to be a slip 'twixt the lip and the throat.

Don Alonzo quickly became aware of what was going on, and, seizing a heavy bottle, he flung it with full force angrily at the dog; and it hit, not the dog, but the dog's champion, happily only a touch, and then fell crashing on the floor of the verandah.

The next instant Montoro's first dash forward to save the dog was followed by a second to save Don Alonzo; for the huge animal had made a furious spring at his antagonist, accompanied by a growl that gave full promise of his intentions. Montoro's most resolute and stern command was needed before the hound was brought to crouch down by his side, with red-lit eyes still glaring at his unrecognized owner.

"That brute shall be shot before he's an hour older," came the surly declaration at last, as Montoro knelt on the stone pavement soothing the animal back into good temper. At the sharp announcement he looked up quickly.

"Then you shall shoot him through me," he said passionately, "as you struck me just now instead of him. He is my only friend out here, and we will live or die together."

Don Alonzo shook himself irritably. He was good-hearted enough if over-indulgent parents in the first instance, and superabundant good fortune since, had not rather spoilt him. Besides, four years' sojourn on the island of Hispaniola had not tended to teach regard for any life but his own; that he esteemed at quite a high enough rate, and he answered Montoro now with angry remonstrance—

"It is all very fine to talk heroics, youngster; but thinkest thou that I am going to be browbeaten into keeping my own dog, to stand in danger of being mauled by it any time its tempers up, as if I were a wretched native!"

Montoro stood up and folded his arms.

"Neither you nor any other man, Indian or European, shall suffer from Doffs teeth. Or, if perchance that sounds too proud a boast, for the first human being that Don injures he shall die. He shall be as a lamb to you now—see—hold out your hand."

With some scarcely-disguised trepidation Alonzo obeyed. Don cast a beseeching glance of remonstrance at his friend; but instead of any encouragement to rejection of the offered fellowship, he got a grave shake of the head; and with a very crestfallen aspect he rose, walked dolefully along the verandah, and put his paw into the outstretched hand, and looked up with mute appeal for forgiveness.

Don Alonzo was wise enough to seal the new compact with a freely-generous gift of more of the coveted grapes. If Montoro for Don, and Don for himself, would engage that Don Alonzo should never feel the sharpness of that animal's teeth, his owner was only too willing that it should live. For it was quite the fashion now to use these powerful dogs out in the new world, not only as terrible aids in battle against the poor, half-defenceless Indians, but also to hunt down the miserable, wholly-defenceless slaves who sometimes dared to run away to die in peace in their native forests, instead of beneath the short-sighted, as well as brutal, taskmaster's lash.

The young Diego had declared that Don should never be so employed, but that declaration Don Alonzo comfortably decided in his own mind was all nonsense. He himself had had qualms about the treatment of the natives when he first came out, but he had long since got rid of all such inconvenient scruples; and so of course would this new arrival get speedily rid of his. Every one did, with the exception of that impracticable idiot of a neighbour of his, that young fellow Las Casas, who had come out from Spain with his head so full of theories and bookish ideas that he had no room in it for common sense.

CHAPTER XVII
GOOD OLD DON

Time passed on. In Spain good Queen Isabella died, and two years later the poor, neglected noble-hearted, pious old Admiral, Christopher Columbus, recommending himself to God, and his two sons, Diego and Ferdinand, to King Ferdinand's tardy justice and each other's brotherly love, also bade a final farewell to an ungrateful world.

And in Hispaniola also time passed on. Many there grieved over the Admiral when he was dead, who had tormented him in every possible way when living,—that is the way with poor, stupid human nature. But he had one true mourner, who had loved and served him with all his heart during the year that they were together, and whose memory for those he cared for was not a short one. Montoro de Diego, amidst his many new interests, felt a very keen pang of sorrow when the news was brought out to the island, towards the end of the year 1506, of the loss the world had sustained.

"Ah! Señor Las Casas," he sighed one morning, some months later; "ah! then, if he had lived, and the queen, you might then have had hope even yet to work some good for these wretched, rightful owners of these lands. But now—"

"Ay, indeed!" exclaimed Bartholomew Las Casas with heaving chest, as he rose and strode hastily up and down his terrace. "You may well pause upon that but now, Diego. For now one might more wisely waste breath in calling upon wolves and wild cats to cease from fierceness, than in pleading with one's fellow-men for mercy, justice, or compassion. 'Give us yourselves,' is the fierce cry that echoes all around us. 'Give us yourselves, your wives and daughters, for our humble slaves; give us your gold, your lands, all you hold most valuable; resign your wills, your faith, your souls into our keeping, and we will give you leave to live as long as unremitting toil and cruelty will let you. But resist us, fight for your country or your liberty, contradict our lightest caprice, and we will shoot you down as though you were so many rabbits, we will hunt you to death with our dogs as though you were vermin or wild beasts.'"

The young man came to a sudden stop, with a face glowing with generous indignation, and literally panting for breath with his burst of righteous wrath. Montoro's cheeks were flushed with sympathy as he said in quick reply—

"It is so. I can but too terribly vouch for the truth of your bitter accusation. But, Señor, your brethren the priests, can they not—"

Las Casas turned upon him with sharp interruption.

"Can they not help me, you would ask? Ay, verily," with indignant scorn; "well indeed do they help the cause I have at heart! This is one of the proclamations allowed by some of those same brethren the priests—'Your souls are doomed to eternal perdition, your bodies belong to those who have conquered your soil!' Much good my brethren the priests will do!"

There was a short silence, and then he continued more calmly, and laying his hand upon a pile of papers, "But after all, Diego, I do hope to work some good for the poor natives. I have written out a strong case for them, and I am intending to return to Spain shortly, there to plead their cause myself."

"And you shall have my testimony, if you will," said Montoro eagerly. "For it is our Don Alonzo's will that I should take a journey to Spain this coming season, in charge of a somewhat richer freight than usual. And if you start not immediately we may go together."

"And Don?" said Las Casas, in smiling interrogation.

"Ay, truly," was the laughing answer, although something of a blush accompanied it. "But in faith," he added the next moment, "it is not only for love of the animal that I have it for my constant companion. Since I have discovered the horrible use to which its fellows are put, I live in fear of a coming day when I may regret having saved its life."

"Then," continued his friend, "you will leave it behind you in Spain perchance, when you return hither?"

"That is so long to look ahead," said Montoro, feeling not a little glad that he was not called upon for an immediate decision.

When it really came to the point he did what he thought much better than leaving Don behind in El Cuevo. He got Master Pedro to transfer all property in it to himself. His services to the old spice-dealer and his son had well merited so much of a reward. And as for Don, he deserved not only a good master, but almost as many bunches of grapes besides as he chose to eat, when, a couple of years later, he was the means of saving Montoro's life and a bag full of gold-dust to the value of many thousand pesos.

Diego's first return journey to Spain proved so successful, owing to his scrupulous honesty and intelligence, that Don Alonzo speedily sent him on a second, and others also most eagerly availed themselves of so upright a messenger to transmit their golden gleanings to their own country.

But, as it happened, with Diego there voyaged also to Spain three ne'er-do-wells. They had gambled away all their slaves, all their grants of land, all their gathered-up spoils, and then, having finally gambled away all their future prospects of wealth in Hispaniola, the miscreants, as mean as they were bad, slipped away from the island and their creditors on the first ship back to Spain.

"And mind ye," muttered one of the number to his companions one evening, as they drew near the end of their two months' voyage,—"mind ye, if we follow that insolent, set-up fellow Diego a day or two's journey up the country after landing, we shall not be losing time, neither shall we have cause to regret having left Hispaniola in his company."

"How so?" questioned one of the two eager listeners doubtfully. "My child yonder, little Bautista, told me when I questioned him some days ago anent Diego's gold, that the bags were to be sent by other hands to Madrid."

"And you credit the tale!" exclaimed the first speaker scornfully. "You'll believe next that the Garden of Paradise has been found."

"And so I will," was the retort, "when the news is given me by Montoro de Diego. He would not lie to save his life, and least of all would he lie to a child."

"By all the saints," sneered the third of the group, "but Don Diego hath a warm advocate in you! Doubtless it were useless to expect you to touch his gold, even though it lay by the wayside to be picked up."

"Doubtless under those circumstances," was the sharp reply, "there should be little left for you to snatch. All the same, he hath shown kindness to my boy, and he tells him nought but truth."

"Well, well," said Almado, the first speaker, more softly, "there is no need that we should wrangle over the fellow's virtues, they sicken me forsooth. Ne'er the less, he shall be a very saint if you will, so we do but get his merchandise. As for the gold that is to go to Madrid, that is but that small part, of what he carries, which is for the king's coffers. Of that I am well assured. So you see thy little son yonder hath been told the truth indeed, but only in part, and maybe to mislead us."

"Umph," muttered Bautista's father, also more quietly. "That may well be."

"Ay," agreed the third of the company, "that may well be."

And for the next few hours they all redoubled their efforts to be on good terms with Don. They flattered themselves, indeed, that he regarded them quite in the light of friends, for Don, like most very strong creatures, whether going on two legs or four, never troubled himself to show uncalled-for fierceness. As long as no one interfered with him or his master, and his master gave him no orders to interfere with others, he maintained the grave indifference of manner worthy of a highborn Spaniard. But woe betide those who should presume upon this calmness.

Arrived at Cadiz, Montoro delivered up the royal revenue to the authorized messengers awaiting it, and then he and his dog and his bags set out on their journey up the country, in company with worthy Master Sancho, who had come to meet him, and two or three other traders from the interior.

"Farewell, my little Bautista," said Montoro; "I shall pray for our future meeting."

"Nay," said the child hurriedly, and with a frightened look round, "do not that, Señor. I love you, you have been good to me, and so I pray the Virgin to grant we may not meet again."

Montoro opened his eyes wide.

"How so, little man? Love me, and yet pray that we may not again cross each other's paths? How is that, tell me?"

But the boy shook his head, and began to tremble violently.

"Do not ask me," he muttered with white lips; "they will kill me. Only keep away from us. They do not know I have heard — —"

"Ha!" exclaimed Montoro, a look of intelligence now taking the place of bewilderment. Then he stooped and kissed the child's forehead, as he said in low tones, "Blessings on thee for thy true heart, my little lad, and my thanks. May the Lord have thee in His keeping, and guard thy hands from sin."

And so they parted, each, as poor little Bautista fondly thought, to go widely different ways, but in reality to take two routes leading to the same goal.

For the first two days' journey inland the party to which Montoro joined himself was a particularly strong one, too strong for the three gamblers to care to meddle with; accordingly they withdrew themselves from notice, until the travelling company was reduced to Montoro himself, Master Sancho and his thick-headed attendant, and a couple of poor-spirited merchants, who would have rather hidden themselves in their bales at the appearance of danger, than tried to defend them. But then—there was Don.

The third day was drawing to a close, when Diego and his companions reached a wretched little inn, the worst on their route, and with considerable grumbling on the part of comfort-loving Master Sancho, they put up there for the night. To make matters worse, the amount of available accommodation was even less than usual, for another party of travellers had arrived before them, and taken the chief and largest room.

However, there was no help for it. Master Sancho had to make the best of a bad bargain, and as nothing would induce him to share a room with Don, and nothing would induce Montoro to dispense with Don's company as a guardian under present circumstances, he and the dog had one room, and the worthy burgess of El Cuevo and the two merchants from Saragossa had to crowd into the other.

"One night," explained Master Sancho to his companions, "that young rascal I've taken a fancy to, persuaded me to share a sleeping apartment with him and that great brute, and in the night I snored,—I'm given to snore,—and the creature didn't approve, and woke me up with a sounding thump of its great paw. And there, behold! it stood reared up over me, with glaring eyes and a growling mouth. I warrant you, I prayed in one minute to more saints in the calendar than I've prayed to in many a long year before."

"Doubtless," assented one of the merchants with paling cheeks. "I have ever thought it a fearful great beast, and unsafe. But hearken! Methinks it is now quarrelling even with its own master. Ah!" with startled breathlessness—"it is shot."

Then there was a sudden rushing all over the inn. Screams, shrieks, shouts, slamming of doors, and above all, the continuous roar of Don's deep growling bark.

At length men and lights were gathered in Montoro's room, and there stood Montoro holding in a firm grip one of the smugglers. But the hero of the fray, and the conqueror, was grand old Don standing with one great fore-paw on the breast of one robber, the other fore-paw on the breast of Bautista's father, who lay weltering in his blood, shot by the other of his comrades in the attempt to shoot the dog.

"But my child, my little son," murmured the wretched, dying man.

"I will guard and care for him," said Montoro huskily.

He had been rescued from misery himself once, now he was the rescuer.

CHAPTER XVIII
DEATH FOR DON

It was the early part of the year 1511, when Montoro, become now quite an experienced islander and man of business, left Don Alonzo's place, Palmyra, one morning for the neighbouring town of San Domingo. The object of the visit was to arrange some important matters with certain foreign merchants, who had lately arrived with tempting offers to the planters for the produce of their estates.

"And don't hurry thyself," said Don Alonzo with unusual consideration. "Take thy pleasure for a few days when thou art in the town, for verily this dog's hole of a place is dull enough to make a man long to shuffle off life with a native's readiness."

"If those same natives should get the upper-hand," answered Montoro drily, "I doubt not they would help you. Meantime, I will trust to find you still in the flesh, and well, when I return, and so—*adios*."

"And for you, fair journeyings and good bargains," said the indolent superior, as he lay lounging in his low chair sipping a cool lime-juice beverage. Little enough of the work he did himself towards accumulating his own wealth.

But, lazy and self-indulgent as he was, it had not escaped Montoro that there was a certain scarcely-suppressed eagerness, and barely-hidden hope of some sort, underlying his present declared wishes for his subordinate's comfort. As Montoro left the verandah and passed through the house he called to his rescued *protégé*, who had proved useful enough to secure himself a home beneath Don Alonzo's roof. No work had seemed to come amiss to him, excepting that of aid to the overseers in the gold mines, in which he had been recently employed. But the brutal task-masters had just sent the boy back, saying that he was no good to them whatever, worse than no good indeed, for he pitied the rascally workers instead of flogging them.

Bautista came readily enough when he heard his beloved Señor Diego's voice.

"Am I to go with you, my Señor?" he exclaimed beseechingly. "Ah! but I will be to you eyes and hands and feet, if I may."

"I prefer to use my own, thank you," answered Montoro smiling, as he patted the boy's head. "But look not so disappointed, Bautista, for if I cannot trust myself to thee, I am going to leave in thy charge one I hold almost dearer. I leave thee guardian of our faithful old Don. And see thou that he comes to no harm, and—that he does no harm. I have guarded him from that sin hitherto; do thou guard him in my absence."

A deep breath, almost a groan, burst from the boy's lips.

"My Señor," he muttered anxiously, "give me some other duty to perform for you. This may be too hard."

Diego frowned.

"I trust not," he said sternly. "It shall be worse for others if it prove so. And remember, you have my orders, and if need be you must declare them."

So saying he nodded his farewell to the boy and departed, leaving Don's new guardian in a very doleful frame of mind, for he knew well enough the cause of Don Alonzo's desire to be a short time rid of Montoro.

The spice-merchant's son was good-natured enough so long as he was crossed in nothing, but Montoro's settled refusal to have Don used as a hunter of runaway slaves had roused Alonzo's spite, and for the past year, ever since the return of Montoro and the dog from Spain, he had been seeking some chance to gratify his malice. Hitherto where Diego had gone the dog had gone, but at last this expedition to the town was arranged, and for various circumstances it was more convenient to leave Don behind.

"And at last," declared Don Alonzo with a malicious chuckle, "at last the brute shall be set to its proper work."

Bautista was in the apartment at the time, as well as one of the overseers, and as a significant warning to him the words were added—"And it shall have its first taste of the flesh of any one, be he Spaniard or native, who betrays my purpose to Señor Long-face."

No wonder the boy desired that some other duty might be commuted to his charge by his patron, in test of his affection. As Montoro rode off with a party of attendants, Bautista made his way to Don, and poured out his fears to an apparently perfectly intelligent pair of ears.

"But all the same, you know quite well, Don," said Bautista reproachfully, "you do know quite well, that in spite of your good Christian bringing up, you would seize a poor redskin by the leg if you were set at him."

"Of course he would, like the sensible thoroughbred he is," shouted a well-known voice not a couple of yards distant. And Bautista sprang to his feet with a terrified look on his face, as he saw the hateful head overseer, Jerome Tivoli, had come up to him unperceived.

The man now stood intently regarding the dog, with a more sinister expression than usual upon his cruel face, and the boy could scarcely restrain himself from flying away from the spot. Nothing short of his loyal devotion to his patron could have kept him there. At last he said huskily—

"It is useless so to examine this dog, for, strong or weak, you can have nought to do with it, since it belongs to the Señor Diego, and he chooses not that it should be used for your purposes."

De Tivoli uttered a short, hard laugh, and his eyes glittered as he said slowly—

"Ah! yes. It is the Señor Montoro de Diego's dog—-his favourite. And verily it is a fine animal, and powerful, and will do a day's work well for us. That dog of a slave Guatchi has run away, and, dead or alive, yon pet of our Señor Diego shall bring him back to us."

Bautista flung himself down again beside the dog, and threw his arms about its neck, as he exclaimed with the courage of affection—

"No! I tell thee no, Señor Tivoli. Señor Diego has left it to me to guard his dog from doing harm, and I will keep my charge."

De Tivoli's thin lips curled; but ere he could reply other footsteps were heard approaching, and Don Alonzo himself appeared upon the scene.

"How now, De Tivoli," he exclaimed hastily. "Why dost thou waste time? The idle rascal Guatchi hath had start enough, I trow, to breathe the dog e'en now; why dost thou delay?"

"It is but for a minute, Don Alonzo," replied the other coolly. "Yon boy declares that, for Don Diego's sake, it shall not be sent hunting."

"And I," retorted Don Alonzo, "swear by St. Jago that it shall."

"And I, in the name of one higher," exclaimed Montoro de Diego, thus unexpectedly making his own appearance on the scene again, "I declare, with Bautista, that it shall not go."

Don Alonzo started slightly, and his face flushed for a moment with ill-restrained annoyance and uneasiness as he saw that set, resolute countenance before him; but he tried to assume an air of carelessness, and to laugh away the matter with an off-hand—

"Why, my mentor, how have you contrived to accomplish the business you had in hand so quickly? What brings you back so soon?"

"Your good genius, I feel inclined to imagine," was Montoro's answer, in tones somewhat quieter than those of his first exclamation. But the fading sparkle in his eyes rekindled as his companion replied irritably—

"Then I wish the meddlesome beast had minded its own business, instead of sending you back here to pull a long face over what I mean to do in spite of it."

As he spoke he walked up to where the dog Don lay tethered, held a strip of cotton cloth to its nose, and then muttering viciously—

"Find him, Don, find him!" pressed his finger hastily on the spring of the dog's collar, and set it free.

The great animal bounded forward. The next instant there was a howl, a moan, and Don lay dying at Montoro's feet; rather, one should say, at Montoro's knees, for the young man had sunk on to them almost as soon as his own fist had fallen with that lightning stroke, and the same hand that had dealt the death-blow was now soothing the poor brute's last agonies. It was Montoro de Diego who had killed it, and yet it was to Montoro's face that the pleading brown eyes were lifted with their last gaze of affection, and it was Montoro's hand that the dying tongue licked with the last breath.

"My poor old Don," muttered Montoro huskily, as he tenderly pressed the side quivering with the death struggle; "poor old Don."

"It's fine for thee to pity the poor brute when it owes its sufferings to thy malice," exclaimed Don Alonzo furiously, and with fingers on the hilt of his dagger, as though they itched to lay his companion beside the animal.

But Diego paid no seeming heed to the show of rage. Maintaining his kneeling position for a while longer, he replied quietly—

"Yes, it once owed its life to me, and now it owes its death to me, and better so than it should have been the innocent cause of suffering to one of our human brethren, for whom the cross rose on Calvary."

And then he rose from beside the dog's dead body, and turned slowly away with a saddened face. In spite of its ferocious nature, the animal had always been most docile with him; and besides, it had been that oft-felt link with his mother's home. How long ago now seemed that first day of parting from his country, when Rachel de Diego's slender fingers had rested for a few moments on the animal's head. Her son would far rather have a second time undergone some peril to save its life, than have had to destroy it for the prevention of a crime.

"Ah, Señor," murmured Bautista, as he crept out on to the verandah after him a few minutes later. "Ah, Señor, you have saved poor Guatchi's limbs from being mangled; but I doubt me you have made an enemy for yourself."

"You were willing to do the same in the same cause, Bautista," was the answer with a grave smile of approval. "I knew not that thou wast so staunchly ranged on the side of justice and mercy. Henceforth we are friends."

The boy sprang forward to clasp the hand held out to him, and said eagerly—

"To follow in your steps, Señor, I began to remind myself that the Indians' flesh had feelings like our own, but my past month in the mines has been a black lesson in horror that I would not repeat to escape the pains of purgatory. These Indians are tenfold weaker than we are, and their sufferings are tenfold more, for they have learnt nothing of manhood to sustain them. You have seen them die here in the plantations, Señor, and that has roused your pity; but in those mines it is not that *some* die, but that *none survive*. A few days of that dismal work beneath cuffs and lashes, and their strength is spent—"

"And then?" came the short query.

"And then," ended the boy with a sort of gasp for breath, "they sink to the ground, and the brutal kick given to rouse them up to continued labour, is the accompaniment of their last breath. It is little wonder, Señor, that I should wish poor Guatchi to get away free, now that he has escaped such toil alive."

The whole fervour of the boy's susceptible nature was aroused, and Montoro felt more than ever convinced that he was in the presence of one whose spirit was akin to his own.

"Hearken, Bautista," he said, after a short pause. "I have within the past few hours copied out part of a commission against the miserable inhabitants of this new world, lately granted by our king, and framed by the greatest divines and lawyers of our old home. Alonso de Ojeda and Diego de Nicuessa bear drafts of this commission with them, and be well assured that they will not spare its execution. But stay; I will read thee the very words themselves, addressed for peremptory orders to these poor heathen, ignorant of the very language in which we call upon them to obey our faith and laws:—'If you will not consent to take our Church for your Church, the holy father the Pope for your spiritual head, our king for your king and sovereign lord over your kings and countries, then, with the help of God,

I will enter your country by force; I will carry on war against you with the utmost violence; I will subject you to the yoke of obedience; I will take your wives and children and will make them slaves; I will seize your goods, and do you all the mischief in my power, as rebellious subjects, who will not submit to their lawful sovereign. And I protest that all the bloodshed and calamities that shall follow shall be due to you, and not to us.'"[2]

As Montoro came to the end of his sheet he folded and replaced it in his pocket, and then, utterly forgetful of his companion in his reawakened indignation, he wandered away from the verandah, and betook himself to the simple dwelling of the good clerigo, Bartholomew de las Casas, who was now finally settled in Hispaniola, by royal desire, as a missionary to the natives.

"But of what use," he exclaimed this afternoon in sorrowful despair to his equally weary-hearted visitor, "of what use, Diego, to waste our time and strength, in trying to teach the sublime truths of religion to men whose spirits are broken, and their minds weakened by oppression?"

"Of what use, indeed," assented Montoro with passion, "to try to teach men to believe in a religion professing itself the religion of love and mercy, while they are slaves to those calling themselves its followers, and who are acting at the same time the part of demons!"

"You speak strongly," said the true-hearted, good Christian bishop. "But verily I cannot say you have not reason. Knowest thou, my friend, that when first we settled ourselves upon this fertile fragrant island, not yet fifteen years ago, the inhabitants numbered above three millions, and now they scarcely amount to fifteen thousand. Scarcely fifteen thousand!" he repeated slowly, and in awe-struck tones, as though he scarcely could endure to recall the awful fact to his own remembrance.

Montoro de Diego looked at his informant with a startled countenance, and then suddenly bent his eyes upon the ground as though he expected to see the 'brothers' blood' crying for vengeance from the soil.

"It is no good," he exclaimed at last. "I will stay in this accursed place no longer. To my restlessness I might have opposed a sense of duty; but to fight any longer against my miserable disgust at the scenes around me is beyond my strength."

The bishop mused awhile before replying slowly, —

"And yet, good example is valuable."

"Elsewhere it may be, but not here," returned Diego hastily. "Else, Riverenza, must your own bright example long since have turned devils into saints, murderers into good Samaritans. What good did your example do, even in the matter of the *repartimientos*? Did your giving up your share of these unjustly and basely-enslaved creatures serve any other purpose than that of impoverishing one who ever uses his wealth for the relief of suffering? Nay, further, your good example on this accursed island worked actually on the side of evil."

"How so?" asked Las Casas. But he looked as though he knew the answer, even before his companion said heavily,—

"Even we reaped some miserable advantage at 'Palmyra' from your renunciation. Some half-dozen poor creatures who had thriven under your mild rule were made over to us to die. But see," Montoro suddenly exclaimed, interrupting himself and springing to his feet, "the day is passing, and I should have been in San Domingo hours ago. I started early enough, but some suspicion that I was leaving mischief behind me brought me back, and now poor Don is dead."

It was only a dog that was dead, but that dog was Don—the dog on whose head his mother's tears had fallen—the dog for whose sake he had once endangered his own life; and with these thoughts suddenly recalled to his mind, Montoro de Diego was glad to beat a hasty retreat from further observation.

Las Casas remained deep in earnest ponderings long after his friend had left him, for he too had begun to think that it was vain to continue his efforts of philanthropy any longer on the island of Hispaniola, and that he would do wisely to exert his influence as protector of the Indians in new fields, less overcrowded with the refuse population of his own country.

Meantime Montoro reached the town, and was instantly accosted by a young man of about his own age, and tall, bright, and handsome as himself, but with a dash of off-hand daring about his person and manner instead of Montoro's lofty dignity.

"Diego!" he exclaimed, as soon as he caught sight of him, "you are just the comrade I most desire in our coming campaign. Throw thy paltry bales into the sea, man, and enrol thyself under our captain's standard."

"But who then is thy captain?" asked Montoro with some interest, "and what is this new campaign? Thou art ever mad, my Cortes, upon some fresh undertaking."

The handsome young notary laughed.

"Better that than sticking to the same spot till thy feet bid fair to grow to the soil, like thy money-grubber, Don Alonzo, yonder. But, I warrant thee, this undertaking now on hand is no mere pastime for a summer's evening. Our captain, Don Diego Velasquez, hath it in commission to conquer an island, the island of Cuba."

"Ay, doubtless," returned Montoro bitterly. "And hath also leave and licence, and perchance it may be even orders likewise, to kill off the inhabitants there, like so many mosquitoes, as hath been done here!"

The other shrugged his shoulders rather contemptuously.

"Verily, Diego, thou and our bishop yonder have been bitten by the same dog. But to comfort thy heart, know that Bartholomew Las Casas is to be invited to go with us to guard thy pets, lest one of us should so much as slap one of their brats to still its overmuch squalling at strange faces. So, what say'st thou now?"

Montoro's face cleared to a smile.

"This is what I say—that if Las Casas goes, then do I go also."

CHAPTER XIX
THE WAY TO TREAT THE REDSKINS

"Montoro! I say, Montoro, I have news for thee."

"Out with it then," came the answer from our friend, who was once more engaged in his occupation of eight years before at Veragua. Houses were built there for a colony that was never founded, and now Montoro and his companions were building houses on the island of Cuba, with a very fair prospect of inhabiting them.

Only one chief had offered any determined resistance to the invaders, and even his followers were not numerous enough to excite much anxiety. He had fled from his native land of Hispaniola to escape the Spanish rule, and now he was brought to bay, and compelled to make a final effort for independence. It had just been decided to send out a party against him, strong enough, as Velasquez put it, "To conquer the rebel once for all, and have done with it."

"And I am to be one of the party," said Juan de Cabrera, excitedly. "And if you choose you also are to have a hand in catching this Hatuey, and helping to make him an example."

"He is that already," replied Montoro gravely. "Would that the poor sheep, his countrymen, knew how to profit by it."

"By my faith," exclaimed Cabrera impatiently, "you are a queer fellow, Diego. Wouldst thou then that these 'poor sheep,' who are as a hundred to one of us, should know their strength, and shoot us down like vermin in a barn?"

Montoro flung down the great wooden hammer with which he had been driving stakes, and came forward, his face set with mingled sternness and sorrow.

"Ay, truly, Juan de Cabrera, less would it shame me that the heathen should thus treat us, than to know that we Christians have acted that hideous part towards them. Hast thou heard of the late campaign in Trinidad, where our countrymen have burnt alive in cold blood—to save trouble!—nigh upon two hundred men and women, and innocent babes scarcely more helpless than their kind and gentle-natured fathers? How shall Spanish tears or Spanish blood, thinkest thou, ever wash out that foul stain?"

Juan de Cabrera turned away for a moment, for he had no answer ready. When he turned round again he said, with an assumption of flippancy he was for once far from feeling,—

"Ah, well, I have not heard this shady tale before, and I don't suppose that it has lost any of its shadows by coming through thy lips. Doubtless it was but a toss up whether our brethren should be killed, or should kill."

"Not so," said Montoro, sternly. "Juan Bono hath confessed, himself, that the unhappy creatures whom he thus repaid had been as fathers and mothers to him, and to all his party; but he had been sent to make slaves, and he made them the more readily by burning part of the population before resistance was dreamt of."

He stopped abruptly, and stooped to pick up his tool. Then once more raising his eyes to his companion's face, he said slowly and quietly—

"That is all; but a ghastly all; and I would to God that the heathen had shot me ere I heard it."

There was a long silence after this ere Cabrera ventured once more to ask—

"But, Diego, for all this thou wilt join us, wilt thou not? Even for the sake of thine own feelings thou shouldst do so to help in the promotion of fair play."

"If I were the Governor himself," said Montoro hastily, "I should exert myself in vain for justice where this unfortunate Hatuey is concerned. He has been as a king in his own land, and now we dare to proclaim him a rebel because he proves himself a patriot, and in the face of despair fights for his country and his people's liberty. No; I will have nought to do with 'catching' this noble-hearted heathen Cacique, and aiding to throw him into slavery."

Cabrera cast a keen, furtive glance at his companion at the utterance of that last word. Evidently, although Diego had heard that horrible Trinidad news, he had not yet heard of the doom pronounced against the troublesomely desperate Cacique of Hispaniola, when he should be once safely caught in the hands of the Cuban governor. As for Don Juan de Cabrera, he had no inclination to give the information. To turn the subject, he said after a short pause—

"Well then, friend Diego, if thou comest not with us, what is it thou hast a mind to? Something nobler, I trust, than wood-cutting, as though thou wert born a boor in a German forest rather than a Spanish nobleman."

"I feel little inclined to boast just now of my Spanish birthright, I can tell thee," said Montoro heavily. "But to answer thy question—Ay; I have other plans on hand than my present employment. I accompany Las Casas on his progress of pacification through the island, and we hope great things from our efforts, both for the natives and the colony."

Cabrera's shoulders went up in a slight shrug, almost in spite of himself.

"It is to be hoped that you and the clerigo have picked your associates carefully for your peaceful expedition," he said, with a touch of scorn. "Otherwise I fear me there may chance some rubs to your tender consciences ere it is accomplished."

"Little danger," answered Montoro, confidently, adding with a smile, "for we have, as you say, chosen our companions with due thought. You see, we have not invited you."

Juan de Cabrera laughed.

"Thanks for the compliment, my friend. I would a hundred-fold rather be found guilty of too much impetuosity, than of a calm, cold-blooded calculation."

The smile died out of Montoro's face as he now exclaimed hotly—

"It is easy at all times for men to sneer at right and justice, and to clothe evil with grand words. In Spain our impetuosity has been a sword in the hand of honour; why is it here a weapon that would be disdained even by the paid tool of an assassin? But there, Juan, I but waste my breath on thee. This is no true impetuosity, no true impulsive daring, that robs and massacres the harmless peoples of these lands; but rather is it the base, despicable, grovelling fruit of cold-blooded reckonings of ounces of gold against lives. By heaven, I—"

"There, there, Toro," interrupted the light-hearted cavalier, with unusual quietness of manner, "do not spend thy eloquence upon an unworthy mortal like me. And for thy solace learn that, although methinks thou and the clerigo draw the line too fine, I loathe some of our doings out here well-nigh as greatly as thou canst do thyself. But adios, for my party will be starting on the Hatuey hunt without me if I do not hasten."

So saying, the gay adventurer departed with an air as jaunty as though he were bound for one of the Court tournaments of Spain, to be rewarded by winning kingly smiles and his lady's scarf. And shortly after his friend Montoro de Diego, with Las Casas, departed on their Cuban tour, accompanied by a number of armed followers, who were intended, by their formidable appearance, to ensure unbroken peace, not to win it after battle. But unhappily Juan de Cabrera's prognostications proved truer than Diego's hopes.

"Well, comrade," said a soldier to a companion at the evening halt of the first day's march; "well, comrade, thou hast then recovered health and strength in time to have another try for fortune; at any rate for such flimsy fragments as our present soft-hearted leaders will permit us to accept. For my part, I had fain that I had been rather sent off after the rebel Cacique. There will be more pickings to be gathered up there I doubt, than we shall be able to find baskets for in this direction. But as for saving souls—"

"As for saving souls," interrupted the man addressed in a deep, fierce tone; "as for that matter, Guzman, we will save our own souls by clearing God's earth of these vile, idol-serving vermin. Joshua was sent forth of old, as Father Gonzalo saith, to rid the world of the heathen, and so have we the like mission now. And for one Andrea Botello will obey."

Guzman stared.

"My faith, Botello, let not the noble Señor Diego hear thee speak thus, or thou wilt most assuredly get ordered back to the settlement again!"

But Botello's eyes blazed with a yet fiercer fire, and his brow grew blacker, as he muttered:

"Against those who have a mission from on high, man's orders avail nought. The commands to slay and destroy, and leave not one remaining, have come to me from authority, supreme e'en over the Governor Velasquez himself. Speak not to me of orders!"

"Nay, then, that will I not," murmured Guzman to himself, as he went off to more cheerful companions. "I will spend no more words on thee, friend Botello," he continued in soliloquy, "so long as it appears that the remnants of thy late fever are yet burning in thy veins. It might chance thou wouldst find thou hadst an order to stick thy poniard into me."

A few minutes later the prudent soldier was consulting with some friends, whether a warning hint respecting Botello's aspirations should not be given to their priest commander.

"But say, then," laughed another, "what need to trouble the good clerigo for nought? What can one man's moody fancies do of harm, with so many against him on the other side?"

"Umph, no," said another, somewhat less confidently; "if all the rest are on the other side; but one fanatic can make an army of disciples, if his feelings be but strong enough."

"Just so," was the off-hand reply. "If they be strong enough, but not if they be the half-delirious fancies of a sick man, who ought still to be in his bed at St. Jago yonder, instead of travelling with us. But come on, let's hurry up to that party of redskins over there; they seem well laden, and for my part I prefer to dine on their providing than on my own, or that of our commanders. They treat us better."

The whole of the little expedition, including Las Casas and Montoro, appeared to be of the same way of thinking, to judge by the way the hospitable and kind-hearted Indians were soon surrounded. Whether owing to the absence of newspapers and telegrams in those days, or to the hopes of the poor inhabitants of the New World that kindness would gain kindness, at any rate in their own case, cannot now be said; but while the refugee Cacique, who had fled from the barbarities of the Spaniards on his own island, was being hunted down in one part of Cuba, in another the gentle, courteous natives were treating their invaders with the most true-hearted friendliness.

"They must, verily, be worse than the tigers of the forests who harm these simple creatures!" exclaimed Montoro one day, as a number of Indians hastened to the new encampment with the farewell offerings of fruit, rice, cooked food, and various little presents as tokens of peace and good-will, accepting smiles for thanks with inborn graciousness.

Las Casas smiled at his friend's ardour.

"I feel now," he said joyously, "that I can afford to smile, for all things here are going forward as I would wish. The natives are learning that there are at least some amongst the white men who have a knowledge of right and wrong. And for these with us, Montoro, thinkest thou not that they have begun to find it pleasant to continue in well-doing, and to awaken smiles instead of tears? For myself, I do hope so, I confess."

"And I," assented Montoro earnestly. "I do believe, my father, that thy noble example has reaped at length the good fruit it has so long merited."

The two friends passed on, nor marked a pallid-faced, fierce-eyed man, who had stood near them, and now muttered between his teeth, gazing after the clerigo:

"Tremble, thou Saul, who wouldst spare Agag, and the chief of the spoil, when thou shouldst destroy! Guard thyself, lest the vengeance that falls upon the enemies of the Cross encompass thee also, as were meet."

CHAPTER XX
THE MASSACRE AT CAONAO

Some weeks had passed, and all had hitherto gone well, when one day, on arriving at the suburbs of the native town of Caonao, Las Casas announced it to be his intention to remain there two or three days, making it the limit of his present expedition, and then to return to the head-quarters of Velasquez, with the report of their doings and adventures.

"Meantime," he said, with the cheerful good-humour proper to his nature when at ease for others—"meantime we will make holiday for the next forty-eight hours."

"And," said Diego smiling, "thanks to our good red brothers here, we can also give our holiday its proper accompaniment of feasting."

"Just so," agreed Las Casas, with an answering smile. "I confess the truth; it was the sight of the abundant supplies of all kinds with which we are provided, that led me to resolve on marking this terminus of our pleasant expedition with something of the nature of a festival. Gather the men for me, Diego, some into the surrounding houses, the remainder may well encamp out here in these gardens, fit for Paradise itself."

"And for yourself, father?" asked Montoro. "Are you bent on other explorations?"

"Not very distant ones," was the bright answer. "I am but about to explore yon temple, and endeavour to use my stammering tongue for God's glory with its inmates. They may now better believe, I trust, that we come as bearers of a message of mercy."

"Truly I hope so," replied Montoro, as he nodded the brief adieu to his friend, and then turned quickly to execute the duties committed to him. In thus hastily turning, he almost knocked over a man who, unobserved, had silently moved up close to the two chiefs of the party, until he stood almost shoulder to shoulder with de Diego.

Diego was about to administer a sharp and haughty reproof to the presumptuous intruder on the society of his superiors, but a second look at his companion checked the words on his lips; and he stood a listener instead of a speaker, as the man uttered, through drawn lips that scarcely moved, a wild denunciation of the Amorites, the Hivites, the Canaanites, the Hittites, the Perizzites, the Gergashites, and the Jebusites.

Those who hear of the matter now may feel tempted to smile, but there was no smile on the countenance of the young nobleman, no feeling of mirth in his heart, as he stood facing the mad fanatic. The man's eyes were fixed in a glassy stare that saw nought then visible; and his eager, bloodthirsty curses against those he denounced as the enemies of God, and of his Christ, made Montoro's blood run cold.

"Friend," he began at last—"friend, rouse thyself. Recall thy scattered thoughts. Those enemies of God's people, and daring breakers of His laws, have perished for their iniquities more than two thousand years ago. What priestly tales from the Holy Scriptures have been startling thy ears of late?"

"He hath been ill, at death's door with malarious fever, but a few days before joining this expedition, Señor," answered another of the soldiers coming forward now, and hastily putting his hand on his comrade's arm, as though to draw him away, but at the same time with an air of secret warning which, at another time, would not have escaped the keen eyes of the young officer. Now, however, Montoro was anxious to get the clerigo's wishes carried out before his return on the scene, and he was more intent on taking a view of the ground around him, as to its capabilities for comfortable encampment, than in noting the actions of individuals.

"See," he said kindly, but somewhat absently, "yonder come our kind Indian friends with supplies of water; doubtless thy comrade is suffering from thirst. Go forward with him, and see that his wants are well attended to."

The man bowed, and quickly pulled his companion on to hinder the word answer he seemed about to give.

"Thou art a very fool, Botello," he muttered angrily, when out of earshot of Diego. "Of what good to rouse us up to help fulfil thy purpose, when thy blabbing lips must go well-nigh to betray it, to the one of all others most keen to hinder it. The clerigo hath some thoughts to spare from his red lambs to his own comfortable living, but this Señor Diego carrieth the vile heathen on his back to his own greatest detriment. Verily, methinks he would far sooner have that sword of thine pierce him than one of them."

Botello turned, with those dull-burning, sullen eyes of his fixed upon his friend.

"If it is thus with him," he said between his clenched teeth, "then will he receive due punishment in witnessing the slaughter of those he thus dares to cherish. But come, the hour has arrived, and the victims."

And suddenly, with a wild cry, he dashed forward towards a group of some hundreds of defenceless Indians—men, women, and children—laden with fruits, and jars of water for their Spanish guests. Snatching his sword from its sheath it flashed for a few moments in the sun, as he brandished it on high, and then, with a madman's howl, he plunged it into the bodies of an infant and its mother who was advancing with a timid smile to offer drink to the thirsty travellers.

Tearing the reeking weapon from his first quivering victims he rushed on over them, dealing death and wounds frantically around him. For some moments he was alone in his dread activity. The Indians were spellbound with the dismal horror. Even his own fellows were awe-struck with the impetus of the hideous onslaught.

But quickly the scene changed. In his fatal career the wretched madman cut down the beloved young squaw of a tall and unusually powerful Indian, before he could fling himself before her as a cover. Baffled of his loving effort he threw himself upon the Spaniard, utterly regardless, in his despairing fury, of the blood-dripping sword. Snapping it with his hands as though it had been a thread from his native cotton plants, he tossed away the pieces, and then, with those sinewy, disengaged fingers, throttled his antagonist, and cast the dead body of the wretched Botello beside that of the murdered Indian.

The red man's ferocious shout of triumph was the signal for answering shouts of fury from the Spaniards. They had looked on while innocent and gentle women and children were ruthlessly slaughtered, but the sight of one of their own number slain was one that aroused all their fiercest feelings of revenge, and ere it could be well said that they had had time for thought swords and daggers were flashing in the light, the fair, flower-bestrewn earth was streaming with blood, and mangled bodies of dead and dying creatures, some still clasping their simple offerings, that pleaded for good-will, in their stiffening hands, were piled in awful heaps around the camping ground.

To this drear, sickening sight Montoro de Diego rushed forward as he saw the tumult that was raging. Guzman, one of the few who remained faithful to his leader's trust in him, flew to the temple to summon Las Casas. The redskins' friend was just issuing from the building when his follower reached it, breathless with haste, pallid with horror, and bespattered with gore from the pitiful victims who had been falling in wholesale crowds around him. The countenance of the clerigo turned pale also as he caught sight of the panting soldier.

"What is it?" he exclaimed. "Our brethren—what of them? Is it a massacre?"

Guzman nodded. He could not speak; one word he managed to gasp out—"Go." For a massacre it was indeed, though not of the nature imagined by Las Casas; not a massacre perpetrated by ignorant heathen of those from whom they had scarce ever received ought but wrong, but a massacre barbarously committed by Christians on those from whom they had received nought but kindness and submissive respect. But Las Casas waited not to learn more from his breathless retainer. He saw the wild tumult surging in the distance; he heard the confused roar of mingled shrieks, shouts, yells, and groans; and whatever was going forward that concerned his company his place was in their midst, to die with them if their rescue were no longer possible.

In a moment of time this decision had darted through his brain, and the next instant he was flying over the ground that intervened between the temple of Caonao, and the open plain where the deadliest of the uproar was in awful progress.

Two or three huts of less pretensions than the houses in the town were scattered here and there. Close to the fighting, dying, struggling multitudes stood one of these wooden buildings somewhat larger than the rest. In it a number of the hospitable Indian women had been gathered, a few minutes since, cooking and preparing food for their cruel invaders. Now a panic-stricken, shrieking rabble of both sexes and all ages was dashing into it, Indians pursued by Spaniards—Indians, as Las Casas perceived at the first horror-stricken glance, with nothing but crushed fruits and flowers in their hands, or wounded infants moaning in their arms, Spaniards with blood-dropping, crimsoned swords. Then he knew all. A groan of bitterest anguish burst from his lips—

"Oh, my God!"

The words were a prayer, an abject prayer to the Most High for mercy. Had the earth at that moment opened her black jaws and swallowed up every Spaniard present, had fire from heaven licked them up and carried them to hell, Las Casas would have felt no wonder. He wondered more that an all-powerful God should spare.

One moment he gave to that groan, one moment to that prayer, and then, throwing himself in the doorway of the hut, he dashed aside a half-frenzied soldier who was entering in pursuit of the wretched fugitives, and uttered a mighty, furious shout:

"Back, Spaniards, back, you dastardly mean hounds, every one of you, or run your swords thus hallowed with the blood of the innocents into your leader's body. I invite you to it, fiends every one of you rather than men, that I may the more speedily close mine eyes for ever on this scene fit only for the shades of hell."

Then he looked into the hut upon the huddled flock of trembling, weeping, wounded human sheep. Some had climbed, for refuge from their bloodthirsty pursuers, to the rafters of the roof, and hung there, with their wild eyes gleaming, through their long black hair, down upon events below, and their white teeth chattering for fear.

The sudden appearance of Las Casas upon the spot, and the change of his usual mild demeanour to one of such haughty, biting indignation, had created a temporary, rapid lull about the spot where he stood. A permanent arrest of the massacre in that direction, he all too fondly believed, and so he began to soothe and reassure the poor creatures gathered together for death within the walls of that humble little dwelling. Some few words of comfort in their own language he knew, and spoke most eagerly, but the deep sympathy of his countenance, his pitying eyes, spoke still more eloquently, and above all, his fame had come before him even here, as a father and friend of the helpless.

Gradually some put back the hair from their faces and ventured to look around them, mothers loosened their convulsive grasp of their children, and the climbers on the rafters swung themselves down to the ground again. But even Las Casas could see that all was not yet achieved for the restoration of peace. At a few hundred yards' distance the horrible, shameful work of slaughter still continued, and once more quitting the hut and its defenceless multitude, Bartholomew Las Casas dashed onwards to repeat his efforts at arresting the wholesale murder of defenceless men, helpless women, the aged and the infant.

"Oh, Montoro!" he ejaculated as to himself, as he neared this fresh scene of horror. "Alas! Montoro de Diego, where canst thou have been to allow such things!"

A voice from beside his feet answered him—"I am here, my friend. Disabled at the first moment. But do not heed me. Hasten to save what poor remnant there may yet remain of these unhappy victims."

Las Casas looked at his half fainting friend, then at the dreadful *mêlée* beyond, and with a hurried—"I will return immediately," he ran on, and a second time hurled his furious commands at his followers to cease their cowardly slaughter of their helpless prey.

A second time the leader's voice and the leader's presence cowed the Spaniards back to order—momentarily. From the rear where the hut lay there suddenly broke upon the air wilder shrieks and yells than had been heard before. Deep oaths and curses of Spanish throats were mingled with the shrill Indian cries, and off darted the soldiers gathered about Las Casas to join their other comrades. They were like so many score of bloodhounds, with the taste for blood so aroused that it could no more be satisfied. Not again could the friend of the Indians reach the doorway of that hut until it had become a charnel-house, so crammed with the dead and dying, that the stoutest heart might turn away from the ghastly task of learning if there were yet any, amongst those heaps of mangled bodies, to whom it might be possible to speak last words of pity.

There had been five hundred living human beings crowded into that building when Las Casas left it ten minutes ago, now there lay there five hundred mangled bodies lying in crimson pools, some already stiff and stark, some writhing in the death agonies, none ever to see the sun in this world again, or to learn on earth that the religion called the Christian faith, which those white intruders came to spread, was not the religion of a demon more vile than any their untaught imaginings had ever dared portray.

A poor mother's despairing wail over her mortally wounded child, had been the slight spark needed to rekindle the blind rage of the Spanish soldiers. A soldier had held a crucifix before the infant's dying eyes, and the mother, fearing fresh cruelties, had wildly dashed it from the man's hand. That was more than provocation enough for gold-seekers who salved their greed for wealth and fame with the plea, that their journeyings were to widen the limits of Christ's kingdom.

Scarcely had the crucifix fallen to the ground ere the murdered woman fell beside it. Many a dead body had the man to move the following day ere he recovered the treasured symbol of an immortal love. All that night the leader of the expedition knelt, alone, in prayer.

All that night Montoro de Diego lay praying, faint and weak from loss of blood, shed at the commencement of the hideous fray in the vain effort to arrest the massacre. Never, so long as Montoro lived, did he hear the name of the little town of Caonao without a shudder, never did he remember the sounds of those women's wails, the sounds of those children's cries of dying agony, without a moan escaping his own lips, and a shivering horror overwhelming him that such things should have been.

One day for a day of burial, and then, in a solemn hush as though a funeral *cortége*, or a train of vanquished fugitives, the expedition formed again for marching, and retraced its steps to St. Jago. Montoro made one attempt to cheer his friend, but the soothing words were hurriedly put aside.

"Nay, nay, Diego. Speak not to me of comfort in our shame and bitter affliction. I came forth confident in my own strength, in my own power to rule man and to guide those under me in the ways of peace, and the Lord of Hosts has thus humbled my presumptuousness in the dust. Speak not to me of comfort; there is none save in prayer."

CHAPTER XXI
THE PATRIOT CACIQUE HATUEY

The march back to the Cuban seat of government was made more rapidly than the march out had been. Then, all had been gaiety and brightness. A band of picked men under a favourite and joyous-natured leader, peace and good-will for their motto, and friendly natives hovering ever around them as they journeyed, to turn each day into one of pleasant feastings.

Now the leader had but stern, grief-stricken eyes to turn upon those under his command, and the men walked on bowed with a sense of well-merited disgrace. Few and far between were the offerings made to them now, and those were bestowed with trembling hands, and countenances marked by abject terror. None of the circumstances of the homeward way tempted the explorers to linger.

But full as was the generous-hearted Montoro's cup of sorrow, it was not yet so full but that it was to be called upon to hold more, even to overflowing.

The shadows of the marching men were beginning to lengthen as they moved along, as though the shades had learnt the art of deception with each hour of the growing day, and wished to startle the whole race of earth's crawlers, beetles, snakes, worms, and their fellows, with the semblance of an oncoming race of giants. The air was full of humming insects, quivering heat, and the rich scent of leaves and flowers.

The Spaniards stepped onwards slowly. They were near the end of their journey now, and their eyes were tired with gazing at that

"Landscape winking through the heat."

A hot shimmer over all things, such as Tennyson had never seen when he wrote a line which almost makes one feel warm even on a cold winter's day.

Montoro was feeling depressed and weary, and sentiments of gladness and regret were pretty equally mingled in his breast as he saw the various roofs close before him of the newly-founded town of St. Jago. But personal sorrow cannot be indulged by leaders.

"Put your best feet forward, my friends," cried Bartholomew Las Casas at this moment. However bitterly he might grieve over recent occurrences, there was still sufficient of the spirit of the commander in him to rebel against the notion of reappearing before Velasquez, Cortes, and the rest of their fellow-adventurers, like a company of whipped dogs; but he need not have troubled himself, for an event was taking place at that hour in St. Jago that absorbed all interests.

Hatuey, the Cacique of Hispaniola—Hatuey, the noble, untutored patriot—had been taken prisoner whilst fighting his last battles for freedom and his country, and Hatuey was adjudged to suffer as a rebel! He was to be made an example of, so the Governor declared—to be the scarecrow to frighten all others of his race and the surrounding nations from daring to perform one of the most sacred duties of mankind. The Spaniards acknowledged it to be so for themselves; but then—Hatuey was a heathen, and had refused to be forced into Christianity at the point of the sword.

Las Casas, Montoro, and their followers were close to the town when Montoro de Diego was suddenly almost thrown to the ground by an Indian woman, who flung herself before him with a wild, heart-rending cry, and clasped his knees convulsively.

Already Diego had become known on the island as a friend of the friendless, an eager helper of the helpless, and this poor, despairing creature had been on the look-out for him, during the past hours of that day, with a gnawing agony of longing that had made the hours seem like weeks. He was her last hope, and now, catching sight of him, she flew forward with a wildness of look and manner that made those around believe her to be mad.

And in truth the favourite wife of Hatuey was well-nigh frantic with dread and horror at the threatened fate of the one she loved.

Las Casas and the whole of the small band of warriors drew around as she poured forth her lamentable tale, with groans and sighs and streaming tears, and the countenances of the two leaders glowed with deepening indignation as they listened. At length Montoro lifted himself up with flashing eyes, and turning to his friend exclaimed passionately—

"It seems that we Spaniards are bent on accumulating sins upon our heads, until the measure of Heaven's wrath shall be attained. Give me your permission that I leave you now on the instant, and hasten to avert at any rate this threatened iniquity."

"If it be possible, with the grace of God," murmured Las Casas; but Montoro had hastened away with the Indian woman before the words were uttered, and was already on his road to the Governor's house. The others followed.

"What! returned, my very esteemed friend Diego?" exclaimed the laughing voice of Juan de Cabrera from the verandah of the Governor's residence as the other approached.

Montoro sprang forward more quickly.

"Well met, Cabrera," he cried, in tones so stern that their ordinary melody was lost; "well met, for thou canst tell me where I may most wisely seek the Governor."

"That can I," was the reply more seriously, "or rather, I can tell thee where thou mayest seek him and find him; but as to the wisdom of the search, verily that is another matter. For my part, I am thankful to maintain my present distance between myself and him just now. And if you are prudent you will remain with me, and ask no further questions."

Montoro strode forward still more hastily, and his face paled with emotion as he asked huskily—

"Toy not with me, Juan. Thou canst not surely mean that yon diabolical act of which this woman speaks is already in progress?"

Cabrera bowed, murmuring at the same time—

"Ah! then thou hast heard. I would have spared thee."

Montoro shook himself wrathfully.

"Exert thyself to spare the deeds, not the hearing of them after. Where is the spot that is to be made foul for ever by this crime?"

Cabrera raised his hand, and pointed.

"But, Diego, stay with me. Spare thyself a needless agony. Wert thou eloquent as the archangel Gabriel himself thou wouldst avail nought to turn Velasquez from his present purpose."

Diego was already going off to the place indicated, but he turned back a moment.

"I am not purposing to use my words on Velasquez, but on his prisoner. This poor creature tells me that Hatuey is offered life on one condition. It shall be my office as a humble suppliant to implore him to accept it."

So saying, with a sign to the weeping Indian woman, he darted off with a fiery speed that gave the poor creature at least the comfort of feeling that she had one with her who sympathized with her hapless misery. They were not long in reaching their destination.

Scattered groups of men and women, chiefly Indians, they came up with first, and then there was a dense crowd around a central space occupied by the Governor, a small group of counsellors, and a tall and noble-looking Indian, so still, so silent, so immovably calm of face, that he seemed rather a life-like statue of a Stoic than a human being.

Yet more central still was a great stake surrounded by a pile of faggots, beside which stood two Indian slaves, who were to feel the bitterest sting of slavery in doing to death their champion.

Had Hatuey been a slave, and assigned this post, he would have joined the victim at the stake rather than perform it; but all are not thus noble-minded. Life is sweet, even with floggings, or rather, death has terrors for all men, excepting such as are steeled by doggedness, or for such as are sustained by the hidden strength from on high, a strength to which the Cacique may now have owed his courageous calm, although his Christian murderers scorned him as a heathen.

But his poor, heart-stricken squaw felt no courage, no grand sentiments of resignation, as she caught sight of her chief and husband being now dragged towards the giant pile, and saw the ropes which were to bind his body to the stake. With a piercing cry she tore a way for herself through that dense circle of pitiless Spanish warriors, and cast herself at Hatuey's feet uttering dry gasping moans worse to hear than any weeping. Montoro de Diego followed her through the crowd, and strode up to Velasquez.

"Señor!" he exclaimed, in a voice that vibrated to the depths of many a callous heart of even those hardened listeners by whom he was surrounded; "Señor, already are we as so many Cains in this land; pause ere you give Satan yet another plea against us in the courts above. Lay upon me what burden or what fine you will, and let me ransom yon grand example to all patriots. Give me his life, that the heathen may learn that Spaniards prize true greatness."

He came to a pause in his rapid speech from breathlessness, and then for the first time gave himself full opportunity to notice his hearer's face.

Cynicism and contemptuous indignation were united in the Governor's expression, but there was no hope to be read there for the success of Montoro's prayer.

There was a sarcastic sharpness in Velasquez' voice as he replied—

"Methinks, Señor Diego, you take somewhat too much upon yourself. I trust to teach Spaniards, and the heathen too, to prize true greatness, in the person of one who knows how to punish those who dare to set themselves in defiance to his country. For the rest, ill news travels apace, and we have heard of the brave doings of your *peaceful* expedition at Caonao. It were a pity that ere you hastened to the rescue of one man you did not spare those hundreds."

"I would have laid down my own life to do so," was the low, hurried answer. "But do not add to my remorse by refusal of this petition."

Velasquez turned himself about to his officers with a scornful laugh, exclaiming—

"Verily, my Señors, 'petition' he calls his demand, backed up by threats of Heaven's thunderbolts for refusal. Humility and arrogance could not well be more perfectly combined."

The great man's laugh was subserviently echoed by some throats, whilst some other of the faces showed shame, or indifference to the spectacle before them.

Montoro de Diego stood yet for some moments gazing with deep, solemn eyes at the Governor. Years before, his father had pleaded for a life with the Inquisitor, Arbues de Epila, and vainly, and had left a true prophecy behind him when he left. So now the son. Turning his eyes slowly from one to another of the group, and then of the wide circle, Montoro raised his hand and cried aloud—

"As that man stands there doomed most basely to a barbarous and cruel death, so may many standing here now, at no long distant date, know what it is to await a horrible death at the pitiless hand of savages."

"He is offered mercy if he will become a Christian," suddenly said the Governor with some change of tone, and an involuntary shudder at the horrible mental pictures conjured up by the denunciation.

Montoro started. Yes; he had forgotten that. He had forgotten there was yet a hope, and that it was to that he had intended to cling when he accompanied the Indian woman to the scene of judgment. Wasting neither time nor words on ceremony, he turned his back on the Governor, and followed the woman to the edge of the faggot-pile, in the centre of which Hatuey stood, already bound to the stake, and utterly calm as ever, excepting when his eyes seemed constrained to rest upon the sobbing woman at his feet.

The priest, Father Olmedo, now stood beside him, exhorting him to change his faith and save his soul. But the admonitions were as though spoken to the wind, for all the heed the Cacique appeared to pay.

The priest, Father Olmedo, now stood beside him, exhorting him to change his faith and save his soul. But the admonitions were as though spoken to the wind for all the heed the Cacique appeared to pay.

"It is useless," said Father Olmedo at last. "I have done all I can for mercy's sake, and for the glory of our most holy faith, but he is obstinate and irreclaimable. He will not hearken to me. He will not be saved. Slaves, light the pile."

The Indians raised their torches, a thrill ran through the assembled multitude, the crouching woman sprang to her feet with a piercing shriek, flinging her arms above her head, and Montoro sprang forward, shouting in stentorian tones to the faggot-lighters,

"Hold!"

There was a moment's pause. Some gleam of thankfulness began to come into the executioners' eyes. The woman dropped her arms to clasp her hands with renewed hope and entreaty. A shade of half-impatient curiosity gathered on the Cacique's face. He had betrayed no agitation at impending death, but this reprieve troubled him. And it was only a reprieve.

The passionate earnestness of Montoro did touch some answering chord in the Indian's breast which the priest had not known how to reach, and, but for that swift-flying news from Caonao, Hatuey might have consented to look forward to the Paradise which Montoro painted in such glowing colours. But, as he listened with some signs of yielding on his face, recollections crowded back upon his mind, and suddenly turning full to Montoro, he asked with startling abruptness—

"But tell me then, assure me of this. There are two of these abodes of bliss, are there?—two of these glorious, sunlit homes of paradise?"

Diego's eyes widened with wonder. So earnest, so eager were the tone and manner of the questioner as he put his singular query, that the answer was not at once forthcoming. He repeated it impatiently.

"Tell me then, and truly, if one of the white-faces knows how to speak the truth—has this gracious Lord of whom you speak provided one Paradise for those of your race, another for His children here? I would know that before I hear ought else, or give my answer to your plea."

Yet again Montoro paused an instant, and then he replied slowly and distinctly—

"They shall be one fold under one Shepherd. Spaniards and Indians who have been good, and loved their Lord, will live there together in love."

As that last word was uttered the Cacique drew himself up to his full height once more, and with curling lip exclaimed—

"In love, you say! Ah! in love such as that which murdered my people in Haiti, and drove me from my home! In love such as that which has hunted me to death, and will look on now to note exultingly if my tortured body writhes! In love such as that which has slain the hundreds of the innocent and the helpless at Caonao! The love of the wild cat or of the rattle-snake! I spurn your love! I hate your love! and will none of your Lord nor of your Paradise. Our gods teach us not such love. Light your fires quickly. I welcome your faggots and their flames. I long to escape from the sight of the faces of the dastard white men to my own heaven, where nought so vile as a Spaniard can ever hope to enter."

Montoro fell back stunned from before the dark face working with mortal hatred. Stumbling against the woman, who once again lay moaning on the ground, he stooped to raise her, and the next moment he himself, with his swooning charge, was dragged back from the lighted pile, and forced by friendly hands to the outside of the wide circle; while Hatuey, the heathen patriot, was burnt to death by Spaniards claiming to do all things "for the glory of the Christian faith."

"And thus," murmured Las Casas as he withdrew, sick-hearted, from the dismal scene, —"thus do they let the light of the Gospel shine, even with a lurid light that makes it to be abhorred."

"As I abhor this land," groaned Montoro. "I have fled from the horrors of Hispaniola, and now I am driven forth once more to find, if it be possible, a land where I may dare without shame to confess myself a Spaniard."

CHAPTER XXII
ANOTHER STORM FOR THE PILOT ALAMINOS

It was the 18th day of February, 1519, an eventful day for many a one besides Montoro de Diego.

The sun was sparkling on the wavelets in the bay, and on the sails of the little fleet riding at anchor in the harbour of the so-called town of Cape St. Vincent, at the westerly extremity of the island of Cuba. The brilliant rays of that southern sun were also shining on an eager assemblage of possibly nine hundred men, who considered themselves quite sufficient for the conquering of great nations.

Dark native faces with smooth cheeks and chins, and surrounded by lank black hair, showed conspicuously amongst the greater numbers of their Spanish comrades. Guns, crossbows, gleaming armour, and a small, precious little troop of sixteen hardly-acquired horses, were also gathered there on the strand awaiting embarkation. And over all waved the great banner of black velvet with its embroiderings of gold.

Many of those stern great Spanish eyes were raised with devout gaze to its crimson cross, set in flames of azure and white, and to its Latin motto:—

"Friends, let us follow the cross; and under this sign, if we have faith, we shall conquer."

Once, as Montoro de Diego lifted his glance to those words, he quietly clasped his hands in silent prayer. But the action had not been secret enough to escape the observation of that scoffing, sharp-sighted Juan de Cabrera, and he muttered flippantly—

"Nay then, comrade, lower your looks a little. There yonder is the sign I follow, and so long as we all hold together and have faith in that, never you fear but we'll conquer, if even that gay-gilt red and black thing should fall overboard."

Instinctively Montoro followed the direction of his companions glance towards the "sign" indicated—a man about his own age, slightly above middle height, and singularly handsome, both in face and figure. His complexion was pale, and his large dark eyes gave an expression of gravity to a countenance otherwise indicating cheerfulness. His figure was slender, but his chest deep, his shoulders broad, his frame muscular and well-proportioned, presenting a union of agility and vigour that qualified him to excel in fencing, horsemanship, and the other generous exercises of chivalry, and to bear with well-known indifference any amount of toil and privation.

This strikingly handsome form and countenance were further set off with all the advantages of rich, well-studied dress, and a few magnificent ornaments of great value. All combined to mark the frank, gay-hearted soldier, the cool, resolute, calculating man, born to command, and determined to be obeyed.

Such was Hernando Cortes, the commander of this present expedition to the mainland of America, which was destined to be so memorable for those engaged in it, and for the world. And such as he was, he possessed the almost unbounded love and confidence, not only of Juan de Cabrera, but of all those now enlisted under his standard. Officers and privates, any or all of them, would have cheerfully laid down their lives for him.

Nevertheless, with some few of them the Cross came first. Gold, renown, adventure, excitement for themselves, honour for their leader, but above all, triumph for the Cross; and so ready ears hearkened to him as he stood there, splendid in hope and beauty and strength, radiant in the clear morning light, and exclaimed—

"My brothers, we are entering on an enterprise that shall make our names famous to after-ages. We go from this tiny bay as the conquerors of nations vaster than our own country, and fit to be the gardens of Paradise. I hold out to you a glorious prize, but it is to be won by incessant toil. Great things are achieved only by great exertions, and glory was never the reward of sloth. If I have laboured hard, and staked my all on this undertaking, it is for the love of that renown which is the noblest recompense of man. But if any among you covet riches more, be but true to me as I will be true to you, and I will make you masters of such as our countrymen have never dreamed of. You are few in number, but strong in resolution; and, if this does not falter, doubt not but that the Almighty, who has never deserted the Spaniard in his contest with the infidel, will shield you, though encompassed by a cloud of enemies; for your cause is a just cause, and you are to fight under the banner of the Cross."[3]

"God grant," murmured Diego, "that that sign of Divine love may wave over scenes less dismal in our future conquests, than it has done in the past."

But with the exception of the good priest, Father Bartolomé de Olmedo, none were in a humour to pay attention to the sigh. The spirited speech of the general had set all the chords of ambition, avarice, and religious zeal vibrating, and the whole force was burning with impatience to set out, without a moment's loss of time, on the promised career of triumphant conquest. Solemn mass was forthwith celebrated by the two priests accompanying the expedition, the fleet was placed under the immediate protection of St. Peter, the commander's patron saint, and, weighing anchor, it took its departure for the coast of Yucatan.

A glorious day for Spain, as men count glory, was that February day of 1519, but so black a day for the unhappy native kingdoms of America that one learns, almost with a thrill of thankfulness, that it was not to be all sunshine for the ruthless conquerors. Bright weather gave place to hurricanes, and the ships were scattered in every direction in that unknown sea. Only on board the general's own ship was a pilot who could pretend to any accurate knowledge of those storm-tossed waters, and even he looked grave, that old Antonio de Alaminos, who had acted as pilot to the great Columbus in his last voyage in 1502, and who regarded the fact as the greatest glory of his chequered life.

In the height of the tempest a voice beside his elbow, a voice singularly clear and sweet even for that Spanish tongue, said calmly, and with no shade of anxiety in the tones—

"Thinkest thou, Alaminos, that we shall live out the storm?"

The old pilot turned, and cast a hasty glance at the speaker's face. It was one worth looking at—a noble face, with the stamp of uprightness on the brow, and a perfect peacefulness in the eyes, even at that moment when Death's lean claws seemed already to have the cranky ship in his clutch, and to be dragging it, and its helpless living freight, into the vortex of those whirlpool depths.

That first swift glance Alaminos repeated with a longer one—one that had a sudden question in it, and a puzzled memory. At last he asked quickly—

"Have you been on board this vessel, captain, since we cast off from St. Jago? Have I seen you, or heard you speak, during the past few days?"

"Never a word of speech hast thou heard from my lips until now, since I enrolled myself under the banner of Hernan Cortes," was the answer, with a passing smile.

"And I have only since yesterday been chosen to form one of the company on board this ship. Nevertheless, thou hast seen me before, good Alaminos, and heard my voice, and then," with another of those fleeting smiles, "thou wast pleased to give me good words in return, as also did our great and grand old Admiral."

Again that keen, swift, puzzled glance from the old pilot's eyes, ere he passed his sleeve over them, to get rid of the sudden tribute they paid to the memory of that same grand old Admiral who had died nearly thirteen years ago. Montoro blinked his own eyelids for a moment before he added—

"Ay, Antonio, it is now within a couple of months of seventeen long years since a lean-cheeked, ignorant boy stole up to thy side one day in these same waters, and asked thee for the first time that question: 'Thinkest thou that we shall live out this storm?'"

"And as then, so now," answered Antonio de Alaminos, with wondering recollection, "the storm begins to fall to calm, even as the words are spoken. Your eyes, Señor, and your voice are the same as then; is the fearless, holy faith the same that made that wise, noble boy so calm and brave in the face of death? or—doth the man but mock his boyhood by the repetition of those words?"

The privileged old pilot put his queries sturdily, and backed them with one of those clear, searching glances that had the faculty of reading men as cleverly as shores, shoals, and quicksands. But the heart of Montoro de Diego had little to hide; the flush that burnt in the bronzed cheeks was the flush of humility, not shame, as he replied in tones so lowered as scarcely to be audible against the wind—

"The man is, I fear, no wiser, no nobler, than the boy could claim to be, but he does hold fast to his boyhood's one little bit of wisdom, in clinging to the fount of all wisdom and salvation."

"Salvation!" exclaimed a voice close at hand from one who had come forward unobserved, and had caught the last word; "ay, indeed, this lull hath been our salvation, I verily believe. Thanks be to St. Peter for his guardianship. I vow the first handful of gold-dust to his shrine, if we ride safely at anchor off the shores of Cozumel by nightfall."

So spoke Hernando Cortes, and as he spoke he laid his hand with friendly familiarity on Montoro's shoulder.

"Dost recollect, Diego," he said, smiling, "how I prevailed upon thee, now six years ago, to be one of Velasquez' followers in the conquest of Cuba? Little we thought then of the time to come, when thou shouldst be a follower of mine for a far greater enterprise."

Montoro's face reflected his companion's smile as he replied—

"Perhaps it were best to beware of boasting until we are beyond Velasquez' reach."

Cortes laughed outright.

"Ah ah! how sorely he repents him already, the poor Governor, that he gave me this command. Verily, Montoro, I think I owe you as many thanks as myself for getting away from Cuba before his messengers could stop us. You are the quickest, readiest fellow I ever saw."

"In flight," exclaimed Juan de Cabrera, sauntering up, and with a mischievous nod of his head. "Will he be as good, think you, captain, at a fight?"

"Stand forth and learn," cried Montoro, as he drew his sword, and flashed it in his friend's face with a suddenness which made that worthy start back against the vessel's side.

Montoro and Cortes joined in a shout of laughter.

"Well, my friend," said Cortes, "thou hast well earned thy answer and received it."

For once the temper of the easy-going cavalier seemed somewhat ruffled as he growled out—

"The beggar brats in the streets of Madrid can be ready enough in their onslaughts on defenceless foes. They are as swift another way when an officer of justice shows his face."

Montoro de Diego restored his sword to its sheath, and stepped up to the angry knight with outstretched hand.

"Forgive my jest, Don Juan," he said with a smile. "You should do so the more easily, inasmuch as you must remember that I did but turn your own against yourself. I have little fear that when need comes either you or I will be found wanting in due bravery."

"And I have still less," added Cortes. "Meantime I confess that I should turn coward, did I find my best friends drawing on me."

Thus cleverly did the Commander of the present bold enterprise heal any little remnant of soreness that might have rankled in the breast of one of his retainers.

With enemies of his own countrymen behind him, and a nation likely to prove filled with formidable foes before him, Hernando Cortes felt anxious enough to have good fellowship reigning in his camp.

"How else," he said a little later on to Montoro, between jest and earnest—"how else, friend Diego, thinkest thou that I shall be able to obtain for our gracious and royal master those 'comfortable presents of gold, pearls, and precious stones,' which are required of us, as proofs of the natives' good-will and the success of our expedition?"

Montoro shrugged his shoulders with some haughty impatience.

"Methinks, Captain, with our countrymen now-a-days it is gold before all things. If possible, no doubt, gold and glory both; but if not, gold at any rate, even with disgrace."

This time it was the handsome face of the Commander that flushed hotly.

"Diego, you use hard words."

"But just ones," was the firm reply; "although I apply them not to you. Left free to the dictates of your own noble nature, I shall not fear the having bound myself to follow you. But" —with a look around, and in lower tones— "there are those in your band may be too strong for you—those whose one article of faith for themselves is, 'I believe in the delights of wealth!' whose one article of belief for the natives of these regions is, 'Beggar yourselves for us, and you shall be saved as future footstools for our feet in heaven. Do otherwise, and you shall be slaughtered here and damned hereafter.' Am I not right?"

For answer Cortes imitated his companion's shrug of the shoulders.

"But I promise you this," he added—"I will make an example of the very first who transgress."

"Thanks for the assurance," said the other.

And then, a disabled barque coming in sight, Cortes went off to give orders as to aiding it to gain the port of Cozumel.

CHAPTER XXIII
A SYMBOL WITH TWO MEANINGS

"Captain," said Juan de Cabrera some few hours after his momentary disagreement with Montoro, and now once more with a smiling countenance. "See, Captain Cortes, I have but stepped forward to remind you that St. Peter hath well earned that handful of gold-dust, you vowed a while since to his shrine. And if you will be advised, you will entrust the gift, with an added pinch or two, to me."

Don Juan de Cabrera had inherited a good fortune from his father, who had been killed during the siege of Zarento in 1501, under the great Captain Gonsalvo. Cabrera was a child at that date; and by the time he was old enough to understand the use of wealth, and to wish to have the spending of some of that he had been brought up to believe he should enjoy, his mother and other guardians had so wasted the greater part, that they were glad to try if they could banish disappointment by filling his brain with other thoughts.

In those days of wonderful and incessant discovery, all ranks were tempted from time to time to try a turn of Fortune's wheel. Even the rich and prosperous frequently left luxury and friends and home, for many a long year, behind them, while they wandered about the world, seeking they scarcely knew what—change and variety, it might be, perhaps—change from slothful ease to the novel sensation of vigorous discomfort. And that they certainly obtained.

But however that might be, when his mother and his uncles and his confessor talked of the glorious voyagings, and journeyings, being now enjoyed by so many of his countrymen, the young Cabrera caught at the bait eagerly enough, and had very soon started off to make a new fortune for himself.

That fortune, however, was as far away from his hands now as when he set out to find it! But he took things easily, and looked bright enough as he stood there, with his laughing face, before Hernando Cortes, offering himself as gold-bearer to the shrine.

But Cortes was in no humour for a joke.

"I will get my handful of gold for St. Peter from St. Peter's namesake," he said sternly, and with his large brilliant eyes fixed on the glum, crestfallen Pedro de Alvarado, captain of one of the vessels, who had contrived to reach the shores of the island of Cozumel before the Captain-General of the expedition.

"And if you make such use of Fortune's favours in the future," said Hernando Cortes still more sternly, "it will prove a bad day for you, my worthy Señor, when you came under my command."

"What has he done?" muttered Cabrera to Diego, who was standing by with a wrathful countenance.

"Done!" was the retort. "Why, done like the rest of our Spanish wolves — spent the first hours of his arrival here in showing the natives what good thieves we make."

"Ay, verily," added the good Father Bartolomé de Olmedo. "And he hath added blows and beatings, doubtless, that the lesson may be the better remembered."

"Or," muttered that Juan de Cabrera beneath his breath, "to make some amends by those gifts for what he hath taken away."

But Señor Juan took some care that his companions should neither hear the words, nor see their author's smile at his own small witticism. He turned away from the groups collected together on the shore, and set off for a short walk inland.

"Whither away there?" questioned a voice behind him a few moments later.

Montoro and the priest had followed him.

"My son," said Father Olmedo, "methinks lonely saunters may be scarcely wise in a strange land at any time; but to indulge them now, when Pedro de Alvarado hath so angered and terrified the people, is too imprudent, I should have thought, even for thy careless courage."

"Say rather, for my careless indifference, father," said the young man with a touch of honest reverence for once. "I can lay no claim just now to brave fearlessness. I had even forgotten there was aught to fear. But see, who goes yonder?"

The three men stopped, as three other men, all Indians, passed them at a light run. One turned a few yards ahead and nodded gaily to Montoro.

"Why, Diego," exclaimed Cabrera in surprise, "surely that is thy man Melchorejo, whom thou hast had so many years?"

"Ay," was the reply, "even from his childhood, when I bound up his wounded hand for him. My slight deed of kindness hath reaped a rich reward since then."

"So it seems," rejoined the other, "if it is to be crowned by desertion, so soon as he has the fair chance of return to his own home."

"But it is not to be so crowned," answered Montoro quietly. "At any rate not now. He has but gone with those poor Indians just taken prisoners by Alvarado, to restore them to their friends."

"And to act as our interpreter from Hernando Cortes," added Olmedo; "to assure the Indians of his good-will towards them, and earnest desire for the maintenance of peace."

"And behold!—behold its emblem," suddenly cried Cabrera with an unusual expression of wondering awe upon his face.

And before his companions could question him, he had sprung forward and flung himself on his knees on the ground, with hands raised in adoration.

"What hast thou?" called Father Olmedo eagerly, and for the moment standing still in his amazement.

"What hast thou found?" called also Montoro de Diego equally bewildered.

And then the two hastened onwards a few paces; in their turn caught sight of some most unexpected object, and also in their turn sprang to their companion's side. One instant the eyes of the priest met those of the Spanish nobleman with an expression of deep rapture in them, and then Bartolomé de Olmedo was about to sink down on his knees beside Cabrera. But his purpose was arrested.

"Do it not, my father," hastily murmured Montoro. And clutching at the priest's arm he drew him sharply back to stand beside himself, where he remained gazing down at a stone cross about three feet high, erected in the outer court of a small temple they had reached.

The priest looked round at him for a moment reproachfully. The next a sort of mingled fear and horror showed themselves growing in his countenance. And he wrenched himself free from the detaining hand.

"Art thou a renegade from the most Holy Faith?" he asked in stern and heart-grieved tones.

"Not so," was the short and absent-minded answer, while eyes and thoughts were still equally fixed, it was very evident, upon that cross.

Father Olmedo was greatly puzzled, but very doubtful, he hardly knew of which—whether of his suspicions, or of Diego. In his turn laying a hand on the other's arm, he said impatiently—

"Rouse thyself, my son, and answer me like a man, and, if it may be, the Blessed Virgin grant it, like a true son of the Church—"

"Which I am."

"May the saints grant it, I have said."

"Why, father, I would vouch for that grave Toro's allegiance to Holy Mother Church with my life!" cried Juan de Cabrera springing to his feet to take part in the question.

There was a scarcely perceptible pause, and then Cabrera added—

"Why do you doubt him, my father?"

Montoro answered the question with quiet gravity.

"Because I hindered him from an act which, although innocent from its ignorance, I feared that his conscience would regret. I have prevented the father from paying adoration to the God of rain."

"What?" shouted Cabrera, retreating from the cross as if he had been stung, but at the same time staring at it with all his might.

"What?" repeated the priest with equal wonder, but more soberly. "What can be the reading of your strange riddle, my son?" he asked in amazement. "You stay me from the due reverence I would have hastened to pay to this most blessed symbol of our faith, and then you tell us—verily, my brain is perplexed—I know not what it is thou wouldst say!"

"I would say only that I have said," was the earnest answer. "Marvellous as it must appear to you, my father, marvellous as even yet it appears to me, it is nevertheless true, that the symbol, to us so sacred as the Christian symbol of salvation, is to these poor heathen people of this world the symbol of the God of rain."

"Umph," muttered Cabrera, eyeing the cross somewhat ruefully. "Father, I ever have so many penances lying upon my shoulders; shall I have yet another for having thus knelt in worship to a heathen god, and will it be a heavy one?"

"I were fain to say 'Yes' for thy levity," came the reply.

"Levity, i' faith!" ejaculated the young Spaniard. "My question arose from no careless merriment, I can assure you. But if I draw not a long face, like Toro yonder, with each word I say, I am ever twitted with my levity."

He turned away in one of his short-lived huffs, while the priest looked at him with no unkindly smile, and said more freely—

"Nay then, my son, pardon me. I do believe that now thou art something wounded in thy spirit, as I myself by now had likewise been, but for the ready thought and hand of our good friend here."

"Good to you, bad to me," retorted Cabrera. "If he could not speak in time to spare me the sin, and mortification, of bowing down to an idol he might have held his peace, and not thus have proclaimed my shame."

"Shame, nonsense," said Montoro good-humouredly. "In my boyhood, when I first came out here under the great Admiral, I and others paid loving reverence to our Saviour before one of these native crosses. And doubtless, He who sees the hearts of men accepted our prayers and praises, for the spirit with which they were offered."

Cabrera's superstitious fears seemed somewhat relieved.

"What sayest thou, father?" he asked.

Father Olmedo paused a few moments. He was a good and merciful man, and a good priest; but his training had cramped his intellect, and he could not quite as readily as Diego grasp at true and noble thoughts. Until now he had felt almost as horrified as the worshipper himself, that Christian prayers should have been offered up at an idol's feet. But Cabrera was impatient.

"Say, father, do you also think that I have placed my soul in no jeopardy?"

Bartolomé de Olmedo must reply.

"Thy soul in jeopardy?" he repeated hastily. "Nay, then, nay; there is here no question of thy soul, my son, seeing thou didst it but in ignorance; and for those who sin in ignorance our Lord hath said the stripes shall be few."

"But still, then, there will be those few," muttered the young Spaniard, eyeing the small cross vindictively, before he turned back to Montoro with the reproachful query—

"Diego, thou couldst stop the father from kneeling to false gods, why wert thou too careful of thy breath to spare me a word of warning?"

Montoro smiled at his unreasonable companion.

"Well thou knowest, Juan, or at any rate can guess, that I saw neither the cross, nor thine intention to do it reverence. The trees hid it from our view."

"And the waters of yon stream shall henceforth hide it from the view of all," exclaimed the discomfited disciple of Rome, as he stooped, and prepared to exert all his strength in uprooting it from its present position. But the politic priest stopped him.

"Hold!" he exclaimed quickly. And then more tranquilly: "My son, we will leave the sacred symbol of our faith standing where'er we meet with it. Only, cleansing it from its past unhallowed memories, we will reconsecrate it to Him who died thereon. Our conversion of the heathen shall thus be rendered easier, by seeing that we also reverence the cross."

Cabrera looked doubtful for a few moments.

"Dost thou not think, father, that, whatever thou mayst do to these crosses, they will still remain to the redskins their god of rain; and that, whatever thou mayst try to teach them, and they may profess, it will be still as the god of rain they will worship them?"

"So I should fear," murmured Montoro thoughtfully.

But the priest said sententiously —

"My son, those questions are for the blessed saints, and the pope."

CHAPTER XXIV
KINDRED FEELING

"He shall be hung; I have said it."

And Hernan Cortes looked very much indeed at that moment as if he had said it.

"As if he had said the whole band of us should be hung," muttered that incorrigible Juan de Cabrera. After a moment's pause he added, "Toro, my brother."

"Thy brother!" exclaimed a companion standing by. "Thy very reverend, great, great-grandfather, thou shouldst say."

"Doubtless," returned the other calmly; "but still my brother in arms, so do not interrupt thy betters, Rodrigo, but hearken. My brother Toro, dost thou not feel thankful that there is no rope in the camp strong enough to hang us all at one go?"

Montoro lifted his proud head high.

"If I were a thief I should be glad," he said slowly, and with a significance little relished by not a few of those about him.

Some of them sauntered off to the neighbourhood of less strict censors. Cabrera laughed. Thieving propensities were not amongst the long list of his faults. But he looked grave again as he said—

"After all, though, it is hard lines upon that unlucky dog Morla, that he should have to be the one to do duty—hanging for the rest of the culprits. A flogging now, or some such penance as that, you know, that—that—"

"That should leave him little the worse after it is over, you would say," said Montoro.

"Just so," was the slow reply, as the young adventurer thought upon some of his own penances in the way of heavy fines, which decidedly did leave him a good deal the worse in pocket, at any rate, whatever might be the case as to person. "But to be hung! That was another thing."

"What was it that Morla stole from the black beggars?" asked Ordaz, who had but just returned with a couple of escorts from a short exploring expedition, during which various little bits of gold had somehow or other found their way into the pockets of himself and his companions.

Ordaz mechanically put up his hand to his neck as he spoke, as though feeling beforehand the sensation of a rope about it. He had angered Cortes very greatly but a few weeks since, by standing up boldly for what he declared to be the rights of Velasquez, the Governor of Cuba, in regard to the present undertaking. On that occasion he had the pleasure of passing twenty-four hours on board one of the ships in irons. There was no knowing whether this resolute, prompt commander might not treat him to something worse now, and so his anxious question—

"What was it that Morla stole?"

Cabrera noticed both the involuntary action and the tone of voice, and answered both with a mischievous—

"Ah, my noble Ordaz, hast heard that the commander thinks of overhauling all our possessions, to see how much each of us has that may help to drown us, if hanging cords run short. Instead of feeling that long neck of thine, thou hadst better learn the Indian art of diving. Morla is to swing for stealing a couple of fowls, thou art as like to sleep beneath the waves for thy golden borrowings. So to confession with thee at once, like a good Catholic."

"Who talks of good Catholics," exclaimed Don Pedro de Alvarado, coming hurriedly up to the group as the men stood gossiping. "There is as good a fighting man, as ever drew sword upon the enemies of Spain, going to be sent full gallop into purgatory just for wringing the necks of a bird or two."

"Or rather," corrected Montoro, "for wringing the fingers of those who held them, is perchance nearer to the truth."

"Well, well," said Alvarado, "put it as you will, most noble and virtuous Señor Diego; but I know this, that the man is a first-rate soldier, and our numbers are small enough already."

"Ay, and if they need diminishing," assented Cabrera, "the redskins are like enough to do us a favour that way when they get the chance, if the horrible air hereabouts do not do it first. Besides, poor Morla hath made restitution."

"Hath he so?" asked Montoro with a more relenting accent in his voice. "I feared that he had killed the owners of the fowls. Otherwise—I do lament his heavy punishment."

"Thou art in earnest?" said Alvarado eagerly, and stepping nearer to the last speaker, who looked hurt as well as surprised.

"Surely I am in earnest. Why canst thou doubt it, Alvarado?"

"Well," was the rather hesitating answer, "to tell truth, Diego, I thought thou hadst of late years given so much pity to our adversaries—"

"Our adversaries!" interrupted Montoro indignantly. "Callest thou these poor, simple, hospitable peoples of this New World our adversaries? That were, verily, to add mockery to our many barbarities." There was a brief, angry pause before Montoro recovered himself, and said more gently—"But there, Don Pedro, I meant not thus to break in upon thy speech. I crave pardon. Thou wouldst have said that I give too much pity to the Indians to have ought to spare for my own brethren?"

"Even so," came the blunt reply.

"And even so it is not," was the answer back. "And I will prove it, by attempting anything thou mayest suggest, for the rescue of this man Morla from his impending fate. What wouldst thou?"

"First to grasp thee by the hand for a true good comrade," was the impulsive reply. "And then—"

"Well, and then? Fear not to tell me thy will," said Montoro more warmly and cordially. "You see, I stand pledged now to help you."

"Yes, I see—I know," said the other stammering, and turning his eyes somewhat cautiously from side to side. At last he muttered quickly in an undertone—"Diego, there are here too many quick-eared listeners; I will seek you in your tent an hour hence. The man is not to die till nightfall."

CHAPTER XXV
MONTORO DE DIEGO TURNS HANGMAN

A good deal within the hour Pedro de Alvarado stepped into Montoro's tent, and with somewhat scant ceremony; for, Spaniard though he was, he felt ceremony and strict punctuality also somewhat out of the reckoning where a man's life was concerned.

Besides, he had just seen Morla sitting bound upon the ground between two guardians, and with the rope beside him, with which he was to be hung so soon as the priest should have been fetched back to the camp to confess him. And the poor wretch had appealed to his superior with a mixture of pitifulness and indignation.

"Ah, Captain! save me from this dismal fate. You should, in very justice you should, for you contented not yourself with stealing skin and bone done up in feathers. And yet you came off with no punishment at all."

"Thou impudent fellow!" exclaimed Alvarado. "Callest thou a furious rebuke before the whole force, and accompanied with threats too, nothing? Thinkest thou that thy beggarly life is worth a Spanish noble's honour?"

Morla was in no great haste to answer this peremptory question; but at last he grumbled out—

"If one has not the honour, I suppose, then, one may at least value the life; and I call it hard lines to lose all one's got."

A grim laugh was the reply to this undeniable statement.

"Well, well, fellow, maybe there I can agree with thee. And yet more; know that I have already given thee more of my thoughts than thou shouldst venture to expect."

The man's eyes brightened.

"Ah! and I am not to be hung after all, thou wouldst say, my Captain?"

"After all, I would say that thou art to be hung," was the curt retort, and with it Pedro de Alvarado turned short round, and went his way. But before he did so he had managed to cast a warning, significant glance at the condemned culprit, which gave the poor fellow comfort in spite of the sinister words, and the brutal laugh of his guardians.

The Captain betook himself, as has been said, at once to Montoro's tent, and was greeted instantly with a ready alacrity that proved time and reflection had not cooled his promise.

"Now, Captain, what wouldst thou?"

Don Pedro had marched in quickly enough, but his tongue seemed unwilling to second the agility of his feet. He paused so long ere speaking, that Montoro said at last, between jest and earnest—

"Perhaps, Captain, your suggestion is that I should substitute my own neck for that of the poor culprit, Morla?"

"And if it were," was the reply, "I verily believe that you would accept it. At any rate, you would accept it as easily as that which I am about to make; that—that— —"

"Well!" rather impatiently.

Alvarado made a dash at it.

"I want you to beg the post of hangman."

Montoro started back with a cry of horror. It was bad enough to him to kill men in fair fight, but to destroy a fellow-creature in cold blood was a thing too horrible to be thought of. He felt stunned, and it was not until his companion had broken into a short, smothered laugh that he could recall his scattered senses.

"Why, Diego," muttered Don Pedro, "you could not look more horror-struck if I had asked you to murder the man, instead of only— —"

"Don't, don't," gasped Montoro. "To me, hanging the man would be like murdering him."

"Doubtless. But I intend not that you should do either, if you please."

Montoro began to breathe more freely, but also to look somewhat angry.

"Don Pedro, this is no time for speaking in riddles, to my thinking."

"Nor to mine either," replied the Captain, with a half-smile. "But to tell you the truth, I am a trifle afraid of you, friend Diego, and I well know that my present proposition must be somewhat unpalatable. But mark you, I only wish that you should request the post of hangman on the present occasion, and not that you should fulfil the duties of the office, when you have it, to its usual end."

"Oh—h—h!" ejaculated Montoro now, with a new light of comprehension beginning to dawn on his face. "But yet," he added, after a moment's pause, "although I am willing enough to plead for mercy in this instance, I fear greatly that I shall sue in vain. Cortes is so resolved on making an example of some one."

"I know that. That is why I only ask you to be appointed executioner, and not to plead for pardon. The wretches to whom the office is now given have a personal spite against their comrade, and will take good care that the fatal decree be carried out to the very letter—that he be hanged by the neck until he be dead. Now I propose that you hang him."

"Hold, hold," exclaimed Montoro once more, with a half-smile upon his face, it is true, but a return of horrified disgust also. "You said I was not to have any hanging to do."

"Well, well," was the answer, "not hanging till any one hung be dead, or even choked. But surely, to save a fellow-creature's life, you will not refuse to put a rope round his neck, will you?"

"Umph!" muttered Montoro, dismally. He did not at all like the alternative. "I would really rather that some one should put the rope round mine. But, by the bye, why do not you ask Cortes to let you have this new kind of honour yourself, pray? Why am I, of all people, to seek it?"

Alvarado lifted his dark eyebrows significantly enough.

"You know the answer, I dare swear, to your own question, Diego. To whom but yourself would our worthy commander be likely to grant such a favour, think you? He knows your feeling for the Indians, and may credit your willingness to avenge them; but for the rest of us—Ah! thou knowest."

Pedro de Alvarado was right enough. Hernan Cortes gave the desired order to Montoro to replace the executioners already appointed, and at the same time he declared very positively that he would have given it to no one else. Secretly, he was intensely astonished and disgusted with his friend for having asked the favour.

"Every man with a hobby is sure to ride it to death," he muttered angrily to Montejo. "Morla must hang, to win us the trust and good-will of the Indians for the present, that our progress towards Mexico be not further hindered or harassed. But to think of a Spaniard longing to kill a Spaniard, for the sake of a parcel of redskins! Faugh! Our Don Diego hath fallen a hundred-fold in our estimation."

That same poor Don Diego felt, foolishly enough, as if he had fallen a hundred-fold in his own estimation when he actually stood beside the condemned culprit, Morla, with the hangman's rope in his hand.

The order obtained, Alvarado had lost no time in hurrying his friend with him to the proposed scene of execution. They were joined on their way by Juan de Cabrera, carrying an empty tub, at sight of which Montoro actually shuddered, to the evident amusement of his companions, who burst into shouts of laughter. He remonstrated impatiently.

"How can you find amusement in what perchance may turn out a tragedy?"

"Tragedy, indeed," exclaimed Cabrera, laughing as heartily as ever. "That element is passed, my well-beloved but too long-faced friend. The comedy is to be played now."

"And thy tub yonder represents stage properties," laughed Alvarado. "The carrying of it becomes thee as would the carrying of a Damascus blade."

"Beware that I break not thy head with it, by way of proving it hath use as well as ornament to boast," was the retort of the light-hearted knight, who ever seemed ready to dance, whether to fun or fighting.

The surly fellows who were guarding the soldier, Morla, were very loth to give up their trust, and it was not until they had received a particularly sharp hint from Don Pedro that their own past, present, and future delinquencies should be visited with the heaviest possible punishments if they did not preserve themselves from his displeasure, that they at length obeyed his commands to betake themselves out of sight and hearing.

"And now, sirrah," said Cabrera, jauntily, "may it please thee to stand up and be hung; for, as doubtless thou canst perceive, the noble Don Montoro de Diego is in haste to be quit of that rough rope, and of his task."

The man thus adjured began to rise from the ground, but still somewhat slowly, and with a dubious countenance. His reluctance grew greater when he saw it reflected on the amateur hangman's face.

"But, my good Señors," he began anxiously, "I thought that surely now you signified I should be released?"

"Yes," said Montoro, with equal anxiety; "verily I think that this play hath continued long enough; too long for yon fellow's apprehensions and my distress. What is to be the end?"

"Why, his hanging," replied Cabrera, quickly. "To that thou art pledged to the commander; therefore proceed to thy task, and for the sake of that very tender conscience of thine ask no further questions. Ten minutes hence thou wilt have light enough to see our plot by. It is very simple."

So saying, he placed his tub on the ground beneath the gallows, and with a solemn shake of the head at the prisoner, desired him to kneel upon it, and to pray that all things might go well with him. To this piece of advice poor Morla paid the greatest heed, as he felt Montoro's trembling fingers adjusting that horrible rope about his neck.

"Ah, Señor, not too tight," he muttered, even yet thinking it more than probable that his noble countrymen might really hang him, in inadvertence, if not in sport.

But they had no such intention. The next minute he felt the tub very slowly and gently drawn from beneath him; his feet naturally went downwards to the ground, which they managed just to touch by the toes, and there he stood, not comfortably certainly, but still not dead—most decidedly not.

"And there thou art to stay, upon the gallows— —"

"Or under it," interrupted Cabrera.

"'Upon' was the commander's word," was the sedate answer. "It best becomes us to keep to that. There thou art to stay upon the gallows for the space of half-an-hour, and then be cut down, and thy body cast outside the camp. But hearken, thou Morla; if I find thy body not again within the camp, ten minutes later, I will find thee a further punishment as a deserter. Don Juan de Cabrera hath consented to hide thee in his tent awhile."

At the expiration of a rather short half-hour, a very tired, toe-aching Morla was accordingly cut down, and Montoro returned to his tent, thankful enough that his good repute had enabled him to save a fellow-Spaniard's life, but also not a little relieved that the unpleasant farce was over, and his new office of hangman come to an end with sunset.

CHAPTER XXVI
CORTES BURNS HIS SHIPS

It was night, and sleep reigned throughout the camp of the Spaniards, for the new city of Villa Rica de Vera Cruz could as yet be considered little better than a camp, in spite of its grand-sounding name, and the crowd of duly-appointed officers with which Cortes had endeavoured to give it sudden dignity.

Even the sentinels were drowsy at their posts, and scarcely feared rebuke, for peace had prevailed both within and without for some days past, at any rate on the surface of events, and Cortes had been indulging in a short breathing space.

Montoro de Diego was in his tent, asleep like his comrades, dreaming of his boyhood, and of the gentle-spirited and lovely young mother who had made poverty and hard usage endurable to him in the past, honour and righteous dealing his firm principles in the present. But his dreams were to be disturbed.

Slowly, and in almost breathless silence, a fold of his tent was pushed aside, and a man crept within, holding back the canvas for a moment, that by the faint light he might discover the object of his search. Then he dropped it again, and moved on the two or three paces in the darkness, until he dropped on his knees beside the low bed on which Montoro lay, and bent his mouth to the sleeper's ear.

"My Señor—Señor Diego," he whispered urgently. "Rouse you, my Señor."

And, with a soldier's watchful spirit, Montoro needed no second bidding to arouse him. Grasping his sword even before he was fully awake, he would have sprung to his feet the next instant, with a shout to banish slumber from the whole band, but that his probable conduct had been divined, and prudently guarded against.

One firm, hard hand was pressed down upon the nobleman's chest, another closely covered his mouth, while the hushed voice beside him muttered hurriedly—

"Nay then, my Señor, nay then. Lie still, and be silent, or you will render my care fruitless. I have come to you with the discovery I have made, before all others, for your prudence's sake, and now you are eager as the Don Juan de Cabrera himself could be, to publish the whole matter to the very winds, methinks."

In spite of this expostulation, which was in truth intended more as a warning than an expression of real belief, its speaker trustfully enough withdrew both his detaining hands at its conclusion, and permitted his companion to rise into a sitting posture on his bed, and to speak.

"Who are you?" was the very natural first use that Montoro made of his power of speech, for he did not recognize the voice, and he could not see the face. However, he was soon enlightened so far.

"I am Morla, the man you hung," was the comprehensive information. "And you were good to me then, my Señor," came the seemingly contradictory statement; "and so for that, and for those other reasons, that you are wise and wary, and have our Captain's confidence, I have come to you with my discovery of a conspiracy in the camp. It is intended by many to forsake the great cause, and, taking to the ships secretly, to flee from this land to Cuba, or to Spain, with evil reports of the expedition and of its leader, to exonerate themselves."

Montoro was startled.

"Wherefore," he demanded sternly, "hast thou not instantly carried news of this base treachery to our leader himself?"

A smile, unseen in the darkness, flitted over the man's face.

"Bethink you, my Señor, what credence should I be likely to gain from our commander, when he learns that I am, myself, a testimony of disobedience to his commands."

There was some plausibility in that reasoning; nevertheless, he yielded to Montoro's desire that he should accompany him forthwith to Cortes' tent, to corroborate the statements he wished made.

Aroused by Diego with the same stealthy caution as had been used towards himself, Cortes was not long in learning the particulars of the cowardly conspiracy, and, even as he listened, his prompt mind had already begun to concert the measures for its suppression.

"But still," he said at length, thoughtfully, "we must be well assured of the truth of these accusations before we publish them, or attempt to punish. From whom, Toro, hast thou learnt all this?"

Montoro moved aside.

"There is my informant, Captain, and—I fully trust him."

A lamp was burning in the commander's tent, or rather hut of palm-branches and native cotton-mats, and as Montoro stepped to one side a man, hitherto unnoticed behind him, came forward into its light, and, falling on his knees before a small crucifix, called it to witness that his tale was true.

Cortes looked at him closely for a few moments and then said drily—

"If it be but as true as that thou wast not hung, friend Morla, then will it be true indeed."

"It had needs be truer than that, Hernan Cortes," returned Montoro: "for he was hung, as I know to my cost, as I had the hanging of him. And at the end of half-an-hour he was cut down, according to thy orders."

"Ah! I see," exclaimed Cortes, with a glimmer of a smile. "And no doubt our worthy Don Juan de Cabrera found it needful to give thee a lesson in hanging, by which thou profitedst. Is it not so, friend Toro?"

Montoro laughed.

"Partly so. But, to confess the truth, Pedro de Alvarado declared that if this Morla were hung to death he should, himself, evermore go about the world feeling as though there were a cord about his own neck, only waiting to be used."

That glimmer of a smile broadened for a moment, but the time was too serious for its cherishing.

"Enough!" said Cortes, with returning gravity. "Rise, fellow, and come nearer. And hearken! Should these charges prove true, well; if false, then will I myself hang thee ere to-morrow's sunset, and thou hadst best make thy peace with Heaven, for I warn thee thou wilt not live to laugh at me as having 'prentice hands at my new work."

The man bowed calmly.

"Ere the morrow's sunset, Captain, I shall have your thanks and praises for my promptness."

And Morla was right. He had gained his dark news from one of the conspirators themselves, who had turned faint-hearted at the last moment, and from this informer all further particulars were quickly drawn. The conspiracy was quashed, Morla reinstated in a post of trust, and the ringleaders punished with death, maiming, or degradation.

The executions had been accomplished, a miserable pilot lay moaning in agony and despair over his footless limbs, others were endeavouring to find some posture of ease for bodies torn and lacerated by fiercely-wielded whips, and the commander of the expedition stood upon the shore, moodily gazing out to sea. He felt those hours to be the crisis in his fate.

A gloom was over the sky, the camp, and Cortes; and a spirit of doubtfulness and disappointment seemed to be brooding in the atmosphere.

Alvarado, Gonzalo de Sandoval, Escalante, Juan de Cabrera, and Montoro, gathered into a group not far from their leader, watched him, and discussed the present position of affairs.

"The conspiracy is put down for the moment," said Alvarado gravely, "but at any hour it may be rekindled so long as we stay inactive in this unhealthy place. And some morning we may rise to find two thirds of the small handful of our comrades gone, and no ships left with which to effect our own escape."

"What would you say, Alvarado," said a voice suddenly,—"what would you all say, in truth, if you did find yourselves thus with the means of escape cut off—with no safety for us but in victory?"

Cortes had suddenly stepped up to them as his comrade and follower had been speaking, and there was so strange a tone in his voice as he put this question, so deep and burning a light glowing in the depths of his eyes, that the little group of men stood as though breathless, gazing at him, and waiting to hear more. The tension on their minds was strained to the utmost.

Having asked his searching question, Hernan Cortes appeared for the moment indifferent as to the answer. Folding his arms across his broad and powerful chest, he once more turned, and gazed out across the waters to where the ten vessels that composed his fleet rode quietly at anchor. They looked well enough to the eye at any rate. And besides, they signified to those few hundreds of men, encamped on that foreign coast, home and life and liberty. While they had those ships to flee to, they felt brave to dare and attempt much. But without those ships, in an unknown world and surrounded by myriads of foes, their case would indeed be desperate. And even so Cortes, in his far-seeing wisdom, wished it should be. He turned back to his companions, and began abruptly as before.

"Comrades, to many, doubtless to most of our brethren in arms, those ships signify home and life and liberty, and yet—I wish you to aid me in burning them."

Montoro and the others of the group gazed at him speechless for one instant, and then cast startled glances around towards the distant camp.

"Yes," said Cortes, answering the looks, "most assuredly it is we who should be burnt before the ships, if some of yon timorous or turbulent spirits heard word prematurely of such intention. But nevertheless, minute by minute, as I have stood here thinking, the conviction has grown upon me that only in the burning of those ships lies victory for us."

"Break down the bridge behind," muttered Juan de Cabrera, "and the mule must go forward."

"Even so," was the reply. "We are few enough as it is for the glorious enterprise on which we are embarked, and shall we allow base-minded churls to force us back to the contempt and ridicule of those who, we too well know, would store up scorning for us? No, no, my brethren, my noble and valued friends and comrades, do you but stand by me faithfully in the future, as you have done in the past, and we will cut off the means of retreat that, for ourselves, we value not, and force all to die with us, or to aid us in winning the splendid triumph that shall shed a glory on us, to endure to the end of time."

He stood there glowing with his own magnificent enthusiasm, and his hearers, carried with him beyond the dictates of a colder prudence, exclaimed eagerly as though with one heart—

"Agreed. We are with you. Burn the ships, and go forward in the names of thy patron saint and St. Jago."

CHAPTER XXVII
MONTORO LEADS A CHANT

"The ships are burnt!" "Our ships are burnt!" resounded on all sides from the Spanish troops rushing from their quarters in that new Villa Rica de Vera Cruz.

Consternation, fear, and fury gave ever-increasing emphasis to that one wild, startled shout, "Our ships are burnt!"

"Said I not well," muttered the discontented priest Father Juan Diaz, instigator of the former conspiracy—"said I not well that this Cortes was leading us like cattle, for his own renown, to be butchered in the shambles!"

Even Father Olmedo, and Morla, and others of his stamp, eagerly watching for opportunities to earn distinction, felt their hearts sink heavily as they repeated that startled cry, "Our ships are burnt!"

For one half-hour it may have been that Hernando Cortes trembled, and that his friends feared for him, and for themselves.

"But after all," said Juan de Cabrera, recovering his usual off-hand carelessness, "one can but die once, and though, as you yourself said, Captain, one would rather die at the hands of others than one's own friends, or one's own countrymen, still, when the breath is once fairly out of the body, I scarcely suppose one will care much what hand drove it forth."

"That is true," replied Cortes, with a sudden return of his usual resolute energy and undaunted bearing, and as another tumultuous shout rent the air throughout the so-called town of Vera Cruz, the Captain-General strode forth from his hut, and with stentorian tones exclaimed to his mutinous followers—

"What means this uproar, comrades? If you have complaints to make, I am here. Make them to me."

"Our ships are burnt, and by your orders," came the reply, but by no means from all throats now, and from none so loudly as before. Some were cowed in the actual presence of that resolute commander of theirs, others were awed into admiration and fresh attachment by his dauntless attitude.

Still, a certain number there were who yet reiterated that reproachful cry, "Our ships are burnt!"

"Yes, comrades, it is true," exclaimed Cortes, in tones as loud and resolute as before. "Our ships are burnt, but not before the foul creatures of these seas had so eaten through them, that they had been water coffins for any who had trusted their lives to them for the voyage back to Spain; ay, or even to our new Santiago yonder. Those who had gone on board them had gone to their death."

"And those who stay here stay to their death," called a harsh voice from the midst of the crowd. "You might at least have given us our choice."

"And so he has, coward," shouted Alvarado. "Stand forth and show thyself, and any others of thy chattering-teethed brethren, and I will gather the bundle of you in my arms as one gathers a bundle of cotton, and fling the worthless bale on shipboard! Faugh! the Captain wants not such as thou to help him on the road to glory and renown."

The tone of this tirade was more scathing in its contempt than even the words, and a momentary hush followed it. None stood forth to accept the untempting offer of its maker.

At length Cortes once again broke the silence. Distinctly, but slowly, and more calmly than before he addressed his assembled army—

"What the Captain, Don Pedro de Alvarado, saith is true. For those who chose flight there is still the means. I desire no unwilling comrades. For me, I have chosen my part. I remain here so long as there is one to bear me company. But for those who shrink from the dangers of our glorious enterprise, let them go home, in God's name. There is still one vessel left. Let them take that and return to Cuba. They can tell there how they deserted their commander and their comrades, and then patiently await us until our return with the Aztecs' spoils."[4]

Cortes ceased, and for some moments there was a silence throughout the small army, broken only by the humming of the insects and the occasional clink of a sword. But Juan de Cabrera never felt much reverence for silence.

"How now," he shouted mockingly, "how now, ye bold cravens! Where are all your voices? Ye were brave enough a few minutes since. Come along with you to the front. Or are ye, in very truth, turned too cowardly even to confess your cowardice, ye miserable crew!"

It seemed so, for there was still no answer from even a single voice, and Cortes wisely changed the question, and in a few moments the whole air was resounding with the enthusiastic acclaim from every throat:

"To Mexico!—to Mexico! Lead on, Captain! Lead us on to Mexico!"

"All the same," muttered a sullen-browed soldier to Juan Diaz the priest, who stood beside him—"all the same, father, you did say that we should be traitors to ourselves if any longer we continued to follow yon upstart."

"Hold thy peace, fool," returned the discontented ecclesiastic. "Knowest thou not that for all things, even for revolt, a fitting time is needful?"

And with that sententious remark the politic priest edged himself away to safer neighbourhood, and resumed the cry as lustily as the truest among Cortes' followers—

"To Mexico! Lead on to Mexico!"

Well satisfied with the change effected thus rapidly in his soldiers' sentiments, the Commander suddenly resolved to give the new-born enthusiasm a safe outlet, and at the same time to further one of his own most solemnly-cherished purposes. He raised his hands to claim silence once more, then his voice. But his efforts were vain. He had roused a new uproar, which, though a joyous one, was universal, and more difficult to allay. Threats to fly might be toned down by some tinge of shame, but offers and entreaties to be allowed to fight needed no restraint. The cry rang on and on unceasingly:

"To Mexico! Lead on to Mexico!"

"To Mexico indeed! To the depths of the sea with you rather, squalling rabble that ye are," said Cortes at last impatiently. Turning to the group of officers about him he added in comic despair: "Can no one befriend me thus far?"

"How far?" asked Alvarado and Escalante together, and with some wonder.

"How far!" repeated the Captain in a tone of increasing irritation. "Why, to the extent of ramming something down those screaming throats, to stop this Babel, to be sure."

Juan de Cabrera gave a delighted leap.

"I have it. I'll set the dogs barking; that will drown them."

"Ay, and thy Captain also," ejaculated Cortes, breaking into a short laugh in spite of himself. "Wilt thou never outgrow thy boyhood, thou madcap Juan? Thinkest thou—"

But his remonstrance died away on his lips, and they curved into an awe-struck smile. From a few feet behind him there arose the first notes of a solemn chant—loud and strong as a battle-cry, sweet as the tones of a silver bell.

Alone and unaided the glorious voice sang on for a few moments, and then Father Olmedo's rich bass joined in, and Pedro de Alvarado's, then the light tenors of Escalante and Cabrera, and the ringing voice of Gonzalo de Sandoval.

For the space, perhaps, of a quarter of a minute the shouting soldiers continued their cry through the chant, "To Mexico! to Mexico!" then, with a startled sensation of thrilling wonder, the foremost ranks caught the sweeter sounds, hushed their own discordant tones, paused, and joined in.

"Hearken!" came the smothered ejaculation of the man Morla to Juan Diaz, who had just come up to him. And Juan the priest gazed at him with wide eyes, and then, accepting this new vent for his restlessness, he too joined in with a tremendous vigour that soon let all ears, that were not absolutely deaf, in the neighbourhood know what was going forward.

By some unconscious impulse the rough company of Spanish adventurers fell upon their knees, and still the solemn chant rose and fell, and swelled again, on that new-found western shore of an idolatrous land, to the glory of the one true God.

Cortes alone remained standing, alone remained mute, with his great, vivacious eyes fixed intently upon the great, earnest ones of Montoro de Diego. By his own fearlessness and iron will he had quelled the mutinous mob, by the power of his voice and the power of his faith Montoro de Diego had subdued it to a noble calm and peace.

The chant ceased; the prayer of Father Olmedo for safety from foes, and unity amongst themselves, was ended, and rising to his feet again Montoro asked in clear, loud tones, audible to all around—

"And now, our Captain, since we have consecrated ourselves anew to brotherhood, what wouldst thou with us? Say on: we hearken."

"Then hear this, first of all," exclaimed the leader with generous warmth, as he grasped his friend's hand, and clasped it between both his own. "Hear this: that from my soul I thank thee for thy Christlike fervour, which has thus taught thee to retune our hearts to reason after their late frantic turmoil. And for the rest," he added after a moment's interval, and more lightly, "Ay, for the rest, the remainder of my speech must wait, for it is ill-rewarded toil haranguing hungry listeners."

"Yea, verily," softly assented that irrepressible Cabrera. "And the more so when the said hungry mortals, not to speak of the dogs, poor starving brutes, can see their victuals waiting for their mouths."

The young cavalier was right, and many other sharp eyes besides his own had caught sight already of the long train of Indians laden with provisions. Pheasants, turkeys, roast and boiled, and very good eating in their native land, even though they were not accompanied with bread-sauce, and were seasoned with neither chestnuts nor veal-stuffing. There were, however, plenty of fresh, sweet maize cakes to eat with them, and enough vegetables to satisfy even a German. Then, amongst the seasonable gifts were fish of all kinds, dressed by those clever native cooks in many savoury ways; plantains, bananas, pine-apples, purple grapes, and even sweet-meats of various sorts made with the sugar of the agave. Beverages also were not wanting, from the thick-frothed, rich, vanilla-flavoured chocolate and cooling fruit-drinks, to the fermented juice of the Mexican aloe, the intoxicating *pulque*.

Altogether the 'victuals awaiting mouths,' as Cabrera expressed it, to put it more in accordance with circumstances, the feast awaiting feasters, was of such quality and quantity as to make it quite as well, perhaps, that Hernando Cortes decided to dispense with his followers' attention for the present.

"To claim a patient hearing for a discourse, while those savoury meats were cooling, really might prove too much for the forbearance of even our good Father Olmedo himself," said Cortes smiling, as he linked his arm within that of the priest, and led him off with him as a companion at the dinner then being carried to his hut.

"'Twould be a deal too much for mine," said Alvarado, moving off in another direction with his friends. "Here, thou Morla,—thou'rt a good hand at looking after fowls, thou know'st,—just hasten yonder and pick us out the plumpest and the fairest-cooked of those good-eating great birds yonder, and thy good patron here, Don Montoro, will give thee due thanks."

"For thy sake, Alvarado, or mine own?" asked Montoro, laughing.

The other shrugged his shoulders.

"I'll not quarrel with thee, my dear Toro, on that point, since thou art very sure to permit me the lion's share of food as the reward of victory, whether won or no."

"Of course he will," broke in Juan de Cabrera, "seeing that for himself he will henceforth live upon an elegant but unsubstantial dietary of air."

"Wherefore?"

"For this simple reason, that time will be wanting to him for any more substantial meal. From this hour henceforth, even to the ending of this campaign, I do authorize, empower, and appoint him to be chief minstrel, on duty unrelieved, to the high and mighty Hernando Cortes, Captain-General and Chief Justice of the magnificent Villa Rica de Vera Cruz. The appointment is splendid, though somewhat empty of—"

"Like thy words—of wit," interrupted Alvarado. "Come, crackbrain, I will allow thee almost as good a share as myself of the viands Morla brings, to silence thy mouth for awhile, for verily thou art the prince of sparrows for a chatterer."

"And also a black-crested cockatoo! Ah! I always did suppose myself a marvel, now I know it."

And so laughing off the emotions produced by the recent great crisis in the fate of their leader and his enterprise, the party of Spanish officers sauntered off to their quarters, and were very soon pleasantly engaged in doing ample justice to the good cheer provided so hospitably by those whom they designated as 'their foes.'

CHAPTER XXVIII
THE GODS MUST AVENGE THEMSELVES

The wooden platters, leaf baskets, and rough earthen bowls brought by the Indians full of good things were not long in being emptied, and then the Spaniards were at leisure once more to indulge in curiosity.

"What think you, father, was our captain about to say to us before the wherewithal for a dinner was so seasonably provided?"

Morla looked anxious for the answer, for although he had caught the infection of the late sudden outburst of enthusiasm, and had shouted as lustily as any one—"To Mexico! to Mexico!" he had a bad foot at the present time, and contemplated with very great apprehension the prospect of a number of days' long marches. But Juan Diaz could give him neither news nor consolation.

"Take a siesta," was the priest's advice. "I doubt not Cortes is doing so himself. And when he hath fed well and slept well, he will perchance think well to inform us of his lordly will, whether half-a-dozen or so more of his betters are to be hanged, perhaps, to do him pleasure."

"Thou the first, for an ill-conditioned, surly knave that thou art," muttered Alvarado under his breath, as he came up in time to hear most of the priest's speech. Passing a few yards farther on he raised his voice, and summoned the little army once more to assemble without delay to hear the proposed plan of future movements.

Within ten minutes the whole force had crowded up together around Cortes, and in breathless silence awaited the coming news. The first words were somewhat startling. They were a repetition of their own at the outset of that morning's tumult.

"Comrades, our ships are burnt."

Then—a long, startling pause following startling words. Men turned their heads slowly from side to side, and gazed into each others' eyes.

Were those words and the silence ominous of evil to come? of passionate accusations or of dark forebodings? But before one could mutter these and many another doubt to his fellow, the words were repeated, and the short speech continued to its end.

"Our ships are burnt. Now we go to burn the heathen gods of this benighted land. We are helpless in our own strength; in the power of the one true God we are invincible. Let us invite His aid and mercy by showing due honour to the most holy faith. We go, my comrades, to hurl the idols from their altars to make way for the Blessed Mother, and once for all to blot out human sacrifices from this polluted land, by raising on high the cross of Him who has become the one sacrifice for all mankind."

The short speech of Hernando Cortes was ended, and although it contained no hint for any one there of gain, of gold, or glory, it went home — straight home from the speaker's heart to the hearts of his hearers.

Intensely ambitious, and burdened with many faults, was that dauntless leader; wild, reckless, and cruel were many of his followers; but in some strange way they held to the Christian faith as they knew it, and were at any time willing to lay down their life in its cause, although none of their sins.

The emotions that closed that day were stronger and deeper than those with which it opened. Even the turbulent priest, Juan Diaz, put on an appearance of satisfaction now, whatever he might really still feel as to the discomforts of pestilent marshes, uncertain commons, and the faint prospect of better things for the future.

"Before all things spread the Catholic faith," was the watchword in that age, of all exploring expeditions, the one universal plea for their aid and countenance. Cortes held to it with the intense fervour natural to his strong nature. So did his followers; but all the same that Merry Andrew, Juan de Cabrera, took occasion during the course of the afternoon to remark to Alvarado—

"Now, my most estimable and dearly-beloved friend, when we get into those heathen temples do the friendly part by me, and just give me a quiet hint where to lay my fingers on any easily-portable little bits of gold."

"If you don't take better heed to that impudent tongue of thine," interfered Escalante with a laugh, "he is more likely to introduce thee to a good cudgelling."

Alvarado himself as usual shrugged his shoulders with calm indifference. Words that would have led to fatal combats amongst those fiery, proud Spaniards if spoken by any one else were uttered by the young, laughing-eyed Cabrera with perfect impunity.

"Did thy mother never think," said Don Pedro with an air of kind pity, "of putting thee in the way of earning an honest livelihood as Court fool?"

"Ay, that did she," was the instant reply; "but thy mother heard of it, and begged of her not to stand in thy light. She said there were so many comfortable little pickings— —"

"Now, now, Cabrera! Hold!" sharply interrupted Montoro; "it is enough. Verily thou dost allow that tongue of thine too much licence. Alvarado, I would a few words in private with you, if you can for awhile forego this youngster's company."

So saying, he linked his hand in the other's arm and drew him away, before amusement should change into anger. And for the next hour and more even Cabrera was deep in converse of the gravest nature with Escalante, Alonzo de Grado, Velasquez de Leon, and Gonzalo de Sandoval.

Not a man in that little camp-city slept much that night, from Hernando Cortes the leader down to the meanest soldier amongst his followers. All felt that they were on the eve of great things. What had gone before was, as it were, drill-work; but now there loomed before them the true tug of war.

"And, in the prospect facing us there is one thing, I confess, that fills me with an almost abject terror."

It was Escalante who spoke, brave, firm, calm-natured Escalante, than whom there was no officer more justly honoured in the whole band for his wise spirit and unflinching courage. And yet now he uttered those craven-seeming words in low, hushed tones, and with eyes filled with a nameless horror that said even more than the words had done. His companions gazed at him in amazement.

"It is well for his present peace," said Cabrera, "that it is thyself and not another that has said that for thee, Escalante."

"Ay, indeed," ejaculated Gonzalo de Sandoval. "But what mystery lies there, Escalante, at the back of thy words?"

"No mystery," was the reply—"nought but a plain truth. The idea of falling alive into some of these heathens' hands in battle, and of then being offered up in sacrifice to their idols, and eaten after in their ghastly cannibal feasts, in very deed seemeth to me, when I think on it, to— "

"Ah! to pluck the heart out of thy breast before those fiendish hands can do it," exclaimed Cabrera, starting to his feet in sudden excitement. "I grant thee, Escalante, one has need to learn a new kind of courage to that we have hitherto required, to hold a stiff face before these thoughts."

"Not the terrors of the Inquisition itself," muttered Alonzo de Grado, "can compare with them."

But Velasquez had had enough, and more than enough, for his part, of such discourse, and flinging back his head with impetuous hauteur, he said indignantly —

"In very truth I marvel at ye all, discussing as though it were a possibility, the chance of a Spanish nobleman falling alive into the hands of a base redskin! Let us turn our tongues to themes that shall be more profitable."

"To pleasanter ones, with all my heart," said Juan de Cabrera readily. "But see,, who comes yonder in such haste?"

"Morla, for a gold button," said Sandoval.

"An easy guess enough," laughed Velasquez. "And none will take thy bet, my friend. Was there ever another man with so huge a head as Morla!"

"Never mind, Morla, it hath brains inside," said Escalante good-naturedly to the man, who had now come up to the party of officers, and stood before them awaiting permission and opportunity to speak. Curiosity gave him them soon enough.

"Brains or no brains, thou hanged rascal," said Cabrera, "what wouldst thou with us. To have another try at thy neck by way of practice for the natives, if they turn restive on their gods' behalf?"

A grim smile flitted for a moment over the soldier's face.

"I thank thee, my Señor, I would rather that practising were undertaken with the Don Montoro de Diego by to witness it, and to make sure that the lesson were not too well learnt. Meantime, I have a message from the Captain-General to the Don Juan de Escalante, to the effect that he will repair without delay to the Captain's tent."

The order was obeyed with alacrity, and when the officer returned, some time later, to his brethren in arms his face wore an expression of mingled elation and satisfaction. The confidence felt in his abilities and integrity had received full proof, for he was to be left in charge of the new city of Villa Rica de Vera Cruz, and of its small garrison, of which Morla was to form one, and of the company of slaves and attendants.

"You will at any rate be safe from the perils of the sacrificial altar, seeing that here you will have neither priests, false gods, nor altars for the sacrifice," said the fine young officer Gonzalo de Sandoval, with just a touch of envy at his companion's elevation to a post of so much trust and honour. But Cabrera looked at the matter in another light —

"Neither will he have here the rich prizes that we go to gather from the golden palaces of Mexico."

"I agree with you," said Velasquez. "Wealth and action, with any peril you please, for me, sooner than poverty and a safe tranquillity."

And so the band of high-spirited young adventurers discussed their prospects gaily, none seeing into the veiled future, nor knowing that the one they thought to leave to such safety was doomed to deadly peril, none dreaming that the remaining days of life of their gallant comrade were so few, and that they were about to bid him a final farewell. But more of that in its due course.

With the first dawn of the morrow after the day of mutiny, clamour, and expectation, the whole camp was astir, and in no long time after, the army was on its way through a country beautiful enough for the Garden of Paradise, to the Indian city of Cempoalla, one of the centres of the civilization of the Western World.

Delighted feelings of new hope arose in the soldiers' minds as they came in sight of fruit-laden orchards in the highest state of cultivation, and gardens evidencing a care and knowledge, in their wonderful beauty and luxuriance, that few indeed of the gardens of Europe could boast in that warlike age.

Hernando Cortes and his men marched on. Cortes himself maintained a closely observant silence, but his officers and men were not so reticent, and on all sides there were exclamations of wonder, at the unexpected signs of an advanced civilization and refinement so utterly unlooked-for in those regions.

And now their progress began to be somewhat impeded by the innumerable processions that met them from the city,[5] some coming to welcome the strange visitors, some coming as sightseers, to enjoy an early view of the new-comers and their marvellous four-footed companions, whom they took, like the ancients of the old world, to form with their riders one extraordinary animal.

"Are we once more fighting on the battle-fields of Granada, think you!" ejaculated Alvarado to Montoro, as he pointed to a long train of men then approaching the Captain-General, and glittering in the sunlight as they came on, clad in richly-coloured mantles worn over the shoulders in the Moorish fashion, gorgeous sashes of every rainbow tint, or girdles, while splendid jewels of gold adorned their necks, their ears and nostrils.

Montoro gazed at them in equal wonder.

"But see," he murmured, almost breathless with amaze,—"see yonder, friend Pedro. Let thine eyes travel on a little farther. Is not yon a singular sight to behold in a country where we had taught ourselves to expect nought but savage wilds, and inhabitants sunk in the depths of a miserable degradation? I feel as though I had fallen asleep, to awake in dreamland."

"And a fair enough dreamland too," replied Juan de Cabrera. "I care not, for my part, how long I may remain there, so I be not altogether smothered with their flowers."

That hope as to the smothering seemed almost needful with reference to the trains of women and young maidens to whom Montoro had directed his companion's notice. Beautifully clad from the neck to the ankles in robes of exquisitely-wrought fine cotton, ornamented with finely-worked golden necklets, bracelets, and earrings, and surrounded by crowds of obsequious attendants, the graceful processions advanced, literally laden with brilliant blossoms, the products of that most lovely country.

Hastening gaily forward, they surrounded the warriors with their dainty offerings. They hung a chaplet of roses about the general's helmet, and wreaths about his charger's neck. As for the yellow-haired Alvarado and the laughing Cabrera, they were very soon converted into tolerable imitations of the English Maypole, or the May-day Jack-in-the-green, their fine Spanish eyes beaming out of the midst of their bright coverings, upon their decorators, with a smiling good-humour that gave little warning of future headlong and annihilating cruelty.

At length the Europeans reached the city, and silence fell upon them as they slowly entered the narrow, crowded streets, and paced along to a temple assigned them by the Cacique for their quarters, during their stay in his dominion.

Not one of the band would have now retreated from the enterprise on hand had he been able. At the same time, for a company of about six or seven hundred men to be cooped up within a close-built town, of whose ins and outs they knew nothing, and in this position to be surrounded by thirty thousand people who might prove to be crafty enemies, was a state of affairs to make even the most reckless feel just a little bit like wishing that they had at least two pairs of eyes, and one of them situated in the back of their heads.

No one saw fit to demur when Cortes announced, on arriving at the temple, that he intended to double the usual number of the sentinels to keep watch at night, and that the whole force was to maintain a constant state of the utmost vigilance, and readiness for any surprise.

"Moreover," concluded the General, with resolute determination of manner, "moreover, comrades, it is my absolute command, on pain of death, that none leave the precincts of our present quarters without my leave, on any pretext whatsoever. I will myself shoot the first who does."

"Umph," muttered Cabrera with a little raising of his eyebrows. "You speak very positively, my Captain. How would it be with your word if you did not get the chance!"

"Just so," returned Alvarado in the same tone. "My fears of being caught hold of by those bloodthirsty idol-priests would do more to keep me from straying, than any threats of being shot if I were lucky enough to get back to camp again. Meantime, here comes a party of well-laden cooks. Whatever other fate they intend for us, it is apparently not starvation."

As those two thus talked together, Montoro de Diego was no little startled by one of the women, with a flower-decked basket of maize cakes in her hands, and cheeks streaming with tears, separating herself with some quiet caution from her fellows, and coming up to him with her gift, and with eyes that besought, with all the power of mute eloquence, for a hearing for some tale of sorrow.

Montoro had been wandering with a vivid interest through some of the numerous apartments of the temple, opening on to the courtyard where the rest of his comrades were assembled, and he was standing within one of the halls, and alone, when the woman caught sight of him. The bringing of the maize bread was but a pretext for an interview.

"Be comforted. Trust me; I will do what I can," said Montoro, with the flush of deep excitement on his face, after listening for a few moments to the poor creature's broken utterances.

Then he dismissed her, and made his way to Cortes, asking a private audience. But the General was in something less than his usual cordial mood. Cortes was preoccupied, and oppressed with many anxieties that night, and little disposed to speech or interviews with even those whom he most esteemed.

"What is it, Diego?" he asked rather hastily—"any news of treachery without or within? For matters of high importance one must have always leisure; for others—I crave your pardon,—they must wait."

Montoro bowed with a certain degree of haughtiness.

"I am not accustomed to seek private interviews concerning trivialities. But,—I will crave your pardon as you have craved mine,—methinks, now

I give second thoughts to the affair, that thou mightest even pronounce my present matter unworthy of your present favourable attention, and with disfavour I can well dispense."

"As I with thine unseasonable anger, friend Toro," said Hernando with grave reproach.

But the angered cavalier had already retired.

"To brood over his fancied causes of complaint against me, no doubt, like the most unreasonable amongst my company," muttered Cortes in a tone of vexation.

Union was so abundantly necessary just now.

CHAPTER XXIX
MONTORO AND CABRERA RESCUE
A HUMAN SACRIFICE

"Cabrera."

"Diego!"

The one name had been spoken with a sort of eager hush in the voice; the second with an accent of startled interrogation.

The hour was about ten at night. Cabrera and Diego had been on sentry duty since Diego's short, sharp interview with the General. One of them had just been relieved, and the other was about to be so, when Montoro called to his friend, who passed him on his way to shelter and sleep.

Cabrera stepped up closer to his friend.

"Why, Toro, what is it? Of all men in the world to hear thee speaking as thou hadst some mystery to whisper!"

"And so I have," came the hurried return.

Juan's big round eyes grew bigger and rounder than ever.

"Well, and if thou hast, there is ne'er a redskin about can understand thee if thou dost but speak fast, and with some of those long words thou knowest so—"

"Hush thee, then," muttered Montoro hastily. "It is from no redskin that I would hide the matter that I have in hand, at least not for the moment, but from the keenest pair of Spanish ears that either thou or I are likely to have met with."

"If thou meanest to hint at our Captain-General by that," agreed Cabrera, "thou art right enough, for I believe that he hears thoughts sometimes, without need of the tongue to give them utterance. But the business grows interesting. I love a plot. I would thou wert about to propose to break bounds, and take a midnight wandering."

"And it is—" a pause at the fancied sound of an approaching footstep. And then he continued, scarcely audibly, "It is even so. Wilt thou join me?"

Cabrera paused an instant, and gave a perceptible start.

"It is death, Diego, by the General's orders."

"I know it. And it is death to a native Christian, my lost Indian interpreter, as a living sacrifice to heathen gods, if we do not rescue him ere the dawn. But there, I should not have asked thee to share the double danger; I will go alone. You will not, at least, betray me?"

"No, nor suffer you to go alone," was the hurried answer. "I would sooner shoot myself. But there comes your exchange. Where shall we meet again?"

"In the hollow there, two yards to the right," muttered Montoro quickly, and then he stood silent and watchful, awaiting the new-comer, as though intent upon nothing beyond guarding his present post.

Two minutes later he once more stood beside Cabrera, at the only spot of the temple's surroundings whence escape unobserved was possible. Montoro's diligent search had discovered it very soon after he quitted the General, and the daring companions had scarcely met before they were safe outside the temple's precincts. There they were joined by the Indian woman, waiting to be their guide to the great temple of sacrifice. On its lofty summit there was a fire burning, and in front of the fire was visible, even at a distance, the great stone, stained with the blood of the countless human sacrifices offered up to the honour of the horrible god of war.

Closely following their guide, and keeping in the darkest shadows of the houses along the silent streets, the two Spaniards went on their adventurous mission of mercy. Suddenly the woman fell back upon them for a few moments with a low cry, and her hand upraised towards the temple's heights. The Spaniards stood still and with their eyes obeyed her sign.

The fire had been replenished, and blazed up fiercely, and there, high up above the houses of the town, on the elevated platform, and illuminated by the ruddy glow, there now stood a group of men. As the Europeans gazed they perceived a stir amongst that group—one appeared to fall; there was a pause, the woman with another shuddering cry dropped her face into her hands. Then a far-off shout fell upon the two friends' ears, and they saw an upraised arm against the glowing background, a hand that held something—

"Is it a head?" muttered Cabrera.

But the woman once more hurried them on.

"But if he is already slain," questioned Montoro sadly, "what can we do more?"

"Perhaps he is not already sacrificed," came the anguished answer in broken Spanish. "There are many to die to-night to please the god; perhaps he still lives, and may be saved."

For that 'perhaps' the devoted champion of the oppressed, and his friend, continued their dangerous route. It might be to meet the fate that, only twenty-four hours before, Escalante had spoken of with such horror. But even if they escaped that, it would but be to receive death at the hands of their own countrymen. Montoro began to be sorely troubled. To save one man he had brought the life of another into jeopardy. After all, it might be that he did deserve Alvarado's accusation. He stood still again.

"Cabrera, I have done wrong."

"Well," was the calm answer. "A thought more wildly, perchance, than might have been looked for from the sensible Don Montoro. Shall we return?"

"You will," was the eager reply. "We have not as yet gone too far for you to find your way back easily."

"Oh—h," ejaculated Cabrera. "And for thyself?"

"I go on."

"Ah! I see. Thanks, my friend, for your dismissal then, but—I go on also."

Montoro clenched his hands tightly.

"It will be a load off my heart, Juan, if you will return."

"Without you?—never. You must keep your load."

They had begun to move on again slowly before this short dialogue was ended; but now a bitter, imploring moan from the poor creature with them helped Montoro to forget all but her troubles, and making a sign to her, they hurried on as rapidly as before.

After all, as far as Juan de Cabrera was concerned, any excitement, even to the excitement of deadly peril, was better than peace and quietness. He rather liked the sensation of feeling as though a dozen or two pairs of those lean, small, redskin hands were stretching out from every doorway to clutch at him, and that he had a sword by his side which should win him freedom. Montoro for the time thought of nothing at all, but his purpose to rescue his native servant from the bloody altar of the horrible war-god Huitzilopotchli.

Arrived at the foot of the mound on which the chief temple was built, the guide paused, and looked at her companions as though with some compunction for having brought them into so great peril; but her regrets were then too late. They had caught sight of a spectacle which had filled them with loathing indignation; and they sprang up the mound, rushed up the great flight of stone steps in the centre of the temple with a fierce shout, regardless of prudence, indifferent to all consequences, and gained the platform just in time to witness the completion of a third awful act of heathen faith.

On a huge block of jasper, with a slightly convex surface, lay the living, human, palpitating sacrifice. Around him were gathered six of the war-god's priests, hardened to their awful office by almost daily custom. Men fitted for such duties they looked, with their wild eyes, their long and matted locks flowing in wild disorder over their shoulders, and their sable, crimson-stained robes covered with hieroglyphic scrolls of mystic import.

Five of these weird, sombre, butcher-priests held down the head and limbs of the victim. The sixth, clad in a scarlet mantle, emblematic of the office, cut open the breast of the sacrifice with a sharp razor of the volcanic itztli, inserted his hand in the wound, and tore away the beating heart from the yet writhing body; the awful trophy was held for one moment up on high, then cast at the feet of the idol to which it was devoted.[6]

All was over before the Spaniards' second furious cry had had power to escape their lips. The next instant that elevated plateau was a scene of wild confusion.

Transported beyond himself, Cabrera had shot down the priest of sacrifice, dashed to the ground, insensible, two of the other black-robed ministers of the dismal faith, and then with his sword cut asunder the bonds binding a group of prisoners awaiting their turn on the jasper block.

Montoro had not been idle. At the point of the sword he had driven the remaining priests into the interior of the temple, flung into the fire the instrument of torture, and the instruments of music used to drown the wretched sufferers' cries, and then, with a far-echoing shout—"For the glory of the one true God!" he signed to the rescued captives, brandished his sword aloft, and, followed by the liberated train, the two Spaniards rushed down from the height, thrust a way for themselves and their bewildered companions through the gathering multitudes, with an impetuosity that bore down all obstacles, and with the happy Indian woman once more for guide, regained their own quarters.

The whole band of their comrades was astir, and within an hour of their stealthy departure Montoro de Diego and Cabrera, with the little group of Indians about them, once more stood in the courtyard of the lesser temple, surrounded by their Captain-General and the whole company of his followers.

CHAPTER XXX
TOO USEFUL TO BE KILLED

"General, I have disobeyed your orders, and I accept my punishment, and acknowledge its justice."

Those words were the first that were distinctly audible above the hubbub and din prevailing in the courtyard of the Spaniards' new encampment. But they were spoken by a singularly penetrating voice, and in cold, calm tones that had an almost incredible power of making themselves heard.

During the last half-hour the moon had dispelled the darkness of night, and was shining in a steel-blue, cloudless sky, with a brilliancy at least equal to the light of many a northern day. In the foreground glittered the waters of the great Gulf of Mexico; to the left the silver thread of a river wound in and out amidst a country luxuriant and fertile as a garden; the narrow streets of the city lay at their feet; above them still gloomed and glowed, like some evil eye, that fire on the summit of the great temple, and over all, away in the distant background, towered the 'everlasting hills' and the snow-crown of Citlaltepelt or Orizaba.

So beautiful, so majestic, so peaceful the scene, could but that agitated gathering of men of the two hemispheres have been blotted out.

Hernando Cortes, tall and stately, bearing his handsome face with a proud dignity, stood with folded arms somewhat apart from the tumultuous throngs, all of whom, in the midst of their other words and thoughts, took time to cast many a searching glance at the leader; but all their scrutiny was in vain. Nothing was to be learnt of the meditations going on in the brain behind that fixed countenance.

Opposite to Hernando stood a man equally handsome in face and figure, equally calm and stately, but with a strange sweet light in his eyes as they rested on the poor startled Indians standing huddled together, scarcely knowing as yet whether to rejoice or no, at their rescue from the hands of the Cempoallan priests.

Montoro's father had died because he dared to plead for the life of the Jew. Montoro had a deep hidden gratitude in his heart, that he had been thus able to offer his life for the lives of these poor helpless Indians. And with this thanksgiving in his heart he spoke, and the babel of confused voices ceased.

Cabrera stepped up beside his companion, saying coolly—

"Well, General, here am I also. I cannot say with Diego that I will acknowledge the justice of the threatened punishment, or that I would accept it, if I could see my way on any side to doing the other thing; but—as it is—"

A shrug of the shoulders finished the sentence, and then there was a silence. The native servant and interpreter crept to Montoro's feet, clasping them, and entreating to be returned to the stone of sacrifice if otherwise his deliverer must die. The native woman hid her face in her robe, and kneeling before Cortes wept there silently.

At last Alvarado stepped forward impetuously, and exclaimed—

"Hernando Cortes, those two comrades of ours have risked their lives to save the blood of a Christian from being poured out to the honour of a heathen god! Is the order of a Spanish leader like the law of the Medes and Persians—one that altereth not? Those two have broken your command; according to that, it is admitted, their lives are forfeited. Can it be that they are to pay the penalty!"

As he concluded with that passionate demand, a sudden brilliant smile for one instant passed over the face of Cortes like a lightning flash. Then it was sternly set as before, as his lips opened to reply.

The soldiers had been subsiding into quietness before, now they were hushed into an intense expectancy that seemed as though it could be felt. The words with which their attention was rewarded were few enough.

"You ask me, Don Pedro de Alvarado, if those two of our Spanish brethren yonder are to die. I say yes, if any of you, their brethren, will shoot them. Montoro, may I crave that private audience with you that I lost this afternoon?"

Juan de Cabrera sprang forward with raised hands, and shoulders almost up to his ears. Even the Indians forgot their apprehensions and laughed. He bestowed a most horrible-looking, wide-mouthed grin upon them, and then drew his face to an almost impossible length, as he continued his way to Cortes, groaning out—

"Oh, General! don't you please to need a private audience with me also? That fellow, Don Gonzalo there, is quite beside himself with longing to try the new gun he hath just received from the armourer. I shiver with fear."

"Then take a doze of sleep to cure thee," was the laughing reply, "and get Father Olmedo to shrive thee first for thy sin of disobedience. I had needs be a schoolmaster rather than a general, to rule great overgrown boys like thee."

Then Cortes turned to a quieter region of the temple, and with his officers held deep counsel as to next proceedings. Although he spared his two followers from the mingled motives of prudence, friendship, and admiration, he felt somewhat bitterly that their romantic act of generosity had greatly complicated the position of affairs. Yesterday he had feared enmity, now he was sure of it.

"As strongly as we hold to our faith," he said gravely, "so I have ere now discovered do they hold to theirs. As resolutely as we would avenge an insult to our Lord, so will these heathen endeavour to avenge the insult put upon their gods of wood and clay. We must be prepared."

As the dawn grew full, Cortes, with his usual decisive energy, determined suddenly to know the worst at once; not to act on the defensive as he had first planned, but to issue forth immediately, and complete the desecration, already so boldly begun, of the heathen altars of Cempoalla.

"We have come hither," he exclaimed in animated tones to his followers, "to burn the idols of this polluted land, and to raise the sacred standard of the cross. Let us delay the glorious task no longer. In the name of the Holy Faith I go."

"In the name of the Holy Faith lead on, we follow you," shouted back the small, undaunted army with one acclaim; and in another minute, in firm, close array, the Spaniards had issued forth from their enclosure.

They had not made much way when an Indian scout flew back to them, with heels winged with fear, to say that the Cacique himself, at the head of his troops, was advancing to their encounter.

"All the better," muttered Cabrera. "Saves our steps, and my boots are something the worse for wear."

But before proceeding to extremities the two leaders called a parley: the Indian chief to expostulate on the violence done his gods in return for his great hospitality; and Cortes to desire that he and his subjects would hear from Father Olmedo a discourse, to prove that his gods were no gods, that it was no more possible to do them dishonour than to show respect or disrespect to an old tree-stump, and to teach them the principles of Divine truth.

With a fine courtesy the Indian Cacique gave consent, even while burning under a sense of wrong; and something he must have gleaned through the interpreter of the required teaching, for he replied with dignity—

"Know this, ye white-faces, that it seemeth to me we have not much to learn from you, beyond that faithlessness that you would have us show to our gods. We too believe in a supreme Creator and Lord of the universe— that God by whom we live and move and have our being; the Giver of all good gifts, almighty, omnipresent, omniscient, perfect. We too believe in a future life—a heaven and a hell. We too believe in the virtues of temperance, charity, self-denial; and that of ourselves, being born in sin, we are capable of no good thing. We too are admitted into fellowship with the supreme Lord of all things by the rite of baptism. The lips and bosoms of our infants are sprinkled with water, and we beseech the Lord to permit the holy drops to wash away the sin that was given to them before the foundation of the world, so that they may be born anew. We too pray for grace to keep peace with all, to bear injuries with humility, trusting to the Almighty to avenge us."

The fine old Cacique ceased, and in breathless amazement the Spaniards gazed at the Indian who had thus made confession of a faith so strangely in accord with their own, so utterly unexpected.

"And with these sublime truths," murmured Father Olmedo with wide eyes, "there is mingled the awful Polytheism, the ghastly idol-worship that revels in human sacrifices. This is verily the devil's work, transforming himself into the likeness of an angel of light that his worship may gain in glory."

Another thought came to Montoro de Diego. Imagination travels as the lightning, flashing from one end of the earth to the other. As Montoro stood there, in one of the flower-decked squares of the Indian town of Cempoalla, his spirit was hovering above the wide piazza of the Spanish city of Saragossa. It was the day, so imagination told him, of an Auto da Fé.

Slowly entering the square came the long procession—priests of the true holy Catholic faith who had learnt 'God is love,' incense-bearers, candle-bearers, and all the troop of satellites.

In Montoro de Diego's dream-ears were sounding the solemn cadences of the chants, as the procession moved slowly, solemnly along. Then, in the centre of the long imposing train he saw a dismal spectacle. Clad in the yellow garments of scorn and contumely, adorned for shame's sake and derision with scarlet flames and so-called devils, limped and crawled along the racked and wrenched, and twisted and scorched victims of the

Inquisition, passing along to be burnt alive, in the name of religion, at those stakes at the four corners of the great piazza.

And as the Romish priest, Father Olmedo, thought of the Indian idol sacrifices, and murmured, "Verily this is the devil's work, uniting sublime truths with the blackest iniquity," Montoro thought of the Autos da Fé, and murmured to himself—

"If the one be the devil's work, is not the other likewise?"

At a future day the same question was asked by an Indian captive in Spain, asked with indignant scorn, and answered by himself—

"Ay, verily. Either both are of the gods—our sacrifices of blood and yours of fire—or both are of the devil. And ye, proud Spaniards, had done well to purge your own land, before ye laid waste our countries, and destroyed our nations, to remove the mote that lay in our eyes."

But we must return to Cempoalla, and pass by dreams and dreamers for the present, for there is once more a sudden sound and stir borne along upon the air. The Cacique and his army raise their heads, grasp their arrows more firmly, and look expectant.

The Spaniards close up together again, lay their hands on their sword-hilts, and wait.

CHAPTER XXXI
ONCE FOR ALL—THEY SHALL CEASE

The number of priests in the capital of the empire of Mexico itself amounted, at the time of the conquest, to very many thousands—five thousand for the immense chief *teocalli,* or house of God, alone.

These priests were gathered together in great establishments, where a most rigorous discipline was maintained, much after the fashion of Roman Catholic institutions. And as with the empire itself, so was it, in a lesser degree, with the empire's tributaries. In those also chiefs and people endeavoured to make their peace with heaven, as in the old world, by such immense endowments of lands and riches as tended naturally to swell the ranks of a race so well provided for, and regarded with such supreme reverence.

The smiling territory of Cempoalla was as well provided as its neighbours, with these numerous ministers of a religion that so strangely blended bloodthirsty superstition with exalted faith and enlightenment.

Juan de Cabrera fondly supposed that in slaying a man whom he honestly looked upon as a murderer of the blackest die, deserving death, he had rid that city, at any rate, of its one hideously-skilful executioner, and, as he put it, "that no more of that sort of work could go on for the present, either in their presence or their absence." But he made a most tremendous mistake.

"The king is dead. Long live the king."

The priest-executioner-in-chief had fallen, before the altar of the god he had served with such dreadful fidelity. He had died yesterday, to-day he had a successor burning with ardour to avenge him by increased sacrifices, to atone for those deferred, and to prove his own consummate skill in the detestable work.

"If only," was his fierce wild prayer—"if only the one invisible, supreme God would grant that some of the sacrilegious, infidel white faces might fall into the hands of the Cempoallan warriors, that they themselves might be offered up as peace-offerings to the insulted Huitzilopotchli!"

Were his prayer granted there was no doubt that the morose and gloomy-natured priest would not spare also to inflict upon the prisoners some prior tortures, ingenious enough in their barbarous cruelty to have excited the admiring envy of the most savage of Inquisitors.

But meantime he had other business on hand—sacrifices truly, but sacrifices drawn from the families of his own nation; and, moreover, sacrifices of such a nature that, had he been as wise as he was ruthless, he would have delayed their attempted offering until those white-faces had left his land. They were just the last drops needed to fill the Spaniards' cup of boiling indignation full to overflowing.

Exquisitely fertile and luxuriant as the whole district of Cempoalla looked to the Spanish eyes, so wearied with the barren tracts of sand, and marshy swamps of their recent station, there had in reality been a considerable time of drought lately, and the Indians were beginning to have fears for some of their harvests. Tlaloc, the god of rain, whose symbol of a cross had so disconcerted Cabrera and Father Olmedo, had to be propitiated.

For some days past a solemn festival had been decreed in his honour. The victims were bought for the altar, the invitation to the faithful was announced, and, although a priest had been slain in the night, the imperious god of rain must not be deprived of his offerings in the morning. Thence the sounds which had so suddenly arrested all speech and movement of the two armies, Christian and heathen, met together in the great square of the city.

The waiting and suspense were short. The sounds of musical instruments and of a wild melodious chant drew rapidly nearer. They reached the square, and the Spaniards turned wondering eyes upon each other.

"The procession of the Fête Dieu!" exclaimed Cabrera in bewilderment.

"One might well suppose so," returned Montoro, almost equally surprised.

Cortes turned with rapid questionings to Doña Marina, the native captive princess and his interpreter.

Passing across the further end of the square, on the way to Tlaloc's temple, were lines of sable-robed priests, trains of flower-decked youths and maidens from the priests' seminaries, crowds of devout worshippers; and in the midst of all, borne aloft in view of every eye, a number of lovely children, tiny creatures scarcely beyond the days of infancy, dressed in bright-hued festal robes, wreathed with flowers, and seated in gay litters, around each of which gathered groups of chanting priests, and the parents who had sold them.

Wide-eyed and dumb with wonder were some of these little ones. And on them the priests frowned. Others, startled, terrified, with tiny, helpless arms outstretched to their miserable, deluded mothers, were drowned in tears, choking with piteous sobbings. And on them the priests cast pitiless smiles, and sang and danced with wilder fervour than before. Those tears were of good omen for the god's acceptance of his worshippers' prayers. Dry-eyed sacrifices were fruitless ones.[7]

But the exacting god was to have no sacrifice that day, dry-eyed or otherwise.

The procession was passing on, when at length Hernan Cortes, with a horror-stricken shout of comprehension, raised his head from Doña Marina, and turning to face his followers exclaimed, in a voice that literally trembled with passion and haste:

"Comrades! look yonder. See ye that sight? See ye those helpless babes, decked out thus bravely as the heathen nations of old were wont to deck four-footed beasts for sacrifice? Those babes are sold for sacrifice by a black, well-nigh incredible bigotry. Twenty minutes hence, without your succour, their innocent hearts will have been plucked from out their riven breasts, as offerings to that blasphemous god who pollutes the sign of our redemption. Say, comrades, shall this thing be?"

The men started a step forward with cheeks aflame.

"No!" exclaimed Alvarado. "By St. Jago and our good swords, no!"

"No!" echoed the whole band, as though with one voice.

"No!" cried Cabrera, impetuously. "Not if we have to put every man in Cempoalla to the sword to deliver them."

And with these exclamations it seemed, for one moment, as though the Spaniards were going to rush forward pell-mell, and effect a rescue. But Cortes raised his hand and checked them. There was time yet to proceed more peaceably. He turned back to the Cacique.

"You see," he began.

"I see there is another of those red-cloaked demons yonder," muttered Cabrera in a tone of bitter loathing to Montoro.

But the low aside formed no interruption to the General, who continued, with determination—

"You see, my followers and I have one heart in this matter. And I, for my part, am resolved that within this hour the idol gods shall be destroyed. Use your authority to stay yonder procession on its further course to sin, and thus hinder bloodshed."

But even before his words were ended it became evident that force must effect, if possible, what persuasion could not do. The Cacique's reply to the imperative demand was a swift signal to his army. It was obeyed as swiftly.

The Indian warriors gathered up from all sides, with shrill cries and clashing of weapons. The priests began to rush on with the litters and their wailing occupants, towards the temple, for the consummation of the sacrifice. The Spaniards, with Montoro de Diego at their head, flew forward, moved to too heart-sickened a pity to wait any longer upon the rule of orders. And soon the whole square and the entire route to the temple was one scene of wild uproar. The priests, in their sombre cotton robes, and dishevelled tresses matted with blood flowing over their shoulders, rushing frantically amongst their warrior brethren, urging them on to the fray, and calling upon them to protect their gods from violation.

All was war and tumult where so lately had been peace and friendly brotherhood.

Cortes took his usual prompt and decided measures. While Montoro led the rescue party, and ceased not his determined onslaught until he had delivered the infants back to arms that, in the new turn of affairs, were stretched out readily enough to receive them again, Cortes, by a bold manœuvre, and the firing off of those terror-speaking guns, gained possession of the great Cacique himself and of some of his principal subjects, including the chief priests.

"Now," he authoritatively commanded once more, and with a better chance of being obeyed. "Now, Nezahualth, you and your people are in my power. Give orders that not another arrow is shot this day, or disobedience shall cost you all your lives."

"The gods will protect us," exclaimed a frenzied priest.

Cortes turned upon him with a cold, haughty glance.

"Did the gods protect thy brethren yesternight? The Spaniards were two to a multitude, and the Spaniards' God gave them victory. Thy god gave his followers up to disgrace and death!"

Whatever effect these words of reminder had upon the Totonac priest, they had a powerful one upon the Totonac chieftain, the Cacique of Cempoalla. With a sudden lowering of his lofty head, he dropped his face into his hands, and exclaimed bitterly that the white men must work their will, and the gods must avenge themselves.

"Even so," said Cortes sternly. "Thus it must be, for from this hour, once for all, their idols shall be destroyed from this city, and the human sacrifices shall cease."

This settled the matter. The Christians were not slow in availing themselves of the Cacique's submission to the inevitable.

At a signal from Cortes fifty soldiers darted off to the chief temple, sprang up the great stone stairway as eagerly as Montoro de Diego and Cabrera had done the night before, entered the building on the summit, the walls of which were black with human gore, tore the huge wooden idols from their foundations, and dragged them to the edge of the terrace.

The fantastic forms and features of these symbolic idols meant nothing to the Spaniards' eyes but outward and visible representations of the hideous lineaments of Satan. With the greatest alacrity, cheered on by Cabrera, the soldiers rolled the colossal monsters down the steps of the pyramid, amidst the triumphant shouts of their own companions, and the groans and lamentations of the awe-struck natives, who forthwith gave up all hopes of the coming harvest in despair.

The work was finally crowned by the burning of the images in the presence of the assembled, startled multitudes. That finishing touch proved a wise one. Hitherto, during the work of desecration, the Totonacs had waited in trembling expectation of some fearful exhibition of their insulted god's great power and glory. But now. Poor impotent deities! they had not been able even to prevent the profanation of their shrines, the destruction of their own representations.

"What think ye of your gods now?" asked Pedro de Alvarado contemptuously, as he spurned a heap of the smouldering ashes with his foot, and turned his scornful eyes upon a group of humbled priests beside him.

"Verily they be fine gods," added Father Juan Diaz, ever ready to hit those who were down. "As able, i' faith, to help ye as to assert their own dignity."

So began the priests and people of Cempoalla, apparently, to think themselves. With bowed heads and dejected steps they left those humiliating mounds of ashes. The day of solemn festival was turned into a day of turmoil and mourning.

The people of that fair land of Mexico had received their first trample under the iron heel of the conqueror. In their abject dejection they aided in the business of their own humiliation.

By Cortes' orders a number of the Totonacs cleansed the floor and walls of the teocalli from their foul impurities; a fresh coating of stucco was laid on them by the native masons, and an altar was raised, surmounted by a lofty cross, and hung with garlands of roses.

"And now, my friends," exclaimed Cortes, addressing the multitudes assembled around the base of the pyramid temple, watching proceedings with a stupefied wonder—"and now, put by your sad thoughts and your saddened countenances, for a brighter day has dawned for you than you have ever known hitherto. I have spoilt one procession, but I will make you full amends with another and more glorious."

With the easy vivacity and changeableness of the semi-civilized nature, the Indians roused up at the Spanish General's new tones of cheerful friendship, and greeted his short speech with shouts of approval, smiles, and nods, which received full reply. Sternness had done its work; he was quite ready now to be as joyous and cordial and brotherly as they would let him. They went from one extreme to the other—from animal-like ferocity to childlike docility, owing to the weakness of their nature. But Cortes, from the dark brows of the resolute victor who would be obeyed, to the courteous, agreeable friend, from policy, and an almost unequalled power of self-command. He promised the procession, and it was soon formed.

Once more Spaniards and Indians assembled in the great square. Side by side, no longer conqueror and captive, but host and guest once more, moved on with calm and stately steps the two leaders, the tall, slender Spaniard, the tall, corpulent Indian chief. Following them came the two armies, in the same brotherly union. Then the Totonac priests, no longer wearing their dismal black garments with those suggestive dark-hued stains upon them, but clothed in white robes, and, like their brother Christian priests, bearing great lighted candles in their hands; while an image of the Virgin, little less roughly made in those days than the idols so lately deposed, but half-smothered under the sweet-scented, brilliant burden of flowers, was borne aloft, and, as the procession climbed the steps of the temple, was deposited above the altar, and a solemn mass, performed by Father Olmedo, concluded the great ceremony, instead of a bloody sacrifice.

"At the same time," murmured Montoro to a companion late that night, as he paced the courtyard of the Spanish encampment—"at the same time, methinks, these poor creatures can but credit us with the cruel insolence of strength, which has destroyed their idols to make way for our own. They had a cross which they adored; we have cast it down to erect our own. They had idols which they reverenced; we have burnt their images but to set up another."

"Even so," replied the good priest, in the same low tones. "My fears go with your thoughts—that they must have strange doubts as to our honesty."

"We preach against idols, and yet have them," added Montoro. "I wonder if our work this day has done much good for the salvation of souls?"

"It has done some good for the salvation of bodies, at any rate," broke in Juan de Cabrera from his sentry post, opposite to which the two friends had paused in the interest of their conversation. "It is thanks wholly and solely to thee, all throughout, Toro, that that hapless little company of babies is alive to-night. And so, my long-faced friend, instead of looking solemn as an old crow, thou shouldst be the merriest fellow in the company."

"Ho, there!" cried the voice of a fourth comer on the scene. "Who talks of merriment, I would know, forsooth, at this sleepy hour of the night, and with never an honest bit of gambling allowed to pass the watch hours by. For my part, I feel glum as a sulky bear."

"Then keep thy distance," was the retort. "For this sultry weather makes me suspicious that my bones may be in a dried-up state, and somewhat too easily crackable, my very esteemed Señor Velasquez de Leon."

Montoro laughed.

"Didst say, Juan, bones or brains were crackable?"

"Both—or meant to," said the young man. "My bones, and Leon's brains. But come, Leon, hast thou not come to relieve guard? for that Toro there, thief that he is, robbed me of my rest last night, and I shall fall asleep on the march to-morrow."

"Better not," replied Velasquez, with a warning shake of the head. "Be advised in time, lest thou mightest get left behind, and then thou wouldst assuredly be raised by the Totonac priests to the honour of the post of one of their lost gods. Thy beauty matches to a marvel that of their striking god of war."

"I'll match him in the striking trait on thee then, at any rate," cried Cabrera, as he raised his arm. But the next instant it was caught, and held fast for a moment in a good firm grip before it was let go.

"How now, my crack-brained schoolboy?" said the laughing voice of the General. "Hast had not enough of brawls during the past day to last thee even over one night? Keep thy blows for the turbulent spirits we may meet on the road to Mexico."

CHAPTER XXXII
ON THE ROAD TO MEXICO

Such magnificent and royal gifts of gold and silver, of precious stones and precious stuffs, of birds and animals, of jeweller's work and the marvellous feather work, feather fans and feather tapestries, costly shields and beautiful embroidery, had been forwarded, by the hands of ambassadors, from the Emperor of Mexico to the Spanish camp, that the Spaniards, from Cortes down to the meanest soldier, had the most exalted ideas of the wealth and power of the new-found empire.

"For my part," remarked Juan de Cabrera one day during the march— "for my part, I have serious thoughts of giving up the worn-out old country, and setting up my tent for the future in this new fairy-land. Gold and fruit and flowers, and food for the trouble of accepting it, are things just suited to my quiet tastes."

Montoro laughed.

"Few of thy friends will doubt thy word for it, Juan. But how about that promise to thy new, bright-eyed bride, the princess of Cempoalla—that she should reign as the queen of beauty not long hence in thine own old city of Madrid?"

"Umph!" ejaculated Cabrera with a slight shrug. "For the promise— well, seest thou it was no vow, bound for honour's sake to be kept—nought but a passing word to a woman. And since she hath me, I doubt not she will have little care for aught else."

"Hearken to him, O ye birds!" cried Alvarado. "Thy vanity doth but outdo thy faithlessness, thou black-crested cockatoo. But knowest thou, I shall be fairly content, for my part, when we are indeed in Mexico's great capital, Tenochtitlan; for I grow tired of this marching with one's head watching all ways at once during the day, and taking sleep at night like a dog, with one eye open."

"Ay, and worse than a dog—with one's hand on one's sword besides," added Cabrera.

Montoro raised his eyebrows as he looked from one to the other of his companions.

"Think ye then, that once in the island city all your cares and anxieties will be at an end?"

"If they do," put in Gonzalo de Sandoval, "I can tell them so thinks not the General himself. Methinks, for all his assumption of cool confidence, that his black locks grow something touched with grey of late."

"And mine also," said Alvarado with a toss of his yellow locks. "But from want of a siesta, and not from any dread of what these poor helpless, red-skinned creatures are likely to do to us."

But even the bold Alvarado and the careless Cabrera felt, a few days later, that confidence, and a feeling of security, were not much more certain of acquirement in a town than amid the uncertain perils of the high-way. Meantime their easy and bloodless victory at Cempoalla had taught both officers and men, for the most part, a good-natured contempt for the natives; and this sentiment was increased by the friendliness hitherto shown them on their route, whenever they were able to come fairly to speech with the Indians.

Alvarado and Cabrera in particular might be pardoned for their impatience, at what they considered something of overmuch watchfulness, for the sunny hair and blue eyes of the one, and the merry face of the other, had hitherto won them smiles and Benjamin's portions from all they met.

However, even before entering a town, the various members of that small army were to learn that their General's prudence was wiser than their own impatience of the discipline.

Between the territory of Cempoalla and Mexico lay the fine little warlike, independent republic of Tlascala, governed by a council elected by their tribes, and united by the strongest bonds of patriotism, and mutual hatred to their powerful and aggressive neighbour, the Emperor of Mexico.[8]

Fierce and revengeful, high-spirited and independent, Cortes decided, as soon as he heard of them, that they were the very auxiliaries to be desired in the contemplated conquest. For every step he now made towards the heart of the great empire, gave him fresh evidence of what an astoundingly bold thing he was doing, in adventuring himself and his handful of enfeebled men in such a magnificent enterprise.

"But with some few thousands of these enemies of Mexico, these Tlascalans," he said one evening towards the end of August, when a halt had been called for the night—"with their aid at our back, Diego, we shall go forward right merrily, methinks."

Montoro looked grave. To say truth, the many human sacrifices he had witnessed of late, and the awfully numerous traces of others discovered along the route, had caused some temporary wavering in his sympathies. Just for the time he was not quite sure if he did not think his Spanish sword would, after all, be well employed in slaying some of the bloodthirsty beings who offered up, in sacrifices to their abominable idols, girls and boys and little children, and then held ghastly feastings on their flesh.

He had begun to feel a loathing indignation for these wretched believers in a gross superstition, which made him a more welcome confidant for Cortes than was usual. He was quite ready to have his five hundred valiant Spanish companions reinforced by a few times that number of the natives. But he had heard news from his interpreter, during the day's march, that made him doubtful if such a reinforcement were altogether so likely as the General appeared to think.

"What does thy face mean, Diego, since thy tongue says nought?" asked Hernando Cortes after a few moments' silence. "Forgive me, but it looks nigh as long as yon merry madcap Cabrera is wont to call it."

Montoro smiled slightly. But he grew earnest enough the next instant as he said—

"Cortes, I fear me that thy face also will lengthen when I tell thee that the Tlascalans are meditating war with us, I believe, rather than peace."

"How sayest thou, Toro?" exclaimed that impetuous fellow, Velasquez de Leon. "Sayest thou the rascals have a mind to feel the touch of a good Toledo blade or two? I' faith, under those circumstances it is for them, not us, to draw the long faces, so I warn them."

"And I warn you," said Cortes seriously, "that it is for both to do so. But what is it that you have learnt, Diego? or rather, what reason is given you for these worthy warriors' bad feeling? They are at such enmity with the Mexicans, that one had some right, truly, to count with confidence upon their friendship."

"And I fully believe would have also had it," was the reply, "had you but given any proof that your sentiments towards this emperor bore any likeness to their own. But——"

"Well?" came the rather impatient query; "but what? Although I have not told the Mexicans themselves such things as should lead them to shut their ways against us, I have let their foes know fairly well that I am ready to aid all complainants to redress their wrongs."

"You have told them so, that is true," said Montoro, once more with a slight smile. "The Tlascalans also admit so much; but, as they say with some astuteness, your deeds are at variance with your words. You have exchanged many valuable gifts with their powerful adversary, you have entertained many of his ambassadors, and you now propose as a friend to visit him in his capital."

"Moreover," put in Father Olmedo, "I learn from your own interpreter, Doña Marina, that they hold us in terrible abhorrence for our hasty and unexplained desecration of the altars of Cempoalla, a place with which they are on terms of peace."

Cortes sprang to his feet angrily.

"That is the best deed I have performed in my life, and it shall receive many a repetition. Preachments are no part of a soldier's duties. It shall be mine to destroy the pollutions of the land; you, father, can take the task of preaching it into purity with such suave slowness as you please. Meantime, to put these rumours respecting those Tlascalans yonder to the test. We will send an embassy forthwith to demand a passage through their territories to Mexico."

"Send me," exclaimed Velasquez de Leon eagerly.

"And me," cried Juan de Cabrera, delighted at the prospect of real action. He preferred using his arms to watching by them, and so did most of his companions.

But Cortes was too politic to accept the offers. The number of his fearless and trusty knights was small enough without risking the lives of any of them needlessly. Some of the chief men among the Cempoallans had accompanied the Spaniards on their march, and of these Cortes chose out four, and sent them to their neighbours, charged with his amicable demand.

Three or four days passed, and those messengers had not returned. Matters began to look serious. Montoro, with his native interpreter, and both in disguise, penetrated some distance one early morning into the unknown dominions. They returned to the camp with the startling intelligence that the ambassadors had been seized as traitors to their country's cause, and renegades from the true faith, and were within a short time to be sacrificed as peace-offerings to the insulted gods.

Instantly the whole camp was astir. The Cempoallans tremblingly anxious to deliver their friends from the indignity of the fate awaiting them; Cortes strongly determined that such a blot should not fall upon his expedition, in the person of his allies.

There was no need to urge despatch in preparations. Each man of the force, native and Spaniard alike, was burning to set forth against the new foe. The foe was equally ready.

But amongst these strange people of the new world were some of the sentiments supposed to belong wholly to the old world's chivalry.

Just as the army was about to set out from its quarters, on that morning of the thirtieth of August, 1519, a long train of people was observed approaching from the distance, bearing an ensign of peace.

Cortes called a halt of his own followers. He and Montoro de Diego, and Father Olmedo, felt most thankful for the turn affairs appeared to have taken, thus at the very twelfth hour. Alvarado and Velasquez, with a good many of their like-minded comrades, it is true, were nothing at all so well contented. They had been living on very short commons the past few days, fare as meagre and unsatisfying as possible, and they regarded the punishment of the unfriendly republicans as a probable means of replenishing their scanty larders.

However, as it turned out, neither content nor discontent had any present foundation. The Tlascalans had also, on their part, it was true, sent an embassage, and a well-laden one. But, although the messengers brought a good deal with them that was acceptable, a request for peace was not one of the offerings.

As the train came near, it was discovered that abundant supplies of food of all kinds were being brought to the half-famished little army. But before they were presented, and to leave no doubt on the Spaniards' minds as to the motives of the gift, one fierce, slim warrior advanced before the company of food-bearers, and with a haughty, undaunted bearing that extorted the respect even of his haughty hearers, he exclaimed—

"See, poor starved-out creatures of a starved-out land, although we refuse entrance to the impious enemies of our gods, we would not that ye should think we grudge, or have need to grudge, you of the bounties that your God, it seems, denies you.

"The Republic of Tlascala sends you food, and in abundance—meat and bread. Eat, and be satisfied. The warriors of Tlascala scorn to attack an enemy enfeebled with disease, faint with hunger. Victory over such would be a vain one. We affront not our gods with famished victims, neither do we deign to feast upon an emaciated prey."

"What a mercy for us," muttered that reckless Cabrera, "since your noble disdain hath led you to feed us thus hospitably."

"For my part also," added Alvarado as quietly, "I would fain try if food will give me back something of the strength of arm their blazing sun hath robbed me of."

"You may well say blazing sun," ejaculated Velasquez de Leon, upon whose excitable temperament the tremendous, continuous heat of the past few weeks had had a peculiarly trying effect. Even the sight of the food scarcely cheered his flagging spirits. Cabrera laid his hand on his shoulder encouragingly.

"Cheer up, friend Leon; I will do the friendly part by thee, if thou wilt, and offer thee up to that aggravating god of rain. Thy dignified person may appease his angry, spiteful idol-ship."

Velasquez sighed.

"I feel well-nigh inclined, Juan, to give thee leave. I have more than once of late had the thought that I would offer up myself."

But whatever might be the voluntarily-endured sufferings of the Spaniards, they were light enough in comparison with those of the poor, brave Tlascalans. Cortes accepted their food, and likewise accepted their challenge, and the following day the two armies met to do battle—the one to preserve its country from the presumptuous invaders' tread, the other to make good its claim to advance where it chose.

Of the two armies decidedly the native one presented the most magnificent and imposing appearance, not only for numbers, but for array.

Far and wide, over a vast plain about six miles square, stretched the enormous army. Nothing could be more picturesque than the appearance of these Indian battalions, with the naked bodies of the common soldiers gaudily painted with the colours of the chieftains whose banners they followed, the splendidly attired chieftains themselves, with their gleaming spears and darts, and the innumerable banners, on which were emblazoned the armorial bearings of the great Tlascalan and Otomie chiefs.

Amongst the most conspicuous of these gorgeous banners were the white heron on the rock, the cognizance of the house of Xicotencatl, and the golden eagle with outspread wings, richly ornamented with emeralds and silver work, the great standard of the Republic of Tlascala.

The feather-mail of the more distinguished warriors, like the bodies of their inferior companions, also indicated by the choice of colours under whose orders they were more specially enrolled. The caciques themselves, and their chief officers, were clothed in quilted cotton tunics two inches thick, which, fitting close to the body, protected also the thighs and the shoulders; over this garment were cuirasses of thin gold or silver plate. Their legs were defended by leathern boots or sandals trimmed with gold.

But the most brilliant portion of the costume was a rich mantle of the Mexican feather work, embroidered with a skill and taste alike wonderful. This picturesque dress was surmounted by a fantastic helmet made of wood or leather, representing the head of some wild animal, and frequently displaying a fierce set of teeth.

From the crown floated a splendid plume of rich feathers, indicating by form and colour the rank and family of the wearer. The rest of their armour consisted of shields of wood covered with leather, or of reeds quilted with cotton, and all alike showily ornamented, and finished off with a beautiful fringe of feather work.

Their weapons were slings, bows and arrows, javelins, and darts. And for swords, a two-handed staff, about three and a half feet long, in which at regular distances were inserted sharp blades of itztli—a formidable weapon, with which they could fell a horse. They excelled in throwing the javelin, and they were such expert archers that they could discharge two and even three at a time.[9]

And yet with all this, and with an almost superhuman courage besides, the poor, noble republicans were conquered. They had not guns, they had not horses, and they had no keen Toledo blades—those cruel blades that cut their hands through to the bone when they grasped them, in their desperate courage, to wrench them, if it might be, from their adversaries' clasp.

And thus, after fourteen days of grand efforts to maintain their hitherto unbroken freedom, and to preserve the soil of their country from the invader's foot, the Tlascalans found themselves at length so diminished in numbers, so broken in strength, and so utterly helpless against the white-faces' wonderful animals and wonderful weapons, that once more an embassage came from Tlascalan head-quarters to the Spanish general.

Once more the stern-visaged Tlascalan warrior heralded a train of men and Indian maidens, bearing various gifts to the invading force.

Even yet the brave redskin maintained his grave dignity of bearing, but it was tempered now with a deep melancholy, as he exclaimed in tones of heart-stirred grief—

"Behold, ye strange and invincible white-faces, our gods have warned us now that to fight against ye is vain. Ye are few, and we are many; but we are slain, and our sepulchres already overflow, while ye all are still alive. We cannot fight against the gods, if such ye be, or against the gods who fight for you."

"You say well," responded Cortes, solemnly. "It is our God and St. Jago who fight for us, and through them we are as rocks to withstand the assaults of all enemies. But if you come to ask for peace, you will find us to be friends as staunch as we are resistless foes."

The warrior lifted his head proudly.

"We come to offer peace, and we bring gifts as signs of good-will. If ye are, in very deed, fierce-tempered divinities, lo! we present to you five slaves, that ye may drink their blood and eat their flesh. If ye are mild deities, accept an offering of incense and variegated plumes. For we are poor. We have little gold, or cotton, or salt; only, hitherto, our freedom and our arms. If ye be but men of like nature with ourselves, we bring you meat and bread and fruit to nourish you."

And they brought them far more besides than all that, for they brought them strong fidelity, clever brains, and arms useful enough against nations armed like themselves, and of no higher grade in the scale of civilization.

CHAPTER XXXIII
THE CAUSE ONCE MORE IN JEOPARDY

A very singular and picturesque affair was the camp of the Spaniards, when they paused, for rest or war, on the march to Mexico.

The gay-coloured cotton hangings of the Mexican manufactures had, in many instances, taken the place of the Spaniards' own rough and ragged tent coverings. All around were squatted groups of the slaves who had accompanied the army from Cuba and the sea-coast—races far inferior to those by whom they were now surrounded, and with very scant ideas as to dress, or any of the other refinements of civilization.

Then there were the gentle-spirited, courteous Totonac allies, evidencing their cultured tastes, and advanced instincts, by gathering armfuls of the brilliant wild blossoms about them to adorn their helmets and their shields; whilst regarding them, a short distance off, stood companies of the more warlike, stern-spirited Tlascalans, looking on at their neighbours' doings with a contempt they took no pains to conceal. They were magnificent enough themselves in their warrior's dress, as has been seen; but, under present circumstances, aught having a festal or light-hearted appearance they fairly well judged to betoken effeminacy as much as refinement.

For the rest, there was little love lost between the Cempoallans and the poverty-stricken, hardy Republicans, and although united for the time in one camp as allies of one commander, they took care mutually not to have too much to do with each other.

As for the Spaniards themselves, who were now but as one to eight of their Indian comrades, they were a lean-cheeked, sallow, hollow-eyed set of tatterdemalions enough by this time. All of them had received more or less wounds in their fierce battles with the Tlascalans, and even Hernando Cortes was only kept up by his indomitable resolution, for what with illness and his doctor, he had been brought to such a state of weakness that he could hardly sit steady on his saddle. Fifty of his poor, overdone soldiers had died since starting from Vera Cruz, and the whole band had at last become more than half doubtful whether any of them would reach Mexico alive.

"And really," grumbled Pedro de Alvarado dolefully one evening, "really I don't much care if I do. I'd just as soon lay my bones out here to bleach as within yon mythical city of gold."

"Mythical, as to the being built of gold, doubtless," returned Montoro de Diego in a cheering tone. "But as to there being a fine city yonder, that you surely do not doubt. Think how hopeful all of you were a while since, when you saw the magnificence of its Emperor's gifts!"

"Ah, well!" sighed poor Pedro restlessly. "I would give him better thanks now for an ounce of good health than for an hundredweight of gold."

"Ay indeed, my Captain," groaned Father Juan Diaz. "There you have me with you. I am but just come hither from shriving two poor wretches, who have bid good-bye to this earthly purgatory to go to that which is invisible, and methinks 'twill be not long before you join them there."

"Nay, croaker," exclaimed a voice between contempt and indignation. "There is many an Indian now living will have cause to wish that thine ill prophecy were a true one, before our friend Pedro rids him of his troublesome body. But come thou with me. I would rather try my hand at putting some spirit into thee, than leave thee to rob our comrades of the measure that is theirs."

And so saying Cortes, who had come up at a somewhat opportune moment, marched off the crestfallen, discontented priest to his own quarters to receive a pretty sharp lecture, spite his reverend profession, before he was released.

All the same, the priest's mischievous growls had already borne fruit, and the following morning, before the tents were struck, the Captain-General had to receive a deputation from the malcontents, who were too numerous to be treated with anger or disdain.

"But you are so foolish!" exclaimed Hernando, indeed trembling at the desperate state of the mighty cause he had in hand. "Ye speak as though it were for my glory alone, to fill my pockets with gold only, that ye have all thus fought and struggled and endured until now! Is it not likewise for yourselves? If our achievements shall be so stupendous and so glorious that they hand my name down to after-ages, will not your names also gain the like renown?"

Cortes put the exclamation as a declared certainty, but his hearers rather accepted it as a question, and a shrunken-limbed, white-lipped soldier from amidst the group rejoined harshly—

"Nay, not so, Captain. Those who live through the battle win their spurs, like enough; but those who die, e'en though it be on the eve of victory, so it be before the battle is decided, think you their names get handed down? Faith, no, then. Fame is like other riches, limited in quantity, and so it is reserved, like many another thing, for those who walk over their comrades' dead bodies to success."

As the man ended his speech he staggered from weakness, and would have fallen forward to the ground on his face but that Montoro, who had been standing beside the General to guard him in case of mutiny, saw the poor fellow sinking, and sprang forward in time to catch him in his arms.

Cortes had been hitherto standing fronting his discontented followers with an air of proud resolve, every inch the commander, and the indomitable discoverer and conqueror, but now his countenance suddenly changed, softened, and his lips trembled. He was the man with a genial temper and a warm heart once more—the very comrade indeed of the meanest soldier in his company, who bore all that they had to bear, eat the same food, and shared all the same privations and fatigues; or rather, differed in this, that he took the lion's share of every discomfort whenever it was possible.

As the exhausted man fell swooning into Montoro's ready arms, Cortes stepped forward hastily, and carefully aided in carrying him to his own tent, and there placed him in the clever care of Doña Marina, the interpreter.

"Poor fellow!" he ejaculated on his return to the waiting deputation. "Poor fellow! no wonder that he speaks down-heartedly, for I find that he has been badly wounded, and has fever."

"So have we all been wounded," said another of the group, but more calmly. "And for the fever, well, I may almost say, and so have we all got fever. And do you wonder, General, that it is so?"

A rather weary smile passed over the General's countenance as he replied,

"No, truly, I wonder not at all. I also have been wounded, as you know, in our late engagements with these brave Tlascalans, and I also have fever. But seeing that we all confess to having suffered so much to reach the threshold, shall we not adventure the one more step to enter the door?"

"If it were a step!" ejaculated the new spokesman. "But as it is, we live a worse life than our very animals. When the saddles are off them they can forget their troubles for a while, but for us! Ah! then, we have no dog's life indeed, but one much worse. Fighting and watching night and day, we have no rest till death steps up to put an end to all."

The speaker's words were hard, but they were uttered so temperately and firmly that Cortes replied to them in the like spirit—

"You are right, my brothers—no animal, no unreasoning beast of burden could endure the life we have borne for these past months of desperate adventure; neither could any animal be so buoyed up with lofty hopes, neither could it have so glorious a rejoicing if success should be the crown at last. Our God has helped us to bear and to overcome, as the gods of the ancients never helped even the very greatest of their heroes. None but Spaniards, my brothers, aided by the Spaniard's God and St. Jago, could have struggled onwards, always conquerors as we have been, a handful in the midst of myriads of foes. And remember—" And as Cortes uttered that word he paused, and looked round upon his followers ere he repeated impressively, "Remember, comrades, whatever adversities we have suffered, whatever trials, we have still ever advanced, we have made no step backwards from our undertaking. But you are all free men. We will all stand here and watch the man who first makes that step in retreat and he shall have no hindrance. I myself will be the first to bid him the 'good speed' of farewell."

"Poor fellows!" murmured Father Olmedo with a half-smile to Montoro. "Our General is indeed clever. Few would have found a way so well to give a choice that is no choice. How can any of them now accept his permission to be gone!"

Montoro's countenance reflected the half-smile of his companion. But at the same time he shrugged his shoulders with the reply,

"Ah, well! as Hernando Cortes himself says, better death with honour than life with disgrace."

Unconsciously he uttered the last sentence aloud, and once more he did the General good service. The poor, hard-worn grumblers heard it, and it clenched the argument already so cleverly managed by Cortes.

"Perhaps you have reason, my Señor," exclaimed one of the malcontents. "If we get home alive with our boasted programme of conquest unfulfilled we shall get nought but scorning, it is probable, till we shall wish that verily we had died with our brethren out here. So for my part, after all, I elect to stay."

"To advance, you mean," cried Cortes joyously, making a stride forward to lay his hand, with a well-assumed air of gratitude and friendly familiarity, on the shoulder of the recovered adherent. "There is no 'staying' for us, my friends. We must continue to advance to our appointed goal, or we must retreat. And I frankly tell you all this, that it is my firm belief that our greatest safety, nay, still more, our only safety, lies in progress."

"How so?" boldly demanded a voice in the crowd. "For honour—well, that may be. But for safety!"

"Ay," replied Cortes. "And for safety too, I affirm. And were it not that the experiment would be too costly I would soon prove my assertion to be well-founded. Hitherto our course has been one of unbroken advance, and victory over one petty state after another, and all have become awed by our strange power. Let us make but one day's journey backwards, as though disheartened or worn out, and the spell would be broken; our enemies, forgetting their own petty squabbles for the time, would unite for the destruction of the common enemy and invader, and by the mere force of numbers we should be overwhelmed as with an avalanche. But now we are once more united, my hands feel strong once more, and I will most surely lead you on, my comrades, to a full and final success."

"Meantime," remarked Juan de Cabrera, in a tone of as much satisfaction as marked Cortes' own voice, "meantime, my very good friends and brothers, I see yonder a party of these worthy redskin cooks advancing in the very nick of time with our dinner. And I confess that, for my part, I would fain for the present put by the questions of backwards or forwards, and stay a while to help clear their dishes for them."

Apparently Don Juan's sentiments were remarkably similar at the moment to those of the rest of his companions, and, after a good meal, Cortes found his band once more ready with alacrity to follow whither he might choose to lead.

Their first destination was the beautiful and sacred city of Cholula—the Rome, as it were, of Mexico. The Tlascalans eagerly warned the Spaniards against approaching it or entering its streets. The Cholulans, they declared, were fair speaking but crafty, making amends to themselves for cowardly weakness by cunning, and the most unscrupulous treachery.

But Cortes was never a man to be easily turned aside from his purpose. The Cholulans sent to invite him to enter their city, but entreated that the hasty-tempered Tlascalan warriors might be kept without in the camp, and Cortes accepted the invitation and granted the request.

CHAPTER XXXIV
AN INDIAN GIRL-CHAMPION

The ancient and populous city of Cholula was reputed of great antiquity by the Aztecs, even when they themselves conquered it from the descendants of its ancient founders. It was the chief seat of the religion of the empire and of its commerce, and was held in the most profound veneration by the Aztecs generally, as the chosen abode for twenty years of their wonderful, benevolent, and wise white god Quetzalcoatl, whose descendants they took the unknown Spaniards to be when they first landed on their coasts.

Poor creatures! they were soon undeceived. These new gods taught them plenty of lessons, truly—such lessons as human nature learns but too readily. But they taught none of the lessons their wise ancestor and so-called god had taught of the arts of peace, and civilization, and wise-living.

But whatever might be the merits or demerits of Cholula and the Cholulans, the Tlascalan Caciques showed such anxiety that the Spaniards should give them a wide berth, that at length Cortes somewhat impatiently exclaimed,—

"Methought the Republicans of Tlascala were reputed a brave nation; but I see now that there are some they fear, and they are the people of Cholula."

The eyes of the younger chieftains flashed indignantly at the imputation, but the grand old centenarian Xicotencatl signed to them to keep silence. He called to him a young Indian maiden, his granddaughter, and in low, impressive tones spoke a few words to her.

As the girl listened the crimson deepened in her cheeks, her chest heaved, and the pair of brilliant dark eyes, she turned upon the Spanish General, were flashing as proudly as any of those belonging to the warriors of her country.

Leaving the apartment for a few moments, she quickly returned with a long leather thong, which she carried to Cortes, and then placing her small, dark-hued wrists together, she made signs to him that he should bind them with it thus.

Hernando Cortes was ever gentle with women, and he looked at the rough leather strap, and at the delicate wrists from which the gaily-embroidered robe had been thrown back, and met the girl's signs with smiling shakings of the head for denial. But it was no good. The young Indian flung back the hair from her low, broad forehead angrily, and stamped her foot. Then pressing her wrists against each other more tightly than before, she again held them up to Cortes with an air of resolution, mingled with something of wistful entreaty he could no longer resist.

"Best see, Captain," said Cabrera, inquisitively; "best let us see what the wilful lassie will be at."

"Ay, indeed," agreed Velasquez readily. "I would fain see what rebuke for your taunt of cowardice, Captain, the ancient white-locks yonder hath devised, and yon maiden is so eager to carry out."

Even Montoro looked curious enough to see what small play was to be performed for their edification. Neither he nor any of them thought it could be anything very desperate, with that slight young girl chosen for the heroine and only actor.

Accordingly, thus urged, and with the small, gold-sandalled foot still tapping restlessly before him on the floor, Hernando Cortes at last set himself to the singular task accorded him, and was not let off, by his small monitress, before he had really bound her wrists together too tightly for her to move them as much as a leaf's thickness apart.

Then she walked with erect head and firm steps back to the old Cacique, where he sat, even that hot day, beside a brazier of burning coals. Old age had chilled the physical nature, although the brave spirit still glowed with the generous warmth of youth.

As his granddaughter stood before him he stooped for a moment over the copper pan of fire. The Spaniards stood at the other end of the apartment still and silent, waiting for what was to come. With all their guessing they had not guessed rightly the nature of the lesson to be taught them.

At the expiration of a few instants the Indian maiden returned back towards them, walking with calm, slow dignity as before—her head erect, her full, crimson lips lying lightly and softly together, and her two bound arms stretched out steadily before her.

At first the Spaniards looked only at her face, and were greatly puzzled. What had been done to her, or what had she done in that short interval to prove the courage of her nation? They could not tell the riddle.

Suddenly the eyes of Montoro fell to her arms, and he uttered a low, pained cry. But he did no more. He seemed as though he could not move; for once his readiness forsook him. His friends looked at him, saw the direction of his eyes, and in their turn they also glanced down at the girl's arms, and in their turn they also uttered startled cries as they did so.

There upon the soft, tender young arms lay a glowing coal, eating its fiery way into the bare flesh. And there came the young and delicate owner of those agonized arms pacing along slowly, with a calm and noble bearing and a proudly-smiling face, the champion of her nation's dauntlessness.

Pedro de Alvarado sprang forward, an unwonted dimness in his eyes, and snatching away the burning fragment with his fingers, he flung it out into the courtyard, and then with hasty gentleness unbound the tortured, swelling wrists, whilst the girl looked up in his face with a pleased, half-smiling wonder at his pity.

The old Cacique turned to Cortes.

"Will the white-face chieftain or his brothers any longer doubt the courage of the warriors of Tlascala? They have seen the courage of our maidens."

"Ay, indeed!" ejaculated Cabrera. "And if the courage of the maidens of ancient times were anything of a match to it I, for my part, feel little wonder that in those days there was a race of Amazons. Little use would there be in trying to keep a wife, after that pattern, in order with a threat of fisticuffs."

Montoro turned a laughing face round from the young Indian girl, whose wounds he was examining.

"Is that the way you try to rule your Cempoallan bride, my Juan? I had scarcely thought it from her looks."

"Ah," was the calm reply, "thou seest, friend Montoro, thou knowest nought of women and their natures. Sour looks and savage ways always put the merry light in their eyes, and the laughter on their lips. I have taught thee a useful lesson, see that it proves profitable."

"When the opportunity shall come," came the answer, but more in earnest now than in jest, "I will surely try to profit by thy teaching, but the teaching of thy ways and not thy words."

And then, summoning one of the young maiden's attendants to accompany them, Montoro went with his docile and grateful patient away to a quieter apartment.

The girl-heroine had been quite willing to bear the agonizing pain with uncomplaining fortitude, but she was by no means loth to have the scorched and blistered sores dressed with a skill and tenderness to which she had been hitherto a stranger. Doña Marina stood by the while, gaining a useful lesson, and acting as interpreter.

As the dressing drew to a close the girl said with a sudden tone of animation, —

"The good white-face seems to think I have done something deserving praise; will he let me take him to see what my brothers, and their companions, bear ere they can enter the noble rank of knighthood?"

Her eyes looked so bright and eager that Montoro would have scarcely cared to refuse the request, even had it been an unwelcome one; but as it happened to agree most thoroughly with his own desires to see, and learn, everything that was possible of these wonderful new-found countries before he quitted them, his assent was almost as eager as the offer; and a few minutes hence Montoro, accompanied by his faithful interpreter, and the Cacique's granddaughter, accompanied, as befitted her rank, by half-a-dozen attendants and Doña Marina, set forth on an expedition to one of the neighbouring temples.

CHAPTER XXXV
THE TLASCALAN KNIGHT'S PROBATION

Fast as her nimble little gay-sandalled feet could move, the aged Cacique's grandchild danced along the well-thronged streets of the fine city of Tlascala, the capital of the Republic.

Friends passed her, and with smiles and nods tossed to her great bunches of roses and sweet honeysuckle. From many a broad, flat-terraced roof sweet-toned, merry laughter floated down, as a well-aimed garland fell over Montoro de Diego's handsome head and rested round his neck, or a brilliant chaplet of bright blossoms stopped its flight on the footway before his feet.

Thither marched along a band of warriors in glittering array, and singing as they marched to the wild music of the instruments. And here Xicotencatl's granddaughter paused a few moments, with the impatient small feet curbed to stillness, and the bright eyes bent to the ground with meek deference. A company of the white-robed, long-haired priests was passing, swinging burning censers as they went, and the clouds of aromatic incense floated like a purple veil through the dazzling, sunlit air of that October day.

The priests passed on, and once more the Indian maiden led her companions on again, showing her rows of little white teeth in gratified smiles as her Spanish companion lingered now and again to admire the beautiful pottery, elegant in design and fine in make as that of Florence, or to gaze in surprise at the fine public baths, or the busy barbers' shops and sweetmeat stalls.

At the entrance of one especially narrow street she came to a second standstill. Montoro very quickly read the cause. About half-way down the street there was a disturbance of some sort going on,—a fight over a bad market bargain,—and the partisans on both sides effectually blocked up the way from every one else.

"Let us take another route," said Montoro.

But his guide shook her head.

"No need," she said confidently.

And even as she spoke two or three of the efficient, well-disciplined Tlascalan police put in an appearance on the scene, and the tumult was quelled almost instantaneously. A half-unconscious wish passed through the Spaniard's mind that the Spanish guardians of the peace were anything like as effective.

But they were nearing the temple now for which they were bound, and all other thoughts were lost sight of for the present in wondering speculations as to what new sights he had been brought to witness. It was thanks to the rank and good-will of his guide, and to the fame of her late deed, which had already spread through the city, that he thus easily gained admission to them.

The temple-in-chief of Tlascala did not, indeed, cover forty acres of ground, with an acre of platform for its colossal summit, like its bewildering giant of a sister at Cholula, but it was of sufficient size and proportions to embrace various ecclesiastical institutions within its limits, under the jurisdiction of the priests—seminaries for the education of children, girls and boys, colleges for the priests, and training-schools for the young knights before their entry into the world and its many strifes.

It was with some parade and solemn ceremony that Montoro de Diego was admitted into its precincts, and only upon the half-pleading, half-authoritative demand of the great chieftain's child. But at length he and his companions stood within one of the great halls, and the chatterbox tongues of the young girl, of Doña Marina, and of the Indian women were hushed to reverential silence.

There upon the pavement, a few yards before them, lay a motionless human figure, emaciated to the last degree, and with a deathly pallidness visible even through the red-lined skin. Beside it lay the gaudy feather mantle, the grotesque helmet, and the copper-tipped javelin.

The figure was that of a very young man, and, so it seemed to Montoro, of one fast dying, if not already dead. He turned with a glance of awed interrogation to his conductor, and was bewildered past all saying, and astounded, when he met her face glowing with enthusiasm and lighted by a pair of eyes brilliant with proud joy.

"See, good chieftain," she murmured, with lips trembling with lofty emotion, "see now that it is not I only of the Tlascalans who know how to endure for honour's sake and our country. Yonder is my brother, the youngest. This is now the fifty-third day that he watches, prays, and fasts in the temple beside his armour, that he may hereafter with due rank and fortitude fight in the Republic's wars."

"Surely," ejaculated Montoro, "surely this youth will never live to fight! Methinks he hath but hours of life left even for peace."

As Doña Marina interpreted this speech the words caught the young knight's ears, and the figure which the Spaniard had taken for that of one in the death swoon had sprung to its feet, and by rapid words, and gestures of indignant scorn, gave swift proof that the emaciated frame was still instinct with keen vitality.

The brother and sister exchanged a few low-spoken sentences, the probationer returned to his hard and comfortless couch beside the armour that he so longed to don, and the young guide led her party away to another part of the temple, where fresh scenes for wonder awaited her amateur surgeon.

These said fresh scenes very nearly led to an outbreak of hostilities, for even Montoro de Diego, for all his self-discipline, had the fiery Spanish blood in his veins, and would imagine himself specially commissioned to set other folks to rights; at any rate to try to do so, whether the effort were wild or sensible.

It is true, however, that the sights to which he was now introduced without any previous preparation were terrible enough to have aroused the uninformed indignation of any feeling heart.

In one of the inner courts the Indian maiden made another pause, and pointed with one of her swathed-up arms to the farther end, where a group of men were collected around a companion, whom they were flogging with a savage force that cut open the flesh at every stroke of the lash.

Montoro winced with sympathy as the great whip fell.

"Ah!" he exclaimed, "use the authority of your father's name to stay that cruel punishment."

The young girl's lip curled proudly.

"It is a self-chosen punishment."

"Self-chosen!"

"Ay, self-chosen. How should the warrior dare the peril of being made a sacrifice by enemies, if he had not fortitude sufficient to bear the rods of his friends? But come, there is more to see, that the white-face may learn that the warriors of Tlascala know how to suffer, and can thereafter have small chance to fear aught that the most cruel foes can do to them."

So saying, the girl once more led the way on to an inner hall opposite to that by which they had first entered. She had, however, scarcely entered it when she turned back again hastily, saying—

"No, not this yet; this is for the last. Come!"

But for once the slightly imperative "Come!" was not obeyed by the white-face as it had been before. His keen eyes had alighted on that which had thrilled him with horror.

"Verily," he exclaimed, "it seems that if ye have many of the blessings of civilization ye have also its curses, even to an Inquisition with all its iniquities."

"What do you mean? what would you do?" exclaimed the girl, half-angered, half-terrified as she saw her companion's perturbed countenance, and could scarcely, with the help of Doña Marina and her attendants, keep him from dashing forward into the dim hall, where a young man lay stretched upon a bier of damp reeds, beneath which burned a great fire of smoking herbs, which were stirred from time to time into greater heat.

Truly the punishment, if it were a punishment, was a fearful one; but the Indian girl laid a firm, determined clasp upon Montoro de Diego's arm as she pointed to the young man on his fiery bed.

"He too is my brother," she said, with stern pride—"my eldest brother. That is his final trial. When he wins through that he will be enrolled in the noble order of our knights. Now you know why the Indian warrior fights well."

"You are a noble race, and worthy of a noble fate," murmured the Spaniard; and many a sigh escaped him as they wended homewards.

And now we must pass on quickly to the occupation of Mexico itself, and there, in that island city of flowers and palaces and temples and turrets, take our final leave of Hernando Cortes, its great, world-famous conqueror.

CHAPTER XXXVI
ACROSS THE CAUSEWAY

Scarcely any one in this nineteenth century, who pretends to the name of traveller, neglects to visit the world-famous and beautiful water city of Italy, the white-robed bride of the Adriatic.

When the Spanish discoverers set out for the lands of another hemisphere they little dreamt that they were to find out there another Venice, even more strange, more wonderful in its sweet, flowery, marvellous beauty, than the Venice on their own side of the Atlantic.

As the rough, way-hardened soldiers of Cortes came in sight of the great Lake of Tezcuco, with its fringe of white, well-ordered, flower-embowered villages, its dark groves of oak, cedar, and sycamores, and its richly-cultivated fields, they involuntarily came to a sudden halt, with first a dead silence, and then the air was rent with a simultaneous burst of ecstatic admiration.

"But behold!" exclaimed Juan de Cabrera with sudden bewilderment; "behold, Toro, the very islands on the bosom of yon fair lake are islands of enchantment!"

"How so?" queried Velasquez, pushing in his eager face between the two. "What new marvel hast discovered, Juan, where all is past belief?"

"Past belief, you may well say," returned the other. "I believe not that Hernando Cortes himself, even in his dreams, hath had thought of what he was to find out here. As I said before, I have cut the old world for aye; my home is henceforth here in fairy-land."

"Well, well," retorted Velasquez, "that is stale news now. Thou'st said that same every time, the past weeks, that thou hast caught sight of bright blossoms, bright eyes, or a palm tree. What hast seen now of novelty?"

"Why, his new home on a moving island," said Montoro, laughing. "Have I not guessed right, Cabrera?"

"That hast thou," was the satisfied answer. "Trust thine eyes, my Toro, to see farther through a deal board than the very wood-worm itself. Thine eyes and thy voice make some amends to thy friends for thy long face and scruples."

"I hope he thanks thee for thy compliment," ejaculated Velasquez, with his more short-sighted eyes roving here, there, and everywhere meantime. "But I do wish thou couldst answer a comrade's civil question, instead of indulging in questionable flatteries. What meanest thou by moving islands?"

"Just what I say," replied Juan de Cabrera, as the group of men moved slowly on down the mountain road towards the vast plain of Mexico, his eyes for the time diverted from the proud island city of Tenochtitlan to the chinampas, or wandering islands, being propelled by their owners from one part of the lake to another, as trade or inclination prompted.

These chinampas might be regarded as the market-gardens of the capital. Originally they were nothing but masses of earth loosened from the shore by the action of the water, and held together by the fibrous roots of the various plants flourishing upon them. Gathering these into rafts, tightly knit together, of reeds and rushes, the Aztecs had made for themselves artificial islands two or three hundred feet in length, on which were grown the fruits and vegetables for Tenochtitlan.

Bright with luxuriant vegetation, graceful with little fruit-trees, and homelike with the pretty little wooden hut of the owner, these moving islands were a feature in the glorious landscape, quite sufficiently noteworthy to excuse Cabrera for letting his attention be diverted by them for a few minutes from more important objects. Even the warlike Velasquez was momentarily charmed into an amused pleasure with the novel sight.

"I tell thee what it is, Juan," he said, laughing. "Our General will thus have small trouble in rewarding his faithful followers with lands and homes. He has but to turn off a score or two of those redskin beggars yonder and put us on, and there we are."

"Yea, verily," exclaimed Montoro in a tone of indignant scorn. "There ye would be. Fresh examples of the base, thievish instincts of the Spanish nation."

Velasquez started forward with flashing eyes, and his sword half-drawn. But Cabrera dragged him back, muttering hurriedly—

"Nonsense, Leon. Thou mightest as well wish to fight that enthusiast, Bishop Las Casas, for taking the Indians' part, as this monk-soldier here. Let him be. He returns to Spain, he tells me, with the next despatches. See yonder. What is Hernando Cortes regarding thus intently?"

"Thy magic islands, perchance," was the reply.

But Cortes had no eyes just then for the mere prettinesses of the majestically-beautiful scene lying stretched out beneath his feet, nor even for the great volcano Popocatapetl towering above it all. His eyes were fixed upon the approaches to that great capital of the powerful empire of Mexico, within which he meant to rest that coming night. As he gazed upon the city, and its approaches, his face told nothing of the nature of his intent thought, but in his heart there was the full confession that his determination was one bold almost to madness.

On the east of Tenochtitlan there was no access but by water. On the other three sides the entrances were by causeways. That of Iztapalapan, built out from the mainland to the city, on the south. That of Tepejacac on the north, which, running through the heart of the city as its principal street, met the southern causeway. And lastly, the dike of Tlacopan, connecting the island city with the continent on the west.[10]

This last causeway, which a short time hence Cortes and his companions were to have the bitterest reasons for remembering, was about two miles in length. All the three were built in the same substantial manner, of lime and stone, were defended by drawbridges, and were wide enough for ten or twelve horsemen to ride abreast.

"But still," as Cortes told himself in the secresy of his own heart, and as some of the more thoughtful of his men also told themselves as they now looked down upon it for the first time, "wide as that causeway was, some thousands of determined enemies upon it in their rear, the thousands of the great city's inhabitants driving them in front, that long causeway might well become the death-blow of them and their exalted hopes."

There was a few minutes' pause. Some would not unwillingly have heard the word of command for a retreat, while there was yet time. But that word did not come. As Cabrera had once said so Cortes always thought: "We must all die, and we can die but once."

The word of command was given to advance, and in no long time after, the army had reached the city of Iztapalapan, where it was finally determined to call a halt for the night, and make a first appearance before the Emperor at a more seasonable hour on the following day.

With the first streak of dawn of the 8th November, 1519, the Spanish general and his troops were astir. A lovely morning, the brilliant beams of the sun gradually fading into dimness the innumerable sacred fires of the assemblages of temples.

The whole city was visible to them. The wide-spreading palace of the Emperor, like a second palace of the Cæsars, comprising many homes, gardens of every description for plants and animals, and aviaries of the most gorgeous description, within the one circle. Then the great redstone mansions of the nobles, their roofs blooming like so many exquisite parterres of flowers. The neat dwellings of the poorer classes, of stone and unbaked bricks, here and there rudely adorned with crossbar wooden rafters. Everywhere gardens, streets perfectly kept and perfectly clean, and terraces.

The whole place was waking up now to a new day. All was gay with business and bustle. Canoes glancing swiftly up and down the canals, the streets crowded with people in their bright and picturesque costumes, fountains playing in courts adorned with porphyry and jasper. Stone footways, revenue offices, and numerous bridges, over which people were hurrying in all directions; whilst the enormous market was already becoming thronged with an animated company of many thousands of buyers and sellers, and commodities of all kinds, from slaves for work or sacrifice, down to pastry, sweets, and flowers. Cotton dresses and cloaks, curtains and coverlids, toys and jewellery of the most delicate and exquisite workmanship. Pottery stalls, graceful wood-carvings, helmets, quilted doublets, copperheaded lances and arrows, feather-mail, and the broad maquahuitl or Mexican sword, with its sharp blades of itztli. Itztli razors and mirrors, and barbers to use the razors and lend or sell the mirrors, hides raw and dressed, and live animals. Fish, game, poultry, and building materials. Flowers everywhere, and also, almost everywhere, in and out amongst the motley throngs, the royal officers of justice to keep the peace, collect the duties, and to see to weights and measures, and good faith and order generally.

This Empire of Mexico, and above all its heart, this fair city of Tenochtitlan, was decidedly no abode of savage ignorance, but rather the region of a civilization but very little lower in the scale than that of its conquerors. The deep astonishment and wonder they felt at the discovery is but reproduced in us, as we read of all these marvels. And the wonder in our minds must but be a hundred-fold increased as we remember that this great and far-advanced nation, was utterly conquered and overthrown by a handful of rough, half-taught adventurers!

Meantime, to return to these same adventurers, with no apology either for having given you Prescott's descriptions of this most astonishing Mexico almost word for word, as he, in his turn, has copied it from the letters of one of the very adventurers themselves who accompanied Cortes, that 8th of November morning over the south causeway into ancient Mexico.

On the causeway, at the distance of about half a league from the capital, the small army of conquest encountered a solid wall of stone twelve feet high stretching right across the dike, and strengthened by towers at the extremities. In the centre was a battlemented gate which was opened to admit the white-faced warriors.

"I confess," muttered Alvarado to Velasquez, who rode beside him, as those gates clanged to behind them, "I confess that I should not think him quite a craven among my brethren who should indeed, at this moment, show a real white-face for once."

Velasquez shrugged his shoulders.

"Well, it is true we have walked into the jaws of death. It but remains to see whether our Captain-General be a wedge strong enough to split them."

"Or, as our Diego yonder would say," returned the other, "to hold them open until we walk out again."

"Bah! for the walking out again," was the impatient reply. "Unless, forsooth, it be to leave but bare walls behind us. As the Lord's people of old had command to spoil the Egyptians, so I believe are we now ordained to spoil the heathen savages who imbrue their land with human sacrifices."

"Well," murmured Pedro de Alvarado thoughtfully, "I know not. But it is true, these hateful sacrifices have made even Diego himself grow somewhat cooler, methinks, in his desire to keep our fingers away from this Mexican pie."

At this point in the short conversation the Spanish expedition was met by a splendid cortege of several hundred Aztec chiefs, sent forward by their monarch, who had at length so far overcome his unwillingness to receive the dreaded strangers as to send these messengers with words of welcome to them, and to announce his own approach.

Having spent a somewhat tedious hour in ceremonious greetings, the route was continued over a drawbridge, accompanied by their brilliantly attired escort, each member of which evidently had studied the art of setting himself off to the best advantage, as well as any dainty Spanish cavalier at the Court of Madrid. At length there came in sight the glittering retinue of the Emperor, wending its stately course along the great, wide, central street towards the foreigners.

Amidst a crowd of Indian nobles, preceded by three officers of state bearing golden wands, was borne the royal palanquin, blazing with burnished gold, and canopied with brilliant feather work, powdered with jewels and fringed with silver.

Having advanced to within a few yards of the Spanish General, the palanquin was lowered, the intervening ground was spread with cotton carpetings; nobles, bare-footed, and with faces bent to the earth, lined the way, and the great monarch Montezuma, clothed with the girdle and ample national cloak of the finest embroidered cotton, stepped forth.

"Behold them!" softly ejaculated Cabrera, as the Emperor stepped to the ground, and the Spaniard's eyes were dazzled by the passing flash of the sandals' golden soles, and the glisten of emeralds and pearls with which their fastenings were beautified.

Montezuma, this monarch who had taught both friends and foes to tremble at his frown, was at this time about forty years of age, tall and slender. His hair, which was black and straight, and of a due length to become his rank, was crowned with a plume of feathers of the royal green, which waved above features marked by a considerable degree of thoughtful intelligence. He moved with dignity, and his whole bearing, tempered by an expression of benignity not to have been anticipated, from the reports of him that had hitherto reached the Spaniards' ears, proclaimed a great and worthy ruler among men.[11]

Such courtly and dignified compliments were forthwith exchanged between the Aztec Emperor and the Spanish commander as might be expected between two such men, and then the Emperor was once more borne back to his palace, amid the homage of his prostrate subjects; while the Spaniards, with colours flying and music playing, were conducted by Montezuma's brother to the quarters assigned to them in the capital.

With royal hospitality the Emperor had devoted to the use of his visitors a splendid palace, built some fifty years before by his own father, and here he was waiting to receive them when they entered, and he completed the ceremony of welcome by hanging a superb and massy collar of golden ornaments around the neck of Hernando Cortes, or 'Malinche,' as with a touch of brotherly affection he now renamed him.

"This palace," he said, with the superb generosity he had already several times shown in the magnificence of the gifts to his 'Brother of Spain'—"This palace, Malinche, henceforth belongs to you and to your brethren. Rest after your fatigues, and in a little while I will visit you again."

So saying, with the most true tact and politeness, Montezuma withdrew, only to evince afresh his thought and kindness by forthwith sending his stranger guests a bountiful collation, and a tribe of obsequious and skilful Mexican slaves to serve it.

Having left his visitors ample leisure, both for feastings and for a few hours' quiet sleep, the Emperor's glittering palanquin once more made its appearance, amidst the fountains and flowers of the courtyard of their pleasant new quarters.

He did not depart this time until he had left behind him substantial proofs of his good-will. Suits of garments for every man of the small army, even including the hated Tlascalan allies, profusion of gold chains and other ornaments, and so many gracious expressions of face and voice, that he left even the most morose or prejudiced amongst the Spaniards deeply impressed with the munificence and affability of one whom they had been taught, by his enemies, to regard as a tyrannical and bloodthirsty monster.

The iron hearts of the rough adventurers were touched for once in their lives; and when, on the next day, they, in turn, visited Montezuma in his royal abode, they beguiled their return march with discourse on his gentle breeding and courtesy, and their new-born respect for this potentate of a new-found world.

Meantime Cortes was not quite so thoroughly satisfied with this new aspect of affairs as might, perhaps, be expected, or as were Montoro de Diego, Father Olmedo, and others of the gentler spirits of the expedition.

Cortes was bent on conquest, not compliments, and the strong position of the Indians and their immense numbers, combined with the growing good-will towards them, and respect of many of his own followers, inspired him with a sudden hurry, and most unusual feverish eagerness to bring matters to an issue.

As a first step to demonstrate his power he treated the inhabitants of the capital to a discharge of the artillery, which the poor terrified people regarded as powers wielded by the white-faces' very gods themselves.

But this was not enough for Cortes. He decided by one great theft, made at once, to gain a bloodless victory. He decided to steal from them their king.

CHAPTER XXXVII
ESCALANTE'S FATE DECIDES IT

"I cannot help it, Diego. It is the force of circumstances. Either we must be the aggressors or the victims. And how, thinkest thou, I could then answer it to myself, were I to see these men, who have with so full a trust followed me, butchered before mine eyes?"

Hernando Cortes was striding up and down the enormous apartment of the palace appointed him for a residence by Montezuma. His whole bearing, his face, his voice, betokened excessive agitation. He had only one companion with him at that hour, Montoro de Diego, and Montoro also looked very sorely troubled.

"We have received nought at the hands of this heathen monarch," he murmured, in tones of heartfelt grief; "nought but the noblest generosity, the most chivalrous respect."

"That is true," was the stern reply. "And we are going to return it with—with——"

"The basest treachery and black ingratitude."

There was silence in the apartment, but for those tramping feet, and the somewhat heavy breathing of the men. At last Cortes turned aside, and came to where his friend sat with clasped hands and bowed head, pondering over the inscrutable ways of Providence. He stood before him, looking down upon him with an expression of impatient sorrow.

"Toro, thou and I have been friends for many a stirring year now. We have never yet had cause to doubt each other's truth. Whatever I do in these coming days, believe, or strive to believe, that I act—I declare it by the holy faith itself—according to what I feel to be the loudest calls of duty."

Montoro grasped the other's hand for a moment. He did believe the assurance, although, to his more tender conscience and more enlightened mind, it seemed extraordinary that a glaring wrong could assume the garb of duty.

As the friends thus stood together the gold-embroidered, brilliantly-dyed cotton hangings before the entrance of the room were hastily thrust aside, and a young Spanish knight entered, and advanced impetuously towards the Captain-General. He paused in some confusion when he had approached near enough to see the two grave faces.

"Well, Velasquez," said his superior, with an accent of friendly encouragement, "methinks thy countenance betokens a whole budget of news. What is its nature? Good or evil? Fear not to speak out. I hold myself ever prepared in spirit to accept either."

Thus encouraged, the young soldier of fortune came a step or two nearer, as he replied with suppressed eagerness—

"It is not news, to be so called, that I bring you, Captain. I come rather as a messenger, I would say."

"Ah!" ejaculated Cortes, with some surprise. "A messenger! And from whom?"

"Well," said Velasquez, more slowly, "I believe that I might almost say with truth that I bear a message to you from the whole of our force now gathered in this island city. We would know, Captain, with your good pleasure, what is the next step that you propose to take for the furtherance of the objects of this present expedition—the spread of the most holy Catholic faith, and the glory of the Spanish kingdom."

"Methinks," said Cortes, with some tone of coldness and hauteur,—"methinks, friend, that we have already not only taken many steps in pursuit of those two worthy objects, but that we have likewise, in some large measure, gained them. What wouldst thou more—thou and those for whom thou claimest to be the messenger?"

The young Velasquez de Leon changed colour somewhat at this address. The buoyant hope of success had made Hernando Cortes even more than usually frank and friendly, the past few days, with his officers. But none knew better than he how to suddenly surround himself with a chill, impassable barrier when he chose.

There was an uncomfortable pause. Cortes broke it.

"Well, Leon," he said, with a short laugh, "say on, man. Methinks thou art but a sorry ambassador. Wilt thou find a readier tongue when I send thee to Montezuma to invite him hither?"

The young knight sprang forward, his colour still further heightened, truly, but with delight now instead of uneasiness.

"Order me on that service, my Captain, this very hour, and if my tongue prove not ready enough, my sword shall make amends."

Cortes turned with a meaning look to Montoro ere he answered, more cordially—

"I do not doubt you; that is to say, if I did not add my hand to thine on its hilt. It is just that over-readiness of my followers to use their swords that ofttimes ties me to inaction. If I took thee with me to yon red-skinned monarch's palace, couldst thou possibly abide by the policy of patience?"

"Put him in my charge, Captain," came a laughing shout from the end of the apartment, and the next moment Don Juan de Cabrera had joined the trio.

"Your charge indeed!" said Cortes, with a shrug of the shoulders. "A monkey tied to a cockatoo!"

"Ah," was the calm retort, "my hair is rather rough, for I broke my comb awhile since on the dog Ciudad's back. But yet, worthy Captain, thy natural history is somewhat astray, as I have remarked before, or I am ignorant if cockatoos are ornamented with black crests."

"I wonder whether thou wouldst still laugh if thou wast beaten black," muttered Velasquez, irritably.

"Perhaps," said the careless-hearted cavalier, "if thou wast standing by, looking solemn enough to tempt me. Dost ever laugh thyself, my Don Velasquez?"

"Not when life and honour lie trembling in the balance," said the young knight, indignantly. And, forgetful for the instant of the leader's presence, he continued—"For you, Don Juan, you seem not to remember that we are here pent up like a stack of wood, ready for the burning when our enemies choose to desire light for their temple's sacrifices."

Cortes bent his face forward swiftly towards the speaker.

"Say then, Leon, do you counsel retreat over yonder bridges while yet there is time? Is that what thou camest to——"

But the commander could not finish his sentence. The Spaniard's deference and decorum were neither of them sufficient to restrain him at such an imputation.

"Retreat!" he exclaimed. "I have never yet been of the number of those who have counselled that. Ere I would join in retreat I would of myself yield me into these heathen butchers' hands, to have my heart plucked out as an offering to their gods."

"But yet, if we stay," was the quiet answer,—"bethink you, Velasquez, if we stay, that may still possibly be thy fate, and that of many of us."

"Not if we make a bold fight for it at once," said Cabrera, grown almost as serious as if Leon's rebuke were weighing on his mind. But, as a fact, he did feel grave enough at their present insecure situation, and, brave as he was, he had a shuddering horror at the thought of becoming one of those dreadful sacrifices.

"Any spark may kindle the fury against us of these savages," muttered Velasquez, "and already our easy sloth is nourishing their contempt."

A return of the former haughty look was quickly visible on the face of Cortes at these words; but ere he could reply to them a noise and tumult without startled all four occupants of the room, and they hastily issued forth to learn the cause.

Montoro was the first to reach the threshold of the palace, and with a low, terrible cry he fell back upon his comrades.

"What is it?" gasped Cortes; and, pushing to the front, he received a ghastly answer to his query.

Spiked upon Indian lances, and held aloft by Indian hands, was an immense human head, crowned with heavy dark locks matted and stiffened with gore. A crowd of Indians, warriors and women, trooped along behind it, rending the air with their yells of triumph.

For the space of ten seconds it might be that the bronzed cheek of Cortes blanched; then he made a dash forward, caught one of the yelling youths, and dragging him back with him to the doorway, questioned him rapidly.

"Whose was that head yonder? Was it the head of an enemy of the Mexicans? a Tlascalan, or whose?"

The Indian boy cringed and trembled in that tightening grip.

"It is not the head of one of the white men here with the great white chief."

"It is the head of poor Morla, whom we left behind at Vera Cruz as one of Escalante's garrison," said Montoro sadly. "I should know it anywhere, and under any circumstances."

"Ay, truly," added Alvarado, in confirmation; "it is doubtless his. I did but save the poor fellow from hanging to leave him to a fate still worse. But what of the rest of the garrison? How comes he to have suffered? What is the meaning of this dismal matter? Was he sent out by Escalante as a messenger?"

All these questions, asked as they were by the lips of Alvarado, were indeed asked by the entire party in their thoughts. Montoro, resolved to know the worst at once, hurriedly obtained permission from Cortes, and, regardless of personal risk, he made his way, with his faithful interpreter, to the strangers, who were still bearing on high their ghastly trophy.

It was with no good news that he returned soon after to his companions in arms. Their saddest fears were realized. The noble-hearted, upright young officer, the beloved of all ranks of his companions, had met an early death with seven or eight of the garrison of Vera Cruz, in a pitched battle with a Mexican general.

"Is that the boasted discipline of this great empire," exclaimed Cortes indignantly, "that we should be cherished visitors of its Emperor, and meanwhile our comrades should be attacked and slain by his officers? What say you now, Montoro? Do you still place implicit trust in these base Indians?"

There was a moment's pause ere Montoro answered gravely—

"Base, I cannot call them, in that they fight for their lands and liberty; but I confess that I do feel now, strongly almost as yourself, that either we must re——"

"Retreat! never!" exclaimed Velasquez de Leon fiercely, interrupting the speaker. "What is thy other alternative, Don Diego, for the first is nought?"

"Ay, the other?" asked Cortes, with some extra touch of anxiety, to which Montoro's eyes replied with a grave, sad smile, as his lips answered—

"The other alternative then, I would say, that is forced upon us for the common safety, is, that some step be taken without delay to make our present position more secure."

Cortes grasped his friend's fingers tight as he muttered in a voice hoarse with emotion—

"Toro, I thank thee for those words. Thou hast strengthened my hands. Thy stern disapprobation of my intent lay too hardly on me. Now I can go forward."

"But meantime," muttered young Juan de Cabrera, with something of a gulp,—"meantime, poor old Escalante hath gone forward to that land whence none return."

Montoro laid his hand for one moment on the younger man's arm, as he murmured earnestly—

"Only free from care and toil a little sooner, Juan. We shall join him. Methinks rest must be very grateful after labour."

CHAPTER XXXVIII
THE DOWNFALL OF AN EMPIRE

The fate of the young commander of the garrison of Vera Cruz, and of poor Morla, effected a speedy change in the sentiments of the whole of the Spaniards towards their Mexican entertainers.

"When the Tlascalans entered upon hostilities with us," said Juan de Cabrera, with a grim laugh, "they fed us up as men feed fowls, to make them fatter eating for themselves; but then, like sturdy, blunt warriors as they are, they told us so, whereas——"

"Ay," interrupted that hot-headed Velasquez, "whereas these smooth-spoken scoundrels here fill our mouths with one hand, only that our eyes may be covered while they give us a dose of itztli with the other."

"Well, well," said Hernan Cortes himself, rather gravely, "it may be so; and verily I hope it is, for I confess I would fain believe that we are but about to meet treachery with treachery, and not true-hearted generosity with cruelty."

The two officers glanced at one another significantly as they moved away out of hearing, and Velasquez remarked irritably to his companion—

"Talk of true hearts, indeed! That Diego yonder is making the General well-nigh as soft-hearted as himself. What is a soldier, i' faith, if he sets up to have feelings for his foes?"

"I will tell thee," said the calm, clear voice of Montoro unexpectedly. "I will tell thee, friend Leon. He is then a true knight, such a knight as our Cid would have called comrades with, and not a rascal. But the General is calling for us. Father Olmedo waits to say mass, and to bless us ere we start."

"Finish your sentence, Toro," said Cabrera quietly, and with a smile, as he passed on with him to the chapel they had fitted up for their own services.

Montoro looked round at his companion with some slight surprise.

"What finish wouldst have to my sentence, Juan? I understand thee not."

The other laughed as he answered in low tones—

"Mind me not, my dear friend Long-face; but thou knowest well that thy tongue ached to say—'ere we start on our kidnapping expedition.' Ah!" with another low, merry laugh, "said I not truly? Thy face betrays thee."

It was indeed true that Montoro de Diego regarded the present intentions of his companions in anything but a favourable light, although, unless they would retreat, he knew well enough that some strong measure was needful under present circumstances.

All he could do now he did. Whilst Fathers Olmedo and Juan Diaz were engaged in the celebration of mass, he offered up the most fervent, heartfelt prayers that the Father of all would have pity upon all His children, that the Almighty Lord of the universe would so order all things that they should further His kingdom upon earth, and His glory.

The mass ended, Cortes at once set out for the palace of Montezuma, accompanied by a trusty band of his officers—the inflexible, sunny-haired Alvarado, the fiery Velasquez de Leon, the intrepid and upright Sandoval, the wary Lugo, Davila, ready-handed, careless and fearless Juan de Cabrera, and the calm, keen-eyed, dependable, noble Montoro de Diego.

Montoro did not, could not, approve of the new, stern step about to be attempted for the conquest of Mexico. Nevertheless, when he unobtrusively placed himself by the General's side, Cortes knew well enough that, should the matter on hand come to bloodshed, Montoro de Diego would die before his General suffered hurt.

Arrived at the palace, the unsuspecting monarch gave his usual gracious and ready assent to his guests' demand for an audience. His oracles of old had foretold the coming of white-faces as gods, or the messengers of the gods, and so he ever treated them with a singular reverential courtesy, even when he had learnt to recognize them as scourges of evil, rather than the bright angels of mercy, teaching and blessing, he had been led to look for and to await with eager hopefulness.

Stationed cautiously, at various intervals between their barracks and the royal residence, were companies of the Spanish soldiers, armed to the teeth, ready to support their General and their officers in case of need. The guns were loaded, and pointed at the palace. Every preparation and precaution was attended to that prudence or foresight could dictate, and with that consciousness Cortes advanced to the undertaking with his usual air of bold, calm confidence.

The poor Emperor was in a specially bright, gay humour. He entered into a cheerful conversation, through the interpreters, with the young Spanish knights, and to prove his brotherly attachment to 'Malinche,' offered him one of his daughters for a wife. He pleased his own generous love of giving, and his guests' love of receiving, by lavishing costly and elegant little gifts upon them after his usual fashion.

Cabrera caught sight suddenly of Montoro de Diego's scornful, curling lip, and eyes flashing with indignation, as Velasquez de Leon bent his head to have a gold chain hung about his neck.

"What is it now, good Long-face?" he muttered, in some slight surprise. "Methought that thou wouldst be well satisfied with this interval of amity."

Montoro turned upon his friend with the fierceness of his ungovernable boyhood.

"I would that yon poor monarch's gifts could burn ye all!" he exclaimed passionately. "The base love of gold hath turned Spaniards into a crew of the meanest hounds that walk the earth. Even a cat would not accept a gift from the mouse it meant to kill."

But Montoro's generous wrath acted as the unintentional signal for the consummation of the proposed act of treachery. His angry words and looks startled the Emperor, and Cortes took advantage of his anxious queries to reply to them in his own way. Suddenly dropping the mask of smiles from his face, he exclaimed sternly—

"Can it surprise you, Montezuma, that my followers should show some tokens of indignation, when their well-loved comrades have been slain by your generals, during the very hours when you have made pretence to grasp their hands as brothers?"

The Emperor's face paled somewhat.

"It has been no pretence, Malinche. I have learnt to love and trust you."

"Then prove your words," cried Cortes, with a rapid glance round at his Spanish officers, who gathered instantly close up about him and the Emperor,—that poor Emperor, who had already, one would think, sufficiently proved his trust by dismissing all his own faithful guards and attendants from the apartment where he entertained his treacherous visitors. "Then prove your words," exclaimed Cortes a second time, striding a step nearer to the trembling monarch. "Trust yourself to our care for awhile. We have been your guests; now be our guest in our quarters, until you have proved your innocence of this cruel slaughter of our comrades. So only will we credit what you say."

Montezuma rose from his pile of cushions, and grasping the embroidered hangings of the wall behind him for support, he replied, with a brave effort at self-command, and with returning dignity—

"Nay, ye white-faces, as messengers from the gods have I received you; but you, as a culprit prisoner would hold me in your power."

"Not would, but will, or as a corpse," exclaimed that hot-brained Velasquez de Leon; and, drawing his sword with unforeseen speed, he had it already touching the Emperor's breast, before Montoro could spring forward and dash it down again.

But the rash, discourteous act had pushed matters to an extremity beyond recall. Even had Hernando Cortes felt any inclination to repent of his harsh purpose, it would now truly have been impossible. After suffering such a gross indignity Montezuma must have consulted his high estate by destroying, or expelling, the handful of foreigners who had dared to inflict it, were he able. Even he seemed conscious of this new aspect of the affair.

"Do you desire to have me in your power that you may kill me?" he asked at length, with a tone of calm despair that touched even Cortes' heart.

He answered eagerly—

"Nay, verily. You profess affection for me; I swear to it for you. But I cannot let my followers be slain with impunity. I have their lives to answer for to my sovereign."

"That may well be," was the answer. "But now they are slain; and although, on my kingly word I declare, without my will or knowledge, I yet profess my deepest grief for the mischance. What would you more, Malinche?"

"That you should come with us now," was the ready answer. "Not as a prisoner, as you put it, but as an honoured guest, surrounded by your own attendants, and free of access to all your subjects as you are here in your own palace."

"And for how long to remain such a guest?" asked Montezuma. He was beginning to waver, not indeed from inward conviction of the truth of the plausible words, but from a growing knowledge that they covered an iron, inflexible resolve; and that he would be allowed no power to summon any of his subjects to his aid from this snare, but at the peril of instant death from that circle of ready, flashing swords. "How long would you that I should thus abide amongst you, Malinche?"

"Until Guanhpopoea and his warriors shall have obeyed your summons hither, to answer for their crimes."

"Crimes," repeated the Emperor. "Their crime, it is but one, Malinche."

"Not so," was the stern, cold answer, while Hernando's piercing eyes fixed themselves with a full gaze upon the monarch's face. "Not so, your Majesty. For one crime, there is the unprovoked slaughter of our brethren. That is for us to avenge. For the other crime, there is the presumptuous warfare waged by your general against those with whom you are at peace, and without your will or knowledge. That is the act of a rebel. That is for you to avenge, that insult to your supreme authority. And it merits—death!"

Before that look, and at that word, Montezuma blanched, as before a fatal blow, and he grew pale as death himself. Even Montoro, in his secret heart, asked himself whether a faithful general were not about to suffer, not for presumption, but for too great fidelity to one who knew the arts of treachery, and of wearing a double face, almost as well as did his Spanish brethren themselves.

One more feeble effort Montezuma made to maintain the dignity of his sovereignty.

"My people will never submit to such an indignity for me, as that I should quit my own royal domain to take up my dwelling with a handful of needy strangers, who have to be dependent on our bounty even for the food they eat."

But this last remonstrance was as vain as all the others had been.

"Your word is law with your people," said Cortes. "Give your orders, and you will be obeyed. I, on my part, swear to you, by St. Jago, that nought now or ever, on the part of myself or my followers, shall lower you in the eyes of your subjects."

And so far, to the letter, Cortes did at least keep his word. From the outward show of respect and deference towards the unhappy monarch he never permitted his rough soldiers to depart, when that golden litter, and the Aztec nobles, had for the second time borne the once all-powerful Emperor of Mexico to those Spanish quarters, which were henceforth to be his sad prison during the short remainder of his life.

Montezuma had been in his gilded bondage but a few days when the noble chieftain Guanhpopoea, his son, and fifteen lesser Aztec chiefs, arrived in proud obedience to the summons, and in like proud, speechless submission suffered the cruel punishment decreed them by Cortes, of being burnt alive. They had but done their duty in trying to rid their sovereign of encroaching strangers, who refused all requests to leave a country to which they had not been invited.

The chiefs were burnt alive in the courtyard of the Spaniards' palace; Montezuma sat manacled in an apartment above, mute with a despair only to be equalled by the shame and grief with which the heart of Montoro de Diego felt bowed to the very dust.

He had saved ere now many an Indian from his threatened fate. This time he was powerless.

CHAPTER XXXIX
HOMEWARD BOUND

"And you must leave us then, Diego—leave us on the very eve of our full and final triumph?"

Hernando spoke with a mingled accent of regret and bitterness. In his reply Montoro hinted at both notes.

"I wish to leave. But believe, my captain and my long-time friend, I shall part with you with grief, and although my conscience forbids my further aiding a conquest and spoliation which I deem unjust, I would not, and I dare not if I would, endeavour to be the ruler of the consciences of others."

Cortes looked at him in some surprise.

"How so, Diego? What sayest thou? Surely thou wouldst make me, and all of us, think as thou dost, were it but possible to thy persuasive tongue."

But the answer came readily enough.

"Nay then, verily," said Montoro, with tones deeper and more earnest than before; "that truly would I not. I am not omniscient. These marvellous and wide-spread conquests and slaughters are allowed by the universal Father, I know——"

"Why, of course they are," came the hasty interruption. "They are undertaken for the glory of the Faith."

"And," muttered Juan de Cabrera, with just a momentary twitch of his lips at the corners,—"and just a little, perchance, for the glory likewise of ourselves and our silk-lined, empty pockets."

But Montoro de Diego paid no more heed to the one interruption than to the other, as he continued with scarcely a pause—

"They are allowed by the Almighty, I know, for against His will there can be nought on earth. But perchance they are also with His will, by His law, and for the spread of the knowledge of His Gospel. What mortal shall dare to judge of this? I, at least, veil my face before the mysterious workings of the Creator; and although I feel my own call henceforth to be to quieter scenes, I judge not those who, with regard to honour and humanity, shall prosecute these wars."

"Then you do not leave me as you left Hispaniola long since, because you believed it given up to the government of Satan and his captains?" asked Cortes, with a touch of anxiety in his voice. "It is not quite so bad as this then, is it, Toro?"

A grave smile overspread Montoro's face.

"I leave you, my friend, because, to my thinking, each nation should be content with its own possessions, and such as it may win peaceably, or in lawful trading; but I confess freely that, since discovery and conquest are now the order of the day, I heartily congratulate these countries that Providence has permitted it to you, rather than to any others, to be the Commander of this, the most glorious expedition of any hitherto undertaken by Spanish arms. Some things you have done hardly, but in much you are merciful. And now, farewell."

"Farewell," returned the other fervently. "Have you any wishes, my Diego, to leave with me?"

Diego retained his friend's hand a few moments.

"Yes—one wish. If, as the days roll on, you have any time and thought to spare to our old friendship, yield it this offering, Cortes—show mercy for its sake whenever it is possible."

"It is a promise," came the low-spoken answer, and the two friends parted, never to meet again on earth.

Hernando Cortes completed his splendid conquest of Mexico; Montoro de Diego wended his way homewards to his mother and his native land, where a surprise awaited him of a most unexpected nature.

The philanthropy and unselfishness which had distinguished Montoro's American career so greatly that in some circles his fame was scarcely inferior to that even of the apostle of the Indies himself, had not, at the same time, very much increased his wealth. This was to be expected; but still, as the Spaniard neared Spain an involuntary sigh burst from him.

"What meaneth that sigh, Diego?" asked a companion.

There came a second half-sigh before the answer.

"I fear it meaneth that I am not as strong as I had I hoped."

"Ah!" said Cabrera sympathetically; "that climate out yonder doth touch—"

"Climate!" echoed Montoro with momentary scorn. "Tush, man! I speak not of climates and bodily strength. It is of the moral powers I was meditating when you caught me in that sigh. I started from our native land eighteen years ago, confident, with a boy's confidence, that a couple of years or so—say half-a-dozen at most—were to send me back to my country so berobed and begirt with gold and glory that I should dazzle all beholders, and walk back to my ancestral halls over the backs of crowds of humble suppliants."

Cabrera laughed gaily.

"Ay, Diego. How like that was to a boyish dream. But now?"

"But now," said Montoro with a shrug of the shoulders, but betraying more sadness than he wished—"but now, there is little need for thee or any one to question. Now, as thou knowest, I return to my mother, able, indeed, henceforth to keep her and myself in bread; but for the olives and the oil and the wine, well, for my purse's length I will trust that they reach not up to famine prices so long as the dear mother lives."

"And where dost thou propose that that same living shall be?" asked Cabrera, with a curious gleam in his eyes, over which the lids were somewhat lowered for concealment.

But such care was a little superfluous. Montoro was so taken up with regrets which for once would have their way, that he paid small heed to his companion's looks. He was thinking of his mother's face, and wondering whether he should read any mute reproach for empty-handedness in the sweet eyes that lighted it. But he had heard the question, and he answered it—

"Have I never yet told thee, my Juan, of the humble home I have long since provided for my mother in the little town of El Cuevo? I hope to join her there within the next fortnight, and there I suppose I shall end my days."

"And there *I* suppose that thou'lt do nothing of the sort," responded the captain with a downright bluntness, that acted as a wholesome tonic to his friend. "Why, Toro, I suppose not that yon wretched little town of El Cuevo is big enough to hold above half-a-score of beggars altogether. How, in the name of St. Jago, dost suppose that, with thy wide sympathies, thou wilt be able to exist in such a narrow field?"

This was a new way of putting the matter, and a very clever one for that moment; and Montoro broke out into a hearty laugh, at sound of which Juan de Cabrera took himself back to the duties of his ship with a growling mutter to himself.

"Well, at any rate, that is some crumb of consolation to a fellow, perhaps, for having to keep a secret that seems sometimes to be burning a regular hole in my brain."

Happily, before that seeming grew into reality Cabrera's vessel arrived safely at the port of Cadiz. Shortly after that he reached the Court of King Charles in safety, and got comfortably rid of that burden of mystery which he found so trying. Better still, he was authorized to have the telling of it to the one it so greatly concerned—his comrade, Montoro de Diego. He also was empowered to tell it after his own desire,—bit by bit,—and found as much satisfaction in this telling, or nearly so, as in telling over his own number of ounces of gold, which proved a goodly sum in spite of his usual honesty, and general carelessness as to golden or any other gains that had not fun for a foundation.

CHAPTER XL
REINSTATED

"Adios, my friend," said Montoro, a couple of weeks after landing on Spanish soil.

"*Adios* for the night, for I am sleepy," returned Cabrera. "But as yet, *adios* for no longer."

"But it must be," remonstrated Montoro. "My business here is accomplished at last, and I am off to El Cuevo with the first dawn of to-morrow."

"Are you so?" retorted Don Juan. "I must surely say that thou art in mighty haste to part company with thy friends, my hasty Señor."

"And I must say," returned Montoro, with a pleased smile, "that thou art as unreasonable as thou art gracious. What thinkest thou the mother will say, whom I have not seen for six years, and then but for a flying visit, if I linger on my road home now?"

"And what thinkest thou," demanded Don Juan, with dry deliberation—"what thinkest thou our somewhat imperious sovereign, the noble King Charles of Spain and Emperor of Germany, will think, and possibly also do, if you disobey the orders of his minister that you remain here?"

"When he pleases to give such orders about his insignificant subject he will be obeyed," was the laughing answer. "Meantime, pending such orders — —"

"Meantime, you have such orders," said again Don Juan calmly, but so firmly that the words began to carry some conviction to his hearer's brain, and he started to his feet.

"Nay, Juan, play not with me thus. Tell me, is there real meaning in thy speech?"

"Judge for thyself," was the reply. And he drew letters from his pocket and spread them before his companion's eyes. "Canst read, Diego?"

The question was not wholly sarcastic. Many a brave knight in those days could read the signs of a field of battle far more readily than the pages of a book, or those written signs conveying thoughts from mind to mind. But, as is well known, Diego could read, and his eyes dilated with wonder as he read the few lines of the two letters now laid before him.

One of the letters ordered that the Don Montoro de Diego should remain at Cadiz until further advice should have been taken about him. The second of them contained the information that the Don Montoro de Diego was to remain at Cadiz until the end of the coming week, and then to proceed, without further delay, to Madrid in the company of Cabrera, his suite, and the Aztec treasure.

Montoro's bronzed cheeks grew pale as his eyes rested on the letters. His first thought was one of dumb despair. Not for himself, for he was toilworn and heartworn, and would have felt inclined to welcome any death just then as the gateway to rest. But for his mother he feared greatly that those orders signified an ominous memory of his origin.

Juan de Cabrera read his friend's face readily enough, and before the reading his own boyish love of tormenting faded, and the mysterious import of the letters was explained.

Montoro de Diego's report had gone before him. The good bishop Las Casas had long since sounded a trumpet for him. Montejo months ago had echoed the blast, and now Cortes, the conqueror of an Empire, and Father Olmedo, the wise missionary of Mexico, had made one of the bearers of their magnificent spoils to the King Charles also the bearer of his own praises.

A few weeks hence Montoro de Diego, with the trembling hand of the sweet-eyed, silver-haired mother, Rachel de Diego, clasped tightly within his own, once more entered the home of his ancestors, from which he had been driven in his helpless first weeks of infancy.

He had sought neither gold nor glory, but only to tread in the steps of Him who has said—'I will have mercy, and not sacrifice.' 'By this shall all men know that ye are My disciples, if ye have love one to another.'

He had sown the seeds of mercy, uprightness, honour, and compassion; and even in those wild, wealth-clutching days he reaped men's honour and a golden harvest.

[1] The wealthy class next in standing to the nobles.
[2] Robertson's 'America,' Bk. III. pp. 193, 194.
[3] 'Hist. Conquest of Mexico,' Prescott.
[4] 'Hist. Conquest of Mexico.'—Prescott.

[5] 'Hist. Conquest of Mexico,' Vol. I., p. 288.—Prescott.

[6] 'Hist. Conquest of Mexico,' vol. i. p. 63.—Prescott.

[7] 'Hist. Conquest of Mexico'—Prescott.

[8] 'Hist. of America.'—Robertson.

[9] Hist. 'Conquest of Mexico.'—Prescott.

[10] 'Hist. Conquest of Mexico,'—Prescott.

[11] 'Hist. Conquest of Mexico,' vol. ii.—Prescott.